TRAPPINGS

Elizabeth Edwards

**ZONDERVAN
PUBLISHING HOUSE** OF THE ZONDERVAN CORPORATION
GRAND RAPIDS, MICHIGAN 49506

TRAPPINGS

1 Days were beginning to get longer again. Sallie remembered that only two months ago she had gotten off the bus in the early twilight. Now, as she gingerly stepped around a large patch of mud in the road, she felt the shy warmth of the pre-spring sun on her face.

Ordinarily Sallie loved the stirrings of spring, the beginning of things, starting each year afresh. She fancied herself to be a sensitive girl — that was how she explained to herself her inability to be among the more popular, less-inhibited girls who set the pace at school. And usually she revelled in the early sunshine of spring. It had a special meaning for her. When she had been younger, oh, say, in eighth grade, she had first noticed the world as a special creation. Spring made her think of her own beginnings, as well as the beginnings of trees, flowers, birds, of all things. Being raised in a religious atmosphere, in a family who attended church regularly and encouraged high ideals, she had naturally attributed her beginnings to God.

On this late winter day Sallie should have been enjoying the sunshine. But today was different. In fact, Sallie herself was different. She was unaware of the sensuousness of the air, of the dull, yet secretly beautiful green of the dormant grass. Her mind was frozen with joyous shock at the events of the close of the day. At last she had a date! At seventeen, a senior in high school who considered herself apart, more mature, and more discerning than the girls in her class who had been enjoying the social whirl of high school, Sallie was finally, actually, going out.

Not that she hadn't been asked at all before, she assured herself. There had been a few early father-will-drive-us dates to school parties. But even Sallie would admit that her escorts to those few occasions *had* been less than dreamboats.

Sallie neared the end of her family's trim blacktopped drive, and turned onto the stepping-stone path that led up to the breezeway. She suddenly realized that her mother would be there, waiting as always with questions about Sallie's day. Mom would be in the kitchen starting a meatloaf or something, looking somehow lonely and forlorn, as if her whole day was spent in preparation for the homecomings of her daughter and husband. Today Sallie wanted desperately to avoid the inquisition. Cam Harris had asked her to a movie less than one hour ago.

"Hey, Sallie!"

Sallie had been running down the hall, coat flying, books askew, late as usual, dreaming as usual, hoping she'd still be in time for a seat on the bus. She had turned her head at the sound of Cam's voice.

"Hey, wait a minute, can ya?"

"Sure, Cam." Her heart had sunk. What does he want with me, she remembered thinking, more help on his Civics paper?

"Say, uh, Sal, I was thinking we could hit a flick this Friday."

It wasn't a question really. Cam didn't need to be concerned about being turned down. He was a member of the "in crowd," that group of superstars who noticed Sallie only when they wanted to pick her brain.

Sallie was speechless.

"Hey, kid," Cam laughed a little uneasily, maybe not so sure after all. "I know it's kinda late in the week, but I didn't think you'd . . ."

"Why sure, Cam, I'm free. I do have more library trips to make, but they can wait. I'd love to." Sallie was breathless, partly from running, partly from sheer surprise. If she hadn't been so surprised, she'd have tried to play it cool, as she had countless times in her dreams.

As Sallie opened the door from the breezeway into the kitchen, she was conscious of a wave of thankfulness she hadn't had time to be cool. Whatever his reason, Cam had asked her out. Who knows, she thought, he may actually like me!

"Hello, Sallie. How was your day?"

Nancy Victor was running water over carrots and scrubbing vigorously. Sallie plopped her untidy pile of books, notebooks, and papers on the counter by the door, reluctantly facing up to the fact that since it was Thursday, she didn't have enough time to savor her secret. She'd have to tell her mother.

She walked to the sink and picked up a carrot. Nancy Victor was smiling slightly as she worked, and Sallie remembered how often she had envied her mother her apparent serenity. Nancy was a slender woman, just past forty, youthful in face and figure, with a shy, girlish manner. Sallie supposed she took after her mother in looks. She knew she was pretty, and the soft, naturally wavy, golden hair that fell half-way down her back gave her the look of a remote saint. Together with her prim manner (also handed down from her mother), her lack of small talk, and a distant sense of humor, this quality of untouchable beauty had been mostly responsible for keeping the boys away.

"Honey," her mother said gently, "if you ever answer me the first time, I'll know you're sick."

Sallie laughed and took a bite from her carrot.

"Mom, you're looking at the most popular girl at North Consolidated High. Anybody as in demand as I am deserves extra attention!"

Nancy Victor looked at her daughter closely. "What's gotten into you?"

"Who, mom, who! Not what. *Who's* gotten into me?" Sallie was suddenly happy. All at once she was filled with the all-enveloping, shatteringly luscious knowledge that her dream had come true! "Mom, I've been asked out! Really asked out. And you'll never guess who! Guess, mom. Guess!"

Nancy Victor felt a warmth stealing around her heart. All the times she had prayed for this. All the times she'd wondered in despair, in the ugly, gnawing despair of the very private person she was, unable to share her fears with her husband, if Sallie would ever come out of her secret world and enjoy the fun of being young. Nancy remembered all too well her own agonies of shyness in her teen-age years. And the fears for her own future as a lonely, rejected old maid were even more powerful for her beloved only child, her Sallie. The relief, the almost overwhelming surge of hope, prevented her from thinking of any names. Who could have made Sallie so happy? Not a shy boy like herself — it would be someone Sallie considered "the most." Sallie had been helping Cam Harris on his Civics paper. But he was a football player, and even said to be seen with girls out of school, more a man of the world than a boy.

"Sallie, I'm delighted," Nancy finally managed. "But I can't guess who! All I can think of is Cam Harris, since he's been here to study. But . . ."

"I know!" Sallie exclaimed. "It's impossible! He wouldn't be interested in me. But he is, mom! It's him!" Sallie stopped whirling around the kitchen and sobered. "Mom, I guess lately I really have been wishing I was like Kay Savage or Julie Smithson — wishing I went places and did things. And since Cam's been coming here to have me help him get his C, I've been wishing harder than ever."

Sallie ran and hugged her mother. "Oh, mom! I didn't want to tell you because it's so wonderful. My chance at last! I wanted to hug it to myself and keep it as mine alone. But it's real. I'm going to a movie with him tomorrow night. And I'm going to have so much fun. If he never asks me out again, I'm going to remember tomorrow night anyway."

Nancy Victor patted her daughter's back as new fears began to stir inside her. He *would* ask her out again! There *will* be a next time!

That evening and the next day at school passed in more of a dream than usual for Sallie. Her father came home, was told the news, and manlike seemed unable to catch the excitement. But Sallie and her mother spent Thursday night going over Sallie's wardrobe, trying to choose something not too dressy yet not too casual. At school Friday, Sallie had confided to her best friend, Cara Ames, her news. Cara, while not one of the really popular girls, had a sparkling personality and an outgoing manner that had brought her dates and boyfriends several years earlier. In her sincere fashion she was pleased and relieved that Sallie had a date.

Now, as Sallie stood in front of her dressing-table mirror in the pink outfit she and her mother had finally agreed upon, she studied her slender form reflected against the dainty pink-and-white rosebud wallpaper of her bedroom, and was pleased. Her fair skin had a glow, and even she could see that she was attractive. More than that, the excited anticipation made her whole being feel alive.

She had ten minutes before Cam was due to pick her up. She had put on her perfume and brushed her hair till it glistened like spun gold. She was ready.

Just as Sallie turned away from the mirror, there came a knock on her door, and Sallie's mother came in.

"You look lovely, dear."

Sallie smiled confidently.

"That's the spirit," Nancy Victor said as she walked to the little stuffed chair upholstered to match the wallpaper. "Sallie, we have a few minutes to talk before he comes. I've always thought it would be like this someday." Nancy laughed a little nervously. "Now, I don't know what to say."

Sallie looked at her mother. Nancy sat in the little chair with primly folded hands, her expression almost as eager as Sallie's. Although Sallie sometimes resented her mother's nearly obsessive interest in her, tonight she felt the closeness brought on by the realization of a shared dream. She knew her mother was as anxious as she was to have this date be a success. Her mother had often said that one success could give her the confidence she needed for further dates.

"I know, mom," Sallie said. "I guess we're both so excited that the dream of having a warm, meaningful discussion before the big moment seems kind of dull! Let's just forget it. Besides, if Cam likes me tonight . . ."

"He will!" Nancy put in.

"Don't be so sure, mom. I can't make small talk or flirt or do any of the clever things other girls do. He'll have to like me the way I am."

"That's why he will, Sallie sweet! When you relax, you are much more charming than the girl who needs small talk. It's just chatter really. You're easy to be with. Remember that, Sallie. Boys like girls who make them feel at ease."

Sallie was about to answer, when Frank Victor's gray head poked in the room. "Hey, you two! I've been calling you. Looks like a car in the drive. There goes the bell now." Frank was a tired-looking man, with sad eyes, the eyes of a man who had given up his dreams long ago. But now even his slightly fleshy face smiled gently at Sallie. "Come on, Toots. Your carriage awaits. I'll let the young prince in."

As her father went to answer the door, Sallie and her mother exchanged a quick hug, and Sallie walked slowly down the hall to the living room. She could see her father introducing himself to Cam, and she admired Cam's smooth handshake and easy acknowledgment. He would certainly impress her father with his maturity.

"Hi, Cam" she said quietly, smiling at him.

In the following pause, Nancy Victor stepped forward and took Cam's hand.

"It's nice to see you again, Cam."

"Same here, Mrs. Victor," Cam replied easily. "Thanks to Sallie's help and your ginger cookies my research has progressed to the point where I feel I might have a Civics paper yet."

Nancy Victor laughed. "My ginger cookies have received some compliments in their time, but I don't think they've ever been given dual honors with a research paper!"

"Is it time we were going, Cam?" Sallie asked.

Cam glanced at his watch. "I guess we'd better. I don't want to miss the cartoon."

Sallie smiled as her father laughed. "That's the best part," he agreed.

"I'll just get my coat." Sallie went to the closet, and Frank and Nancy Victor stood to one side as Cam helped Sallie with her coat.

"Have fun," Nancy said as they went out the door.

"We will," Cam said. "And I'll bring her back safely."

At last they were settled in the car and Cam expertly backed it onto the road. Sallie was suddenly tongue-tied as she knew she would be. She tried to relax against the cushion and thought of a question.

"Is this your car, Cam?"

"This junk? It's a good, economical family car. Sorry, sis, I don't have wheels of my own. I — uh — wrecked them and Pops says I have to buy my own next time."

"Well, it's comfortable anyway."

"Yeah, it'll get us there. Boy, one good thing. Your dad didn't give me the third degree. I can't hack a girl with a heavy father."

Sallie was surprised. She'd never seen Cam like this. He was always the polite, smooth gentleman — so much so that some of the guys at school considered him too much of a "dude." Cam seemed nervous tonight, Sallie noticed, and that knowledge served to relax her. She felt the tightness around her heart ease a little.

"Dad's not that kind, Cam. I'm the only one and they care too much for me to play that role."

"Suits me fine," Cam said as he turned onto the main road. Sallie lived in a new subdivision of medium-priced ranch homes and split-levels. Her father had finally felt they could safely afford a new home, and her mother had wanted to remain close to the city where Frank worked as branch manager for a bank. Their subdivision was called Hilltop Acres and would eventually be well landscaped and have swimming and golf. As yet, the roads were constantly muddy, though blacktopped, from the construction machines. Most of Sallie's life had been spent in a small, older house in a poorer section of the city, though she still attended the same school. That had been what she had begged for. She was too shy to face moving as a senior.

Cam stopped at a traffic light. "You're quiet," he said.

"I always am. I was just thinking about where I used to live. Where do you live, Cam?"

"In the fabled community of Verdant Woods — not too far from you. Pops is a 'success,' you know, and we have to live in the 'right place.' "

Sallie laughed.

"You're a real happy fellow tonight," she said.

"Sorry, Sal. I'll try to be my usual debonair self."

"That's okay, Cam! I just never knew you were, well, sort of anti-establishment. You always acted so much the opposite."

Cam started the car moving as the light turned green, and glanced at Sallie. She was smiling gently, her face looking concerned. He longed to touch her long, silky hair.

"I know," he said. "I've always been the dude, right? But you know, Sallie, the dude always dates the right girls. And you're not one of them."

Sallie felt crestfallen. What a mean thing to say!

"I know I'm not," she faltered.

"Hey!" he interrupted. "No insult intended, sis. I'm fed up with those cool chicks! I'm fed up with being a dude! You know, you helped me on my paper and I saw you were *real*. None of this big talk. I just liked you and wanted to know you better. But you'll have to take the real me! For your folks I'll be a dude, but I can't hack the role any more."

Cam parked in a slot near the theater entrance and turned off the engine. He turned and looked closer at the fair-haired girl beside him.

"Hey! You're crying. Listen, I'm sorry I was so blunt. I thought you'd see I thought you were better . . . !"

"I always cry, Cam. Don't apologize. I've always been so afraid of dates, and I know I'm not a flirt or the popular type, so I'm just a little sensitive." Sallie opened her purse and wiped her eyes with a tissue. "You can be yourself with me, Cam. I like you the way you've been at my house and at the library, and I'm glad you got fed up!"

"Hey, we better go or we'll miss the cartoon."

Sallie laughed, feeling a surge of joy. I *am* having fun, she thought. He likes me! He likes *me*.

After Sallie and Cam left, Frank Victor let the jovial mask slip from his face, and sighing deeply, he turned to go back into the living room. Nancy stood transfixed, staring at the door. She wished somehow she could guarantee the success she had assured Sallie would be hers.

"Come in here, Nancy," Frank said quietly from the depths of his leather armchair.

Nancy turned and looked at Frank. She saw a tired, defeated man who looked at least ten years older than his forty-five years. She wondered what she would do with herself until Sallie got home. Years ago she would have wanted to try to talk to Frank about her feelings, her hopes and fears — then they had been for herself, now they were for Sallie. But she knew it was useless. Frank had never understood her emotional nature, and somewhere along the way she had given up trying. She walked to the couch facing the front window and sat down. Her knitting was lying where she had left it that afternoon on the coffee table. With a sigh she picked it up and resigned herself to another long, tedious evening of silence.

Frank read his newspaper, aware of his usual sense of having failed Nancy. He knew she was worried about Sallie, but he also knew he couldn't help her. Long ago he'd realized life was just one struggle after another, and he felt he'd lost most of the battles, or at best just held back the enemy a little longer. There had been a time when he'd had hope, when he'd dreamed of climbing the ladder to success at the bank, but that had gradually been killed off. Now he accepted the dismal truth — he would never rise above branch manager; he would never gain the success he needed to be the source of strength Nancy wanted. Again Frank sighed, shaking his head. Sallie had looked so happy tonight! It made his own heart ache with remembered hope for a life full of dreams come true. He looked over his paper at Nancy. She was knitting absently, the needles seeming to move by themselves, her face set toward the window, waiting.

Somehow, at some point during the movie, Sallie discovered that her hands, which had been lying gently clasped in her lap, had separated, and now one was covered by Cam's big, football-calloused one. The movie was nearly over, and they had enjoyed the swift-paced action as the plot had unfolded. They had exchanged looks of surprise and fear at various times, but Sallie couldn't recall when his hand had covered hers. It didn't matter, except it was the sort of thing you wanted to be aware was happening. Her hand felt warm and moist beneath Cam's, and as she stole a glance at his absorbed face, she realized he, too, was unaware of this development. For Sallie, she did a bold thing. It was as if all her hopes and dreams would grow out of this moment. She turned her hand over, slowly, and clasped Cam's, giving it a little squeeze.

Cam turned, and for a moment unhindered by the usual walls of shyness, torn down by the shared excitement of the film, their eyes locked in a look that stirred Sallie to the depth of her being. The look held, and then, Cam squeezed her hand in return and they both smiled.

13

The movie over, they settled back in the car, in the same places they had sat before, but not in the same way. Sallie felt relaxed and comfortable with Cam now, something she had never thought she would be with any boy. And Cam, his large frame folded into the too-small space behind the wheel, was quieter, not so aggressive.

"You want something to eat?" he asked.

"If you do," Sallie smiled in return.

"How about McDonald's? We can eat in the car."

"I love their French fries."

"Who doesn't?" Cam laughed.

Five minutes later they were parked at McDonald's, and walking hand in hand to the counter.

"Two Cokes and French fries," Cam told the skinny boy behind the counter.

Sallie found herself staring at the boy's bony neck and large Adam's apple. It bobbed up and down as he relayed the order to a girl filling bags of French fries. He looked about sixteen and very comical to Sally in her relaxed frame of mind. I'm going to get the giggles, she thought wildly. Right here in front of the poor kid.

Just then Cam looked at her and seemed to sense her mood.

"Some apple, huh?" he whispered in her ear.

"Shh!" Sallie managed to maintain a pleasant smile while Cam paid the bill and picked up their order. "Let's get out of here before I die," she said in a fierce whisper.

When they got to the car, Sallie let the laughter come, gales and gales of it.

"It's not funny!" she sputtered. "He's a perfectly ordinary kid. I just became fascinated with his neck, and when that thing moved I thought his skin would pop."

When they were finished eating, Cam started the car and headed for Hilltop Acres.

"How long have you lived in your new pad, Sal?"

"Almost a year now. We used to live on Elm Street, in one of those quaint little houses. I guess I still miss my upstairs room. But mom wanted a new house for a long time."

"Yeah, I know what you mean. Pops is a senior partner now in a big-deal law firm. So naturally we have to live in a country club estate. You know, I really can't see why they bother. They always have to play the role, you know?"

Sallie thought of her father, who for years had been a teller at the bank, and of the skimping that had been their life style. She remembered her mother's envious comments concerning their friends' homes. Then, a little

14

over a year ago, her father had been promoted to branch manager. He hadn't seemed too happy, but her mother at last had the prospect of a new house. No country club estate, but a good imitation, and cheaper since it was in a new subdivision, as yet unestablished. She, too, had wondered why the prestige had been so important. She had given up her cozy room for a perfectly decorated pink-and-white domain.

"I know." she said softly. "Daddy doesn't even like his job any more. Of course, he's just a bank manager, nothing big like your dad, Cam, but since we've been in the new house, it seems like they have nothing left to hope for."

"Yeah. My folks are bored, you know? Bored with all their fancy clothes, their vacations, and most of all with each other."

Cam turned into Hilltop Acres, negotiating the broken patches of asphalt.

"Are they going to fix this?" he asked.

"Oh, I guess, when they get done building. At least we got our lawn in last spring, so we're not in mud." Sallie was disturbed by Cam's casual attitude toward his parents, as if nothing really mattered. She had always thought her parents were happy with each other, and assumed that most people were.

"Don't your folks like each other, Cam?" she asked shyly.

"Hey, what gave you that idea! I just said they're bored. You know, you gotta have a little new experience." Cam smiled rather bitterly. "Mom spends all day doing the same stuff. Pops does, too. Me and my little brother — you know, Mike — we keep 'em riled up some. But, come on, Sallie, everybody knows the fire goes out after a while. The point is having a good time while it lasts."

The car drew to a stop in Sallie's driveway. Cam shut off the engine, and turned toward Sallie.

"I thought being married meant growing more in love, didn't you?" Sallie asked, her eyes questioning.

"Uh," Cam looked at the innocent girl beside him, her fair skin luminescent in the moonlight, hair shining — oh, that hair! — and thought of some of the girls he'd been out with who had no illusions about anything any more. He licked his lips and reached out a hand, gently caressing her hair. It was soft. So soft, you could forget all about the ugliness in the world for awhile.

"I guess sometimes it does, Sallie. I guess I think with the right person it does mean that," and then, abruptly his hand slid down to the back of her neck, gently cradling it. "Come here."

Sallie was frightened, her heart hammering madly. His stroking her hair had been so teasingly gentle, now she knew he was going to kiss her. She hadn't really been prepared for this. Somehow, she had expected the

15

evening to end — successfully, as her mother would say — with no really new thing happening, nothing to test her ability as a girl. She had never kissed a guy before. She sat and stared at Cam, unable to move.

"Hey, kid," Cam said softly. "You're scared. I won't hurt you. Come on."

His hand brought her gently toward him, and frozen from any thought, she felt herself sliding slowly across the car seat. Cam's smiling face was coming closer to hers.

Sallie closed her eyes, and thought incoherently that the reason you closed your eyes when you kissed was because you couldn't stand to watch. Forever, it seemed, nothing happened. Then, at last, she felt Cam's lips touch hers, gently moving on her mouth. Without thinking, her arms moved around his neck, as his other arm pulled her closer.

After a minute, Cam lifted his head. Sallie lay still in his arms, her heart still now, strangely calmed by the soft caressing of his lips.

"Hey, kid, I think you liked that," Cam whispered.

Sallie opened her eyes, and looked into Cam's so close to her. I'm falling in love, she thought. Oh, I hope this isn't the end.

"Yes," she whispered back. "It's very nice. I guess you can tell I've never done it before."

Cam felt a thrill run through him. Ironically, he thought, he'd never kissed a girl like Sallie before either. He bent his head and did it again.

After that first date, the days began to form a sort of pattern for Sallie. There were the days Cam called or came over, or they went out, and the days he stayed away. Sallie's dream world became less vital to her, as more of her secret wishes worked out through Cam. She began to blossom the way girls do who believe they are cherished. At school she found she had more confidence with girls like Kay Savage and Julie Smithson; and, too, those girls seemed to take new note of her. She was no longer a decorative, but unaccountable, wallflower. The girls began to admire the way Sallie dressed.

Sallie became the late bloomer who so often shocks the other girls, who have been dating for several years, into wondering why they had been in such a rush.

At home Sallie's mother was delighted. Nancy Victor became more mellow and serene than ever. Word got around. At her church circle meeting, Mrs. Savage remarked on how poised Sallie had become.

"And Kay says that darling Cam Harris walks her to every class, and waits for her after school."

Nancy relished every compliment for Sallie as if it were her own. At last! One of Nancy's secret dreams was reaching fruition. Nancy's own romance (really her only real one) had come much later, after she was working at the bank, when no one noticed. Oh, the joy of it all! To be the mother of the talk of the school.

Even Frank was pleased. Somewhere in the back of his mind there still stirred an errant hope that life might be good after all. Throughout his life Frank had hoped that by being a decent man, doing the proper things, performing his duties as husband, father, church man, and generally sticking to the straight-and-narrow, would eventually lead him to success. He would be revered, respected.

Of course, Frank hadn't made it. At least not good enough for Nancy and himself. As an elder at church, he was successful enough to feel properly superior, but at home he often let his defeated ego show. Ah! But Sallie. She was so sweet! He had always known it. And good! Who could ask for a better daughter? She got good marks at school, she was serious about church (not one of these rebellious hippie-types like some he could think of), and she was so beautiful. Yes, Frank thought, his daughter was beautiful. He wasn't jealous of Cam, no, Cam just proved it — the whole thing. Cam was a football player! How Frank had envied those football players in his day. Cam was well known for his finesse with the girls. He knew how to choose.

Even Cam's parents were happy about the budding romance. After all, Martha Harris thought, Cam was eighteen, going to the university in the fall. He could very well get serious about a girl (at last!), and who could ask for a nicer daughter-in-law? Mrs. Harris had often worried that something might, well, "happen" with one of those other girls Cam had been so involved with. And he wasn't setting his fifteen-year-old brother a good example, tearing around town with girls older than he, drinking, and wrecking his car. As Mrs. Harris sipped her mid-afternoon martini, she wondered what might have become of Cam if he hadn't met this sweet little Victor girl. And she did have lovely hair! Mrs. Harris envied her that pale, natural blond. Mrs. Harris' own hair was beginning to show the wear of too many so-called gentle rinses. No doubt about it, Mrs. Harris could think of worse things happening than Cam's marriage to the Victor girl, even if they were engaged for a few years.

Of course, Harrington Harris was too busy at the office to really be bothered with such triviality as high school romance. Besides, he had his own affairs to be concerned with. But when he was home, putting in his hours as dutiful husband and father, he had occasionally seen Cam bring Sallie by the house. Why just last week, the weather had been almost like summer and the two had dared each other to jump into the icy pond on the tenth fairway behind their house. Spunky little girl! She'd jumped in! Of course, Martha had been horrified.

"They'll catch their death! It's not even April yet!"
"Oh, come on, Martha," Harry had said. "Surely you must have

done something exciting at least once for no reason at all. Even *you* must have."

In fact, if Martha had been more like this cute little Sallie, she'd have been able to hold him. Sallie was quiet (Martha could learn something there!) but not stupid, and she had a marvelous figure — of course, youth always did appeal to Harry, especially now as he was approaching fifty.

Even Mike Harris, Cam's younger brother, was taken with Sallie. From afar, the half-grown, gawky Mike, with the beginning of Cam's too-rich good looks, dreamed about her. He was young and inexperienced concerning girls, but his dreams of Sallie helped him build his wobbling ego.

And Cara Ames, Sallie's petite, raven-haired girl friend, was delighted. Cara was one of those genuinely generous people. She had always hoped Sallie's true worth would be known before high school days were over. She had often been asked why she bothered with Sallie, who was so shy. But Cara hadn't listened. In fact, she even tried to fix Sallie up with dates, though Sallie would have no part of that. Yes, Cara could now smile with a full-bodied, I-told-you-so gloat!

It seemed everyone was pleased or impressed or reliving their own youth in Sallie and Cam's romance. But no one enjoyed it more than Cam. Cam had never before been interested in a girl like Sallie, and he was enjoying the new experience of having to carefully, gently, lead her along the path of love. It gave him a new thrill — better than a fast car, or a fast girl. Each kiss from Sallie was a trophy won, and it held more meaning than those of girls in his past. And Cam was aware of the adulation they were receiving as the most romantic couple at school. He felt protective, and liked it. He had been tired of being a dude — a real swinger. Now he was a mysteriously attractive man. Yes, a man! Only the most developed, the smoothest of the guys, could take Sallie out and make it pay. And was it paying! He enjoyed being with her, he really liked her silence, and yet her sometimes wild release — like the day they'd jumped in the pond. But it paid more than that. Cam could respect this girl, and so he could respect himself.

To everyone the growth of their romance was sweet in the heartbreaking way of early love. But to Sallie it was more than sweet. It was heaven on earth! It was all her dreams come true! All her prayers answered — and so marvelously! She was popular! More than that, she was an idol, the image of true love. And though there were times that Cam's off-hand nature bothered her more sensitive one, she was usually too involved in the joy of being catered to by her mother, father, friends, and most of all Cam, to worry about it. Only in fleeting moments, on rainy days, did she question why Cam cared for her. She simply assumed most of the time that Cam meant what he said. He liked her! Her! Sallie Victor! She didn't really care about the stir they were causing. She only cared about the beauty of it all. And as the days lengthened into spring, as the weeks flew by, as the final months of high school drew to a close, Sallie lapped up and absorbed all the fun and enchantment she had desired for so long. As graduation and the senior prom approached, she pretended — no, she believed — it would go on forever.

Sallie was completely, wholly, blindly, in love.

3 One morning in late April, a Saturday, Sallie awoke to the tip-toe of spring rain. For awhile she lay quiet in the still unfamiliar white French provincial bed, luxuriating in the warmth and softness of body-heated permanent press sheets. She lay perfectly still, letting her eyes roam around the room. Her dressing table was cluttered with her purse, a play program from the night before, the love note Cam had sent her fifth period, and the usual array of perfumes, makeup, combs, and brushes. In comparison the dresser that matched her bed looked neat. Draped with a pale pink embroidered cloth, it held a clock radio, one small picture of her family on a picnic when Sallie was thirteen, her piano-shaped music box that played "Somewhere My Love," and the imitation Dresden Shepherdess lamp. From where she lay, she could see across deep rose broadloom to the satin drapes of tiny pink-and-white check, and out the window. Her view overlooked the rear of the house, and she could see the tops of the tree-row left by the bulldozers to divide one string of lots from the next, and to give the development a semblance of heritage.

Sallie stretched, enjoying the pleasant sensation of tingling muscles. She glanced at the alarm clock on her bedside table. Ten minutes to ten! She smiled to herself as she berated her laziness. Last night had been a delight. She wriggled her toes against the sheets. After the school play Cam had taken her to the Hickory Inn, a really fashionable restaurant. They had sat in a dimly lit alcove and exchanged long looks of adoration. They had hummed a little to the piano music that floated out of the bar. It had been dreamy! Then they had come home and walked silently up and down Sallie's street, for once dry, and enjoyed the soft spring air and the myriad stars in the midnight sky.

Sallie counted in her head. There had been twelve dates with Cam now, counting last night. Counting all the study dates, casual visits to each other's homes, and the times Cam had driven her home from school, she had been with him fifty-five times! It was almost unbelievable!

Sallie sat up and swung her legs over the edge of the bed. She ran her fingers through her hair, encountering many little snarls, not entirely from a night's sleep.

She remembered coming into the quiet house, her mother and father long since having gone to bed. She and Cam, feeling warm and close from their quiet walk, had gone into the living room and sat on the couch. Cam had immediately begun playing with her hair and kissing her. He seemed more urgent than usual and Sallie had felt an answering urgency deep inside her. Somehow their perpendicular position ended up horizontal, as softly, insistently, Cam had kissed and held her.

It had been wonderful! How much she had missed! Never had she considered getting carried away with a boy, but after last night she could see the prospect was not frightening. She had actually longed for Cam's hands to stray a little more.

Sallie stared out into the misty rain. Everything looked soaked through, but in the west it was breaking away a little and a washed-out snatch of blue showed through the clouds. Deep inside she guessed she was at least a little concerned about the growing passion between her and Cam. She had read the books on how to maintain a healthy relationship with boys. She had heard the warnings of becoming too involved too soon. If not from her mother, who seemed to assume Sallie was too innocent to have any real danger from that quarter, then from the youth minister at church and health class as school. Oh, yes, she had been warned. But of what? There had been no trouble stopping last night, and if she had wished for more contact — a little more — what was the harm of that?

Sallie took her lacy duster from the closet, and putting it on, went out into the hall.

"Good morning, sleepy-head." Her mother smiled as she came into the kitchen.

Sallie returned her smile and felt suddenly grateful. She was so lucky! She had everything she could want — nice parents, a good place to live, clothes, a future with a terrific boyfriend!

"Hi, mom," she returned sunnily.

"Have fun at the play, Sallie? Here, have some orange juice while I fix you some eggs."

"It was super, mom! Cara was great. She really stole the show with her funny faces!" Sallie sipped her juice and sat down at the breakfast bar, picking up the morning paper open at the women's page where Nancy Victor had been reading.

Nancy came over from the stove where she had been draining the bacon. "Look at this dress, Sallie. Isn't it just beautiful?"

"Yeah, mom, I was looking at it, but look at the price!"

"Oh, well, dear. I think we can manage that. You ought to have something really special for the prom — you didn't go last year, after all, and you'll remember it all your life.''

Sallie remembered last year. She had gone out to dinner with her folks and pretended she didn't really mind. The next day Cara had called and told her what everyone had worn, who had danced with whom, how Amy Carter had thrown Joe Hollis's ring at him right in front of everyone . . . .

''I guess we could go see it, mom. I was hoping we could get my dress today. Prom's only two weeks away.''

''I know,'' Nancy said as she set down Sallie's bacon and eggs and toast on the bar. ''And you may need shoes dyed to match.''

''What's dad doing today?''

''Well, of course he won't be home till three or so, but if we get going we can be back by then. I'll leave him a note just in case.''

Nancy poured coffee for Sallie.

''We could have lunch in the Blue Room — you always like that.''

Sallie ate her breakfast and nodded absently, thinking of how in six weeks her high school years would be over. Prom, graduation, the parties would all be things of the past. With a little pang she wondered if her relationship with Cam would be, too. Of course not! They hadn't really said anything, but surely he must feel as she did — that someday, after college or at least after a few years, they would marry.

''Mom, do you think Cam will meet someone else when he goes to State in the fall?''

Nancy paused in her wiping of the stove. She *had* thought of that, of course. It *was* possible. Aloud she said, ''He'll meet lots of girls, Sallie — all kinds. But you'll meet different boys, too, when you go to Pleasant Valley. The real question is whether you two really care for each other.''

''I think we do, mom.'' Sallie remembered the way their bodies had responded to each other last night. That must be the real thing!

''Well, if you do, meeting other people will only make it truer.''

Sallie finished her breakfast.

''I'll get dressed, mom. Unless you want me to help clean up.''

''Go ahead, dear. I can finish here before you're ready anyway. Do hurry a little, will you?''

Sallie laughed. ''No hour primping sessions, I promise. I can do that before our date tonight. Thanks for the breakfast, mom.''

They found that the dress in the paper was all wrong for Sallie. So they shopped around the mall, and finally found a floor-length, pale aqua, princess-cut gown. The shade brought out Sallie's pink-and-blond coloring, and enhanced the peculiar blue of her eyes.

''I love it, mom!'' Sallie exclaimed. She felt like a princess, only more real. She couldn't believe all this was happening to her.

By the time they had enjoyed creamed chicken on rice at the Blue Room, it was past two. As they drove home, Sallie and her mother discussed whether or not she should have her hair done for the dance. They finally decided against it. Sallie's naturally wavy hair looked best when just washed and brushed to a gleam. She would find a small hair ornament, and wear her curls cascading down her back. Secretly, she didn't want to put it up, since Cam liked it down.

The remainder of the afternoon Sallie spent on her homework. She was going over to Cam's that evening, and tomorrow was Sunday school and church and youth meeting at night, so she didn't want to put it off. She finished in time to enjoy a leisurely bath and spent a good deal of time trying on outfits. She finally selected a sunny yellow pantsuit.

When Cam came, Sallie was still finishing dressing. As she came into the living room her father and Cam were discussing reports from the spring headquarters of their pro football squad. She was pleased that Cam was still unfailingly the gentleman with her parents, though at times his lightning changes in mood with her were unsettling. He always talked with her father, making a real effort to enter into conversation with him.

"I don't think Groton is living up to his promise," her father was saying from his chair. "Last season he was fast and good, but from what I've heard this spring, he's losing his speed."

"He's still a rookie, don't forget," Cam replied. "He's bound to be inconsistent." Cam was sitting on the couch. He heard Sallie come in and turned his head. His eyes took her in appreciatively.

"Hi," he said.

"Hi, Cam. Say, dad, I forgot to ask you. We're having a discussion on family living tomorrow night at Youth — it's part of a series. I'm discussion leader tomorrow night and I wondered if you could talk for a few minutes on budgets and stuff. You know, the money side of family life."

Frank Victor was also appreciating his daughter's beauty. She looked so slim in that yellow outfit. Of late, he had felt happier than he had in a long while, and no small part was due to Sallie's newly won success. A few months ago, he would have dutifully agreed to her request, but with no pleasure, feeling that he was less than an authority on finances. Now, despite his dead-end feeling about his job, he was deeply pleased.

Aloud Frank said, "Of course. I think I have some pamphlets at home here I can let the kids see, too."

"Great, dad. Are you ready, Cam?"

"It seems to me I'm the one who's been waiting," Cam laughed. "Was it worth it?"

"Go fish somewhere else, beauty. You know what I think."

Sallie felt the now-familiar thrill in her stomach. In his off-hand

22

way he was telling her she was someone special.

Sallie grabbed a sweater from the hall closet.

"What time will I be home, Cam?"

"Early tonight. Mom and Pops have a party after dinner. We can watch the tube for a while, but I work tomorrow."

That was good, Frank thought. The boy didn't just loaf on his father's handouts. He knew Cam was saving for a car. That meant he had ambition, goals.

"Okay, Cam," Sallie said. "Guess we'll be home by eleven, dad."

"That's good. You were out late last night."

As Sallie and Cam rode to his house, they talked about the prom. Sallie was excited about her dress.

"I'll be so gorgeous you won't be able to take your eyes off me."

"or my hands."

"Cam!"

"Cam!" he mimicked her.

"There are other things to think about, you know."

"There are?"

Sallie laughed. "You aren't really *that* one-tracked."

Cam let his gaze slide over the length of her as they pulled to a stop in his driveway. He remembered how she had seemed to move last night in such a way as to encourage his hands to roam. The very sight of her was enough to set his thoughts racing.

"Maybe not all the time, kid. But you do a real good job of making me that way."

That night after Cam's folks had sent them into the den as the guests for the party began to arrive, they sat close together on the couch. As the noise of the party grew louder, they felt more and more alone, as if no one was anywhere near.

The TV was on, with shows that Cam and Sallie didn't see. The Harrises entertained their guests, letting the liquor raise everyone to a state of hilarity. Once, a bleary-eyed man poked his head into the den.

Sallie was reclining with Cam alongside her, their arms wound around each other.

"Oops!" he said. "Thought this was the bathroom."

For a moment Sallie felt guilty, as if they'd been caught doing something wrong. She sat up stiffly, trying to tuck in her blouse.

"Hey, kid," Cam said. "No harm done. That's one of my pop's partners. He's so blotto he can't say his own name let alone yours."

"That's not the point," Sallie said, but she didn't know what the point was. She felt confused, mixed-up. She was stirred by the closeness and kisses, but she wondered if maybe they were going too far.

It seemed that Sallie must have lain awake most of Saturday night trying to quiet her conscience. As she lay in her bedroom, she wondered how it had come to happen. That was the disturbing part. She hadn't decided it *would* happen. To be honest, the previous night's passion had put her in such an anticipatory frame of mind for more of the same, that perhaps in the back of her mind she had decided to allow Cam's hands to wander more.

For the first time Sallie was afraid of where they were drifting. And she seemed to lack the will to stop them. She knew it was up to her to slow things down, but she was desperately afraid of losing Cam.

Often, before she met Cam, she had been disgusted by the way some girls became hysterical at the prospect of losing their boyfriends. Now, she was one of them.

She thought of talking to her mother, but immediately discarded the idea. How could she say, "Mom, Cam felt me. What should I do?" Besides she knew her mother would be horrified by what she'd allowed already.

She thought of talking to Bill Dudley, the youth minister at church, but he was too young. She'd die of embarrassment. And Rev. Crumm, the senior minister, was too old. He seemed to only understand her parents' generation.

It never occurred to Sallie to offer up her problem in prayer. Always before she had found God to be a comfortable presence in her life — a sort of safety net if she ever needed it. She had easily, and with very little doubt, answered questions of creation, the divinity of Jesus, and she had an average comprehension of the theology of sin and Christ's sacrifice. But none of it seemed very real or of any practical help on present-day morality. There were times when Sallie breathed a prayer before a test, or even before a date with Cam.

"Let it go okay, God. Please." And it had gone all right most of the time. But let's face it. Now it was question of whether or not she should become physically involved with a boy she loved very much.

Yes, Sallie was in love with Cam. She knew it. She had waited too long — not even knowing that she was waiting, dreaming away the days — not to recognize the dependent adoration she felt for love.

Girls at school had talked about it. Pretending not to pay any attention she had stood with Cara in the little cliques that gathered in the halls.

"Jim kisses me like he means it. Boy, I'll tell ya, *I* do!"

"Don't you think you *owe* the guy you love something? I mean he gives up a lot to stick to you."

"Well, I think you've gotta keep their respect. Now I let Carl go just so far and that's it!"

Well, wasn't that the trick? Sallie tried to arrange her body more comfortably between the sheets. How could God help her draw that hazy line? Why, in the Song of Solomon all they did was play around with each other— and it sounded so beautiful, so holy. And David had lots of girl friends. What did God think of that?

She really couldn't imagine God thinking anything about what had happened tonight. He had made their bodies the way they were, and it seemed logical that many girls before her had let someone other than their husbands touch them.

Sallie's stomach gave a lurch. She hadn't thought of that. Suppose she and Cam broke up? Would there be another boy then?

It seemed she was getting nowhere. She couldn't bear to think of Cam's leaving her. That was the most important thing. If she kept him from leaving her, eventually they'd get married. The thing to do was to learn the trick of going "just so far."

As Sallie fell into a restless sleep, her confused mind kept trying to work out how far that limit was. Her dreams were chaotic, and kept her in a state of anxiety, so that it seemed she didn't sleep at all. Where do you stop? Where do you stop? For Sallie the question had no answer. She trusted no one well enough to discuss such intimate things, God included. She was like a small child lost in a large department store. There were too many rooms and passageways to be able to select the right one. And like a lost child, looking everywhere for its mother, she hadn't the sense to stand still, or to go back to familiar territory.

4 The days before the prom flew by. There were the shoes to have dyed, the hair ornament to find, and schoolwork to complete as the seniors were rushed through their classes so they would be finished a week ahead of the rest of the school. The prom was May 15, graduation, June 7. Sallie became so busy trying to wrap up term papers and prepare for finals that she scarcely had time to think. There was to be special recognition for the seniors in her church on Graduation Sunday and she had to find a white dress for that. The time went by so swiftly Sallie was hardly aware these were the last days of her high school years. In the rare moments when she had time to reflect, she felt a combination of joy and sadness for the finish of those years, forever over but never forgotten.

The senior girls had pajama parties practically every weekend. The girls with boyfriends left home for their dates with overnight cases and no deadline to be back. They straggled in from midnight on at one girl's house or another. Hilarity at the parties ran high, and in those last sweet days confidences were exchanged in the wee hours of the morning that were later remembered with a sense of shock. A feeling of it's-now-or-never reigned supreme. Cara Ames got engaged and all the girls raised their eyebrows.

"Do you think she's . . .?"

"No! They never get engaged. They just turn up married."

A few did turn up married, still slim and girlish but with the ripe look of realized womanhood.

Oh, those were glorious days! Nancy Victor watched Sallie flit here and there.

"Dear, don't you think you should take a little rest today?"

But Sallie didn't want any rest. It was wonderful! She was one of the leaders in those last hectic days. As a member of the scholastic honorary, she had been selected to give a speech at graduation. At the pajama parties she was among those who exchanged confidences.

And all the while she and Cam were getting in deeper and deeper. Those first days of wondering were gone. She had irrevocably made her decision. She thought she had learned the trick — let him have a little for quite a while. It seemed to satisfy him, and more and more she found their relationship had become richer. She felt very grown up and in control. All the girls did. They talked with condescension about their mothers.

"Well, of course, my mom and dad are divorced, so mom has dates. But can you imagine them . . . ?"

"Yeah, well, my mom's so noble she couldn't possibly even remember when she wasn't."

In the quiet of family rooms and bedrooms stuffed full of slender, sure young girls, when their parents were long asleep, they discussed and categorized everything. They knew what they were doing, just as thousands of young girls had known before them. They admired each other's slimness, their young bodies unstretched by time and babies, and vowed that life would make sense to them. They would bend it to their wishes.

And Sallie was swept along by the tide, sometimes leading, always enjoying, forgetting any warnings she had heard. She looked with contempt on those unfortunates who had to get married, or who, even worse, were too ugly or too fat or too shy to have to do anything. Her life was perfect. If anyone had bothered to tell her otherwise, she wouldn't have listened anyway.

Frank Victor did worry.

"Nancy, this is the third night in a row she's been out. If it's not Cam, it's those confounded girls."

Nancy smiled, "But, Frank, she only has a few more weeks and it's all over. Let her enjoy it."

"I don't like it. She's not used to all this. She used to be such a quiet girl."

Nancy placed her hand on Frank's arm. Lately she had felt more tender towards him than she had in a long time. It was so wonderful to watch Sallie, to feel a part of the excitement!

"It's all right, Frank," she said. "Sallie's a good girl. She's never had this much fun before. If she goes a little overboard, it won't hurt — for just a while. Don't spoil it for her."

So Frank was cowed into silence again. Wearily, he receded into his own concerns. There was no point in arguing with Nancy when she was like this. And secretly, he was proud of Sallie's poise, of the way she rode the crest of the wave.

Cam came often. He and Sallie took long walks, not talking much, just walking along slowly in the woods on the golf course near Cam's house. The trees were tinged with green, the earth heady with scent. They lay on mossy patches and kissed gently.

At last Cam had said something. It had been while they were in the woods. Sallie was sitting on a fallen tree, playing with a tight-furled mayapple, her hair falling across her shoulders in a ripple of gold. Cam had suddenly realized how different this girl was. She was a mystery to him — one moment quiet and shy, the next laughing and brazen. She could raise his desire to a fever pitch, but when she gently pushed his hands or his mouth away, he obeyed. Always before, there had been only forward progress with his girls, none of this come-hither-until-I-say-no.

Cam looked at the girl on the log, and to him she was a vision.

"I love you, Sallie." He had never thought he would say it. He'd figured that would be his ultimate tactic to persuade her to have sex with him. But now he wasn't sure he wanted that with her.

"Oh, Cam, I thought you weren't the serious kind! I thought you'd never say it."

"Hey, kid! It just came out! You're so different. I feel so different . . .!" Cam stopped in confusion.

Sallie got up and walked to him on his mossy bed. She reached out her hands, never feeling more sure. This was it! He was in love with her, too!

Cam grabbed her hands and pulled her down with him. For Sallie all doubts were erased. This love was sacred, and she had nurtured it by her careful give and take.

The day of the prom came and Sallie was happier than ever. The whole day was spent in preparation. She bathed leisurely, she washed her hair three times, she lay on her bed for a rest so that she could go all night. Her dream-come-true got better and better. If there had been questions of right and wrong, of whether she was becoming too involved, they had been smothered by the happiness. With each passing day she was more convinced of the wisdom of her course. She felt sure her happiness was the reward. By now, Sallie had discovered the pleasure she herself felt to be enough reason to allow Cam some freedom.

And always, ever-increasingly, she was more convinced of her own ability for self-control. It was delightful to let the leash on her emotions out a little more each time they met. It was marvelous the way Cam could be led, and then artfully put off. From her talks with the other girls, she knew this was the game they played, also. She hadn't really answered the question of how far to go, but the answer didn't seem to matter any more. Sure of her own strength, she knew she could stop if she wanted to.

The last days of high school are head-turning at best, and Sallie's head was already so bound up with her love for Cam, that any direction she chose seemed sure and safe. She loved it! The all-encompassing, overwhelming power of it! Her better-than-a-dream real life!

When Sallie finally got up from her rest, not actually having slept, she was so excited she couldn't eat dinner. In less than two hours Cam would come for her, looking big and handsome in his tux. It was unbelievable, but true! She was loved! And by a boy any girl would want for herself.

The prom was even better than she expected. Cam came for her at 8:30 and they arrived just as the gym was beginning to fill. Girls in lovely long gowns floated about on the arms of tux-clad boys. Everywhere were flowers — bowers over the doors, on the tables, banked around the bandstand, a huge centerpiece on the buffet table. The barrenness of the gym had been disguised by yards, miles probably, of crepe paper, carefully executed scenarios depicting garden paths with borders of flowers. In one corner was a gazebo, secluded by more flowers and potted plants. Overhead was a large multicolored light that rotated, spraying varigated streams on all.

"Oh, it's more beautiful than I imagined!" Sallie exclaimed as she and Cam approached the receiving line.

"Not bad," Cam agreed.

They greeted the teachers and chaperones, and walked out into the central area to find a table. The tables were arranged as if separated by garden paths, with dance areas in between.

"There's Cara and Tim," Sallie pointed to a table at the far end of one court. "They're saving us a place at their table."

Cara was waving madly. Her white dress, scattered with embroidered red roses, accentuated her dark good looks. Tim stood beside her wearing a welcoming smile on his big, pleasant face. Tim was also a football player, but not so revered as Cam, a big, jolly boy with nondescript features whose warmth of personality made him well liked.

"Oh, you're scrumptious, Sallie," Cara said as they came up.

"You, too! Wow, you look like a picture!"

"No need to flatter them," Tim remarked. "They do it themselves."

Cam laughed and seated Sallie. He was feeling rather ridiculous in his fancy get-up.

The girls discussed the other girls' dresses and greeted their friends. The boys mostly talked sports and cars.

They danced and sat and exchanged outlandish stories with their friends. Toward the end, one of the guys pulled a streamer, bringing down a cascade of kleenex roses on the dancers. After that, the boys were all over the tables tearing down the streamers while the girls collected flowers for souvenirs.

Cara was having a post-prom party, and at midnight they decided to leave. Cara and Tim went ahead to get set up. When Sallie and Cam got there, the guests were already arriving. Kay Savage was sitting on her date's lap tickling him, when they walked in.

"Hi, Sal!" she shouted. "I'm drunk!" She went off into a gale of giggles. Bob Warner, her date, flourished a half-empty bottle of whiskey.

"Hey, man! Where'd you get that?" Cam went over to where they were sitting.

"My old man. He's got cases of this stuff. What's a few missing?" Bob whipped out another bottle, still full.

"What about Cara's folks?" Sallie asked nervously.

"Hey, Sal, they groove. They've gone out," Kay replied, tipping the bottle to her lips. "Here have some."

"No, thanks." Sallie was feeling increasingly upset.

"Well, I will," Cam said taking the bottle. He wiped the neck expertly with the sleeve of his rented tux, and took a swig.

"Oh, I'll try it, too." Sallie didn't want them to think she was a prude. She had worked too hard to overcome that.

"Ugh!" she said as the hot liquid rolled down her throat.

"Hey, kids, here's some *good* music." Cara came in with an armload of records. Then she saw the bottle being passed. "Hey, come on, you guys. Mom would have a fit. She's as loco on booze as she is on drugs."

"She's not here, Cara," Kay said. "Don't be a spoil-sport." She gave a gentle hiccup.

"I mean it, Kay. Drink later if you want, but not here." Cara's small form stood staunchly holding the records.

Bob took the bottle from Kay.

"We'll do that, Cara." he said. "May as well make later right now."

Sallie watched thankfully as Kay and Bob left with the bottles. She envied Cara her cool, Who-cares-about-them-anyway? attitude, wishing she knew when to say no.

Cam was bored. More kids came and the party progressed into a quiet after-dance jam session. At two, Cara's parents came home from the wedding they'd attended in another state. Mrs. Ames made sure they had enough to eat, and went off to the bedroom with her husband.

Sallie sat with Cam in a little love seat, trying to sort out her feelings. The dance had been wonderful — just perfect. But the episode of the liquor bothered her.

At last Cam whispered in her ear, "Let's get out of here."

They went to an all-night restaurant and had coffee. The waitress smiled at them and Cam snickered at her interest. Sallie was suddenly fed up with his sarcastic attitude.

"Why can't you just be nice?" she whispered fiercely.

"Look, kid. This scene is not for me. I'm doing it, aren't I?"

"Yes, but you seem to want to ruin it for me."

"What about me, huh?"

"What about you? If it hadn't been for you I wouldn't have taken that drink."

Cam laughed.

"A little more wine, my dear?" he said nastily. "Sometimes you kill me, you really do. If it weren't for me, you'd be sitting home right now."

"At least I wouldn't be so disgusted with myself. Look at Cara! She's not afraid to say no."

"And you are, huh? Well, Cara's a Miss Priss. That jerk Tim can't play football, let alone pick a woman."

Sallie felt deflated. The whole evening was spoiled. She looked down at her coffee, wondering why she felt so mixed up again.

"I guess, this is all so new to me. I know most of the kids drink, and do a lot of other stuff. I just don't like it, that's all. I thought we were different."

Cam thought of the day in the woods when Sallie, cool and confident, had aroused him to a fever pitch. Always playing, leading him on. For the first time, he thought how she really couldn't be as sure as she acted. She had been in control until now. In control of him! Toying with him but keeping him at arm's length. Letting him touch, but not take. Well, who was in charge around here anyway?

He stood up. "Let's cut this joint, kid. Come on, dry your eyes. No harm done, huh? We can kiss and make up, okay?" He gave her his most charming smile. "No more booze on dates, right?"

Sallie smiled through her tears. He was a dear, after all. "You do understand," she said.

"Sure, kid. Come on."

They drove to their favorite spot, and made up very thoroughly. It was exciting, like a secret rendezvous in Victorian days. He kissed her deeply, becoming more ardent than ever before.

"No booze necessary," he breathed in her ear. "Just this, Sallie, Just plenty of this."

Sallie was out of control and she knew it. The whole night had been too much for her. She felt his hands become more intimate, and she felt her own confused thoughts blur into oblivion as she grew more and more relaxed.

Her dress was a little rumpled when she got home, but she couldn't think of that. Her mind was filled with surprise at how simple it had been. No huge pain, like she'd heard. It had been simple, and Cam had been so grateful.

"You're great, Sallie," he kissed her once at the door. "You know that, don't you?"

"I love you, Cam. If I hadn't . . ."

"I know, kid. But it's okay. You said yourself, we're different."

"Yes!" Sallie answered eagerly.

Cam kissed her once more.

"Good night, kid."

"Good night, Cam."

Sallie let herself into the quiet house. The prom was over.

5

Sallie didn't question the latest turn of events. By now she was committed — for better or worse. There was no sense going over the old guilts and doubts again; she had at some point decided that nothing took precedence over Cam. He was her god. And even if he were a false god, Sallie's course was taken.

Cam still came often to the house, but usually he suggested they take a drive or a walk, and the evening or afternoon would end in their lovemaking. Only now, Cam was careful. He'd been so mad the night of the prom at being played for a sucker, that he'd been careless. And, too, up until that time he hadn't planned to follow his usual pattern with Sallie. He had thought of himself as the experienced man-of-the-world, preserving through chivalry her virtue. But virtue is virtue, and he had little patience with it. So from then on he came prepared.

When he was fifteen his father had taken him aside.

"Say, son, you're getting to be a man now."

"Yeah, Pops. I'm not getting any younger."

"When I was your age, I got pretty involved with the girls." Still do, too, Harrington thought gleefully.

"Sure thing, Pops. Me, too. Got nice little things to offer a guy."

"Yes," Harry thought of Clarissa, his latest. Very nice indeed.

"Well, you've got a responsibility, son."

And he had told Cam that if he were going to do it, he should use some protection — always.

Well, he had slipped up once in three years. Not bad.

Cam's mother had ineffectually tried to teach Cam morality. Too late as usual. When he was seventeen, she'd corralled him in the kitchen.

"Cam! You're getting a little wild, son, don't you think?"

"Come on, mom, I know what I'm doing."

"Cam, I just wish you wouldn't be out so late. And some of your girl friends aren't fit company. You have an example to set for your brother." Martha took a swallow of her pre-golf cocktail. If only she had had the courage to speak up sooner.

"Ah, come on! Lay off, can't you? Mike's got two good examples already. Let me do my own thing, okay?"

"Cam!" Martha was hurt. She'd done her best, hadn't she? Sticking with Harrington had taken its toll. She downed the rest of her drink.

"All right, Cam. I'll leave you alone. Someday you'll wish I hadn't."

Well, that day wasn't coming, Cam thought as he drove home after a meeting with Sallie. Yet the thrill wasn't as big now that Sallie had yielded to him.

"Cam, you *do* love me?"

"Hey, kid, you know it, huh?"

"Yes, but I've always been told that what we're doing will wreck it."

"Hey, baby, the thing that wrecks it is the piece of paper."

"Not always, Cam. It wouldn't for us."

"Well, don't sweat it, okay? We got a good thing going. Let's enjoy it, kid."

But, despite his glib agreement to love, Cam was getting itchy. There was a cute girl at Pops' office. He could see her after hours.

As Cam began losing interest, Sallie became more desperately in love. Or so she thought. By now she was caught on a merry-go-round with no stopping point. She had gotten involved because of love, and now that she was so involved she *must* be in love.

Sallie pushed everything out of her mind but her dates with Cam and the final preparations for graduation. She and her mother found the perfect white dress for the occasion. As Sallie tried it on at the store, Nancy thought she had never looked more wholesome and innocent. What a fine daughter she had!

Sallie walked the double line, behaving on the surface as cool and innocent as ever, but in her desperation, growing more and more daring with Cam. Somewhere along the way, she had forgotten to be happy. It was no picnic, this juggling act. At school, she was still the cool leader, and one part of

32

her still enjoyed the adulation. At home she was the daughter of a month ago. That was tough. Being happy and so sure of her success. Her parents didn't make it any easier.

"I suppose you heard about Candace Jones — I think she's a year behind you at school," Nancy said one day.

"It's terrible. I feel so sorry for her. She's just sixteen."

"Yes, her mother's awfully broken up. Of course, they're getting married." Nancy sighed and shook her head sadly, "These forced marriages just don't work very often. It's hard enough without that. Thank goodness you have more sense than Candace."

And Frank, watching his daughter, was proud of her clean prettiness. He knew it was her decency that was most important to him.

"Just always be my little girl," he told Sallie late in May as they were planting beans. "Be your sweet innocent self." Frank wiped his brow with an old hanky. The sun was hot. Somehow, he must see to it that Sallie's dreams didn't get blasted. "Always be decent, Sallie. No matter what."

Sallie hid her face, putting the little seeds in the ground. Put one down, move two inches, put one down . . . What would he think decent was?

"I am decent, daddy." She was in love!

"I know, honey."

But with Cam, there was no sham. At times she was ashamed, or afraid someone would come and catch them. But usually, he was the only one she could relax with. She thought that was because they were in love. It didn't occur to her that because they shared a secret, they could trust no one else.

Graduation Sunday dawned clear and sunny. There was a gentle June breeze when Sallie went to her window and breathed in the fresh air. School was over — exams written, papers graded, the last mad rush for good times finished. After today they would all embark on new lives — some to jobs, some to more school, some to marriage.

Sallie stood at the window in her shortie pajamas.

"Mr. Brockton, teachers, parents, and fellow students of North Consolidated High School. As a member of our school's honorary, I have been asked to speak on its behalf. There is no higher goal, no worthier cause . . ."

The words of her graduation speech, carefully prepared and memorized, flitted through her mind. She saw the newly leafed trees sparkling with early morning dew, the rows of lettuce and peas in the garden. She felt the pleasure of just being young and alive — more a spiritual pleasure than sensual.

"In conclusion, let me say that Honorary has helped shape my own personality, always pointing the way to the higher ideal. It was well worth the extra hours of study and personal restraint. Thank you."

That would be this afternoon, by the looks of the weather, on the football field. This morning she had church, the presentation of New Testaments, and a dry, uninspired sermon by Rev. Crumm. He would urge them to continue in their high aims and always maintain the "faith of their youth," one of his favorite statements. It seemed to Sallie that Rev. Crumm would have done better to expand the faith of his youth a little to include a few new ideas.

She smiled, and stretching, turned away from the window. She went to her closet to get out her new dress. Hanging on her closet door was the church calendar.

With a sinking feeling Sallie noticed the tiny x marking the due date of her period. It was on the previous Sunday — May 30. She was late! Not unheard of in the past, but there had been no dark possibilities then. She froze with her hand on the knob unable to tear her eyes away from the little square that was May 30. Over and over she read the little verse that accompanied that day.

"Keep my commandments and live" (Prov. 7:2).

Somehow, Sallie dressed. Through a haze of panic, she put on the sweet lace dress, brushed her hair, and tied a blue ribbon around it, Alice-in-Wonderland style. Now was not the time to think about it. She must get through the day.

Getting through the day proved easier than she expected. There was no time to spend worrying about her latest problem. Breakfast was a rushed affair so as to get to church in time to line up. At church, the excited whispers and giggles were contagious, and Sallie persuaded herself she was just one of the girls. Each passing moment seemed to push the reality of the little x farther back in her mind.

Rev. Crumm gave a long, dry sermon as Sallie had expected, geared to the parents of the seniors rather than the graduates themselves. But, unexpectedly, Rev. Dudley added a few words.

"By now you are beginning to believe all you've been told — that the future is yours for the asking and all you have to do is keep on the right track. But don't forget," Bill paused and seriously looked into each shining young face, "don't ever think you will find the right track easy, or even obvious. Sometimes the right decision for one would be wrong for another. And some of you will try hard to maintain high ideals and goals, only to end up miserably failing. I would submit to you, ladies and gentlemen, that the test of the strength of your Christian convictions will be found not in your successes, but in the dark hours of despair."

Sallie's mind couldn't register the meaning of his words. To her, success or failure were one and the same in difficulty of management. As a wallflower she had shrunk from reality, and as the popular late-bloomer she had found reality to shrink from her, becoming less and less discernible. It seemed to her that the difference between success and failure lay not in what you did, but in how you did it. She could not imagine despair being any more difficult than delight, for both distorted reality. To her, there was no reality outside of her own mind.

As the New Testaments were solemnly passed out, as each senior filed past the altar, Sallie felt more and more lost. She could not seem to find solid ground. As she walked to the front of the sanctuary, she was conscious of a floating sensation as if the whole thing were a dream. Her brain was reeling with the words on the calendar: "Keep my commandments and live!" and the apparent contradiction of Bill Dudley's words: "Don't ever think you will find the right track obvious." Life was so confusing! She had wanted to do the right thing! Oh, God! What was right? Was she going to pay now for doing what had seemed right?

Sallie shook hands with Rev. Crumm and took her little black bound book. Somehow she found her place again. Just follow along, sit down when the rest do. On the way back down the side aisle she saw her parents. Her mother was wiping her eyes with a tissue, smiling proudly. Her father was looking happier than she'd ever seen him. Sallie reached her seat just as her legs folded beneath her. Through eyes misted by tears she couldn't shed, she reached for the pew in front of her, supporting herself. She mustn't faint! Oh, the look on her father's face! If only she could be proud, too.

It was over. They were filing out to the last hymn. Sallie's feet seemed to move more readily. There would be a break now, dinner, and a little time before the graduation ceremony. She smiled and joined in with the other kids, congratulating each other. She stood for pictures with her parents, a strained smile plastered to her face.

At last they were home again, her mother taking off her hat, complaining of the early June heat. Her father remarked on Rev. Crumm's sermon.

"Good advice to remember."

"Yes, daddy."

"Young Dudley made a good point, too."

"He's rather deep for me," Nancy said shredding cabbage.

"Failure is always harder than success to live with."

Nancy smiled, "Well, Sallie's a success now. Let her be a good Christian as a success for a while."

Sallie picked at her food. The fried chicken was like paper in her mouth. The jello salad slid down easiest.

"Are you nervous about your speech, honey?" Nancy asked.

"Of course she is," Frank said. "It's a big day for her."

Nancy and Frank talked happily about how proud they would be.

"Three hundred in her class," Frank said. "And only three speeches."

Nancy scraped plates and served strawberry shortcake. "Well, after all, Sallie was one of the best students and nobody could fault her character."

"Excuse me." Sallie stood up.

"No dessert, dear?"

"I can't, mom. Just too excited, I guess."

"Of course," Frank said. "Rest awhile. We don't have to leave for an hour yet."

"I think I will, daddy. The dinner was wonderful, mom."

In her room, the door shut, Sallie stood in front of her closet. The *x* was still on May 30.

"There's your reality, Sallie," she whispered. "No matter what you think, what you want, you can't change that."

She lay on her bed. Once she had been two weeks late.

"I must be just late again. For the sake of staying alive I must believe that."

She turned on her side, staring at the wall. Supposing she wasn't just late, what then?

Sallie flung herself out of the bed and walked to her window. Everything was the same outside — the same trees, the same garden, the same sunshine streaming down — just like in the morning. No more dew to sparkle though.

She would simply have to talk to Cam — before her speech. She couldn't do it otherwise. He would reassure her. He would know what to do.

The day was easier than she expected, simply because in her first panic there had been no possibility of going on. But the mind has a way of cajoling itself into carrying out the impossible. For as long as possible, she would hold off the truth. She would not worry or try to reason. She would take one step at a time and the next step was Cam. He would prove her fears groundless.

Sallie felt a calmness steal over her, a numbness akin to anesthesia. Reality was only in her mind — no success, no failure, no right path, no wrong turn. There was no need to think beyond Cam.

The hour was up. Before long Sallie would see Cam. He would solve everything. How silly she was to become so upset!

Sallie checked her hair and makeup, straightened her dress. She looked normal. Everything would be all right.

For awhile, everything *was* all right. Her parents were seated in the stands in a good location to see and hear the proceedings. Then she looked for Cam.

He was talking with some of the kids right inside the gym door, where the seniors were lining up for the processional. He saw her coming and detached himself from the group.

"Hey, kid. Where've you been?"

"Had to get my folks settled."

"Yeah, you want them to get every advantage of your speech."

"Please, Cam. Don't tease me today."

"Hey, what's with you? Why so glum on the big day? Hey, baby, the big bore's almost over."

"Cam, I have to tell you something."

Cam stopped looking around, as if searching for a more interesting pastime. "What's that, kid?"

Sallie took a deep breath. There was no cool way of saying it.

"I'm late," she said.

"I know, kid. So you made it in time still. So don't sweat it."

Sallie gritted her teeth to keep from screaming.

"I don't mean that! My period, you idiot. I'm late for my period."

For a minute Cam felt as if he'd been doused with cold water. He'd just met a cute girl he'd never noticed before this morning. Now he'd been trying to think of a painless way to end things with Sallie. She was getting to be a drag. What he didn't need were complications!

Sallie was standing with downcast eyes, pale and scared.

"Hey, kid, haven't you been late before?"

"A few times. Once two weeks."

"Well, doesn't excitement sometimes cause that?"

Sallie brightened. Of course! All the last-minute activities, the strain and excitement had held her up.

"It can, I guess."

"How late are ya?"

"A week."

"Well! Kid, don't sweat it. You know I've been careful."

"All but the first time."

Cam felt a twinge of something like fear. He'd worried about that. It sure was dumb to get so mad that he didn't get prepared. He looked at Sallie's face and wondered why he'd gotten so upset over it. Sure, she was pretty and sweet, but he'd really been crazy about her. That's why he'd become so mad. He'd never felt that crazy about someone. Well, most likely it was the excitement. One time, for goodness sake! One lousy, careless move. Yet he smiled in remembrance. It had been great!

Sallie thought he was smiling at her, reassuring her.

"I guess one time wouldn't hurt," she said.

"Naw, don't worry about it, kid."

Sallie let out her breath slowly, feeling the numbness ease a little. It *would* be all right.

The speech was a success. After the ceremonies, after the three hundred diplomas had been passed out, all the teachers on the platform congratulated her. Even some of the parents she knew told her how much she exemplified the ideals of Honorary. Mr. Henson, the advisor of Honorary, said she'd carried on the "fine tradition established for years." She had been a good choice, none better could have been made.

Sallie felt proud at last. The thing was to carry on no matter what — to keep up appearances. She had discovered a lot of self-pride in these last months, pride at her ability to walk the double line. Well, didn't everyone have things to hide? Didn't everybody perfect an act for the world to see? If only she'd been smarter. Whether to have sex or not wasn't the question any more. It wasn't what you did that counted, but how intelligently you handled it. Like Bill Dudley said, the right decision wasn't the same for everyone. And she probably was just late, that's all.

That week Cam called Sallie twice for dates. She was a little worried about that. She'd thought he'd see more of her with school out. Of course, he was working more now.

"Why haven't you called, Cam?"

"Hey, kid, I'm a working man!"

"I've missed you."

"Yeah, me too! How about a drive, okay?"

Of course, he was ready. They had a new pattern now. No need to go to a movie, or out to eat. They got right to the point. No messing around.

As Cam held her, Sallie wondered how it had come to this. She didn't really think of their love as sacred any more. When she wasn't careful, the thought would steal into her mind that Cam wasn't in love with her either. Maybe he never had been.

This struck panic to her heart. She returned his kisses with feigned passion, never daring to question him.

Nancy Victor noticed subtle changes in Sallie. She wasn't so bubbly any more; she seemed withdrawn, even more than before Cam. Sallie had little interest in her future at Pleasant Valley College — just agreed with whatever she or Frank said. It seemed that after graduation everything had gone flat. Sallie was no longer the effervescent schoolgirl of the spring months, and as the fizz seeps out of an uncapped cola, the vicarious joy faded from Nancy's life, too. Somehow, she had to stop it! She couldn't bear for this sweetness of love to end!

Frank settled back into his old routine. He suspected things were cooling between Sallie and Cam. Oh well, what had he expected? He just hoped she hadn't gone too far with Cam. She tended to be wholehearted, like he was. When the break came, he hoped she wouldn't go to pieces.

The break didn't come yet. For the weeks of June Cam saw Sallie often enough to keep everyone happy. He saw the new gal, too. But, let's face it. He could depend on Sallie's willingness. Once she'd given in, she'd been a pushover.

The days went by, Sallie shopped for college clothes, helped in the yard and garden, worked several afternoons a week at the bank. The calendar no longer hung on her closet door. She'd put it in her drawer. She didn't need its reminder. The numbness had returned, and with it, a kind of dull acceptance. As the days passed she knew there was no mistake in her first fears. The sweet, hot days of June, the lushness of the grass and flowers, the lethargy that usually possessed her in summer were all unnoticed by Sallie. Each day brought her closer to the truth, the unavoidable reality.

Lying under the trees with Cam, feeling their two bodies mesh with familiarity, she cursed her stupidity. The whole thing would be so pleasant, if only *she'd* thought to be careful. But, of course, that night had been strange and unsettling — she'd been out of control. Only recently had she seen things with clarity.

Her faith and her upbringing no longer mattered; she realized that. At some point she'd had a weak link in the chain. Suffice it to say she'd wanted the dream-come-true of Cam more than anything else. She'd put him above all else, and that had been her undoing. She felt Cam's release, his murmured words of love — no, sex! She should have put herself first. She could have had it all! The admiration of the kids, the respect of her parents, the fun of unhindered sex with Cam!

With a shock Sallie sat up. What had she become? How had this happened?

"I'm pregnant, Cam."

Cam lay stretched out immodestly, his eyes shut. It was good to have Sallie when he needed her. Why couldn't she be quiet and let him just relax?

"Cam!"

He opened his eyes. She was standing near him looking very alluring, her hair a halo around her face.

"You're beautiful, kid."

Sallie looked with fury and sudden hate at the boy who had brought her so low.

"I hate you!" she said.

Cam sat up in surprise.

"What'd I do?"

"What'd you do!" Sallie spat. "I'm pregnant! Do you hear? You selfish fool! Don't you care? Haven't you noticed no interruption in your fun?"

Cam stood up shakily. She was right! There'd been no interruption, no put off. He swallowed hard.

"You could be wrong," he said.

"No chance!"

"You been to a doctor? Maybe you're sick."

"Be nice, wouldn't it?"

Sallie was crying, the tears running down her cheeks. She pulled on her sweatshirt and jeans.

Cam felt foolish suddenly. He could hear a golfer shout "Fore!" not too far away. Quickly, he got dressed. So this was where it got him. One dumb move!

"There's something to do, Sal," he said.

Sallie was leaning against a tree, sobbing silently.

"What's that, superman?"

Cam turned her around, looked steadily into her eyes. Had she thought him handsome? *This* brute?

"An abortion, kid. It's easy. I heard Pops setting one up for one of his girls."

Sallie flung herself away from him. She looked with disgust at the mossy bed where she'd just been used.

"You really are something, Cam."

"Don't be so righteous on me, kid! You sure haven't held back."

"I was stupid! I thought I could play the game and win! Well, I lost."

Cam tried to touch her.

"Aw come on, Sal! An abortion will fix everything! Then we'll be more careful — like we have been!"

Sallie jerked away from him again.

"Take me home," she said.

"You won't tell your folks?"

"What's wrong? You afraid daddy has a shot-gun?"

Cam blushed.

"I can't marry you! We both got big futures."

"Sure, Cam. Take me home, okay?"

6 Nancy Victor heard Sallie come in. It was mid-afternoon in early July. The sky was darkening with a thunderhead, the air was sultry. Nancy was sewing a hem, sitting in the living room and sipping iced tea. She had watched with mounting disappointment the slackening of Cam's visits, Sallie's taciturnity. Without being an interfering mother she could see no way to help. It seemed that, after all, the romance was just a case of puppy love.

Nancy sewed, while Sallie said good-by to Cam.

"I'll call you tomorrow," Cam said.

"No, don't."

"I want to see you again, kid. We can talk . . . "

The door slammed shut. Nancy put down the dress she was working on. She turned as Sallie came in and sank exhaustedly into Frank's chair.

"What's wrong, dear?"

Sallie wondered what she should say. Nothing? Everything? I'm going to have a baby, mom?

"I guess it's over."

"But, dear, I heard Cam say he wants to see you!"

"Don't I have an opinion?"

"But Sallie! You said you loved him! Surely you're not so light with those words!"

"I was mistaken."

Sallie stood up.

"I'm going to take a shower," she said, turning her back on her mother.

"Sallie! There must be some reason! I've sensed the change. Oh, how I've wanted to help!"

Sallie spun back around.

"Mom, it's too late! It was too late a long time ago. You can't help! Just let me alone awhile. Please!"

Nancy looked at her distraught daughter. What could Sallie be saying? They'd always talked about things until recently. Was there to be no explanation?

As Nancy watched, feeling the disappointment deepen, Sallie walked out. In a few minutes she heard the shower running, running. With a sigh Nancy picked up her sewing. She had so hoped that things would work out for Sallie and Cam. He seemed to be such a nice boy! And such a good background, too! Maybe it was just a spat, a lover's quarrel.

Nancy sewed, while Sallie tried to wash the disgust away. At last, it seemed, she saw Cam for what he was. She had been beguiled by the romantic first awakening of love — or what had passed for love. She had been carried away by her success! Well, never again! She'd learned her lesson! If ever she let a boy near her again, and now the very thought made her sick, she'd be very careful to protect herself.

For she realized bitterly that she was the one to pay. It would do her well to prevent that ever happening again, to be very wise, to let innocence go.

Unfortunately, this time it was too late for that.

Sallie lay on her bed as the pale light of dawn filtered into her room. She hadn't seen Cam for a week now, and her heart seemed to have died

41

within her. The first bitterness of having recognized Cam's true character had hardened into a firm resolve. She was no longer wildly angry and resentful, but as the anger cooled, it was replaced with a new cynicism.

Not very successfully, she had avoided her mother's questions. She had little concern for how she appeared to her parents now, and she realized her silence portended some ominous event to them. It was as if Nancy and Frank tiptoed around the house, awaiting the dreadful day that could not be held off. Still, she didn't think they actually understood what was the cause of her total withdrawal. They whispered together about her, and Sallie sensed merely a deep concern. They must have written her attitude off to a broken heart, a lost love.

Actually, Sallie was never less in love. There were no dreams now, no building castles in the air. And there was no romance. To be exact, there was nothing.

Sallie's mind seemed to have closed on one fact: a baby grew within her. She knew she should go to the doctor to be sure, but then the cat would be out of the bag.

As she lay on her bed in the early hours of brightening day, she seemed to believe that if she just waited long enough the problem would go away. The void of her mind had lost its ability to function, as though the harshness of reality had crippled the mechanism that made it work. No more dreams. No more thought at all.

Sallie got up, and felt sick. It had started this week, that churning nausea. It was worse this morning. She was not going to be able to swallow it.

When Sallie was finished vomiting, she leaned against the cool tile of the bathroom wall. She felt a little better.

"Well, Sallie, now we have the answer."

Sallie looked around. Her mother was standing in the doorway, her wrapper drawn tightly around her. Her hair was mussed from sleep, and her eyes were sad with understanding.

"Oh, mom!" Sallie ran to her mother, flinging her arms about Nancy's neck, clinging. "How could this happen?"

"Last week, I knew," Nancy said, standing stiffly, unable to return Sallie's embrace.

Sallie unwound herself, stood apart from her mother.

Nancy seemed to realize she had failed her daughter. She lifted a hand and patted Sallie's arm.

"How far are you?"

"Seven weeks."

"I guess there's no point in asking why." Nancy's mind was screaming: How could you do this to us!

"Why!" Sallie wrung her hands. "Why! I was in love! It seemed good. No, that's not why! Who knows why?" Sallie sat down on the edge of the bathtub, dropping her head in her hands.

"No, dear! Please, don't be so broken-hearted! I can't bear it." Nancy knelt and put her arms about her daughter. I'm dreaming, she thought. This can't be happening. Not to my Sallie! She was so innocent!

"What's all the commotion about?"

Sallie lifted her head and saw her father past her mother's shoulder. Nancy released her, and turned. Both just stared, mute.

"Why are you crying so early, sweetie? Is it about that Cam? He's made you unhappy, hasn't he?" Frank was tired. The past week had been tough at the office, and coming home was like visiting a mortuary. All silence and whispers. He wished one of them would tell him what the trouble was. They both just stared. Was the boy worth such lost looks?

Sallie dragged herself to her feet. Nancy tried to hold her back, but she shook off her mother's hands and went to her father.

"Daddy, there's no easy way. I'm going to have a baby."

Frank stood still. Sallie's sweet face with unspoken pleading, swollen by tears, swam before him. How could this be?

Sallie was good. Good! He uttered an oath.

Sallie shook her head, tears streaming.

"No, daddy! He wanted it, yes, but I did, too! If I hadn't . . . Oh, daddy, please, try to see! I wanted so much to belong to someone, to be loved . . ."

"We loved you! Couldn't our love keep you decent?"

"Frank!" Nancy's voice shook with fury. "Stop it! Can't you see she's half-crazy with grief?"

Frank stood unsteadily, registering his wife's words. It was impossible, of course. They were all in some kind of a cruel charade.

Nancy put her arm around Sallie.

"We'll have some breakfast," she said. "We need to think."

They all picked at the eggs and bacon Nancy fixed, breaking their yolks, and trying to act as if they were eating. Mostly they were silent, each lost in his own private limbo.

Sallie felt relief. Yes, relief! At last they knew. She saw now how she had been so panic-stricken she was incapable of coming up with a plan. Now her parents would help. In the midst of her agony over her predicament, she was grateful to share the burden.

Nancy was heartbroken. She had blithely assumed Sallie would never get into this sort of trouble. That's why she hadn't dwelt too much on sex. It had seemed unnecessary with such an innocent. Now, belatedly, she accepted the fact that innocence and inexperience can be a deadly combination.

Frank was angry. One more example of the unfairness of life! How he had hoped for himself and seen those goals missed. How he had transferred his need for hope to Sallie! She had seemed to be the realization of all things good. Now this! God had no concern, no real interest in them. If He had, He would have prevented this!

At last Nancy stood up, signifying the end of the mock-meal. Sallie rose quickly to help clear away the dishes. Frank remained seated, thinking.

The boy should be held responsible, he thought. It wasn't fair that Sallie must take the whole responsibility.

Finally, Frank rose also.

"I'm going to call the Harrises."

Nancy turned from the sink.

"You can't! Not yet!"

"Why not?" Frank roared. "I want that boy made to pay."

"Daddy, wait, please," Sallie pleaded, running to his side. "I can't marry him."

"What do you mean, girl? You're pregnant with his baby, aren't you?"

"Yes, I . . ."

"Then, what else can you do! You aren't going to disgrace us any more."

Sallie crumpled into a chair, shaking her head.

"No, daddy, I'll go away. I'm out of school . . ."

Nancy came over and put her arm around Sallie.

"You won't go away," she said.

"You're darn right she won't," Frank said. "She'll marry him and bring some decency to the thing."

"Decency!" Sallie screamed, leaping to her feet again. "Decency! Haven't I lost decency by my association with Cam? I made a mistake, daddy, yes, but I won't give up my chance to overcome it by linking myself to him." Sallie turned to her mother. "Oh mommy! Make him see! Please! Cam doesn't want to marry me — and he knows! Why do you think I won't see him? Why, when he called, wouldn't I talk to him? I told him and he told me to get an abortion! If he was forced to marry me, he'd hate me. Don't you see? It would be hell for us all!"

Sallie sat down again, needing the support of the chair.

"And I already hate him! He made me forget everything. Oh, I must have wanted to put his wishes first, but now that I know what he is, I can't marry him, no matter what! I can hardly bear to *think* of him."

"You should have thought of that before!" Frank said. "His parents have a right to know, too!"

Nancy went to Frank where he stood at the door of the dining room near the phone.

"Frank," she said patiently, "you don't want to make it worse than it already is. Let's sit down and talk reasonably."

Frank glared at Nancy. "You always are reasonable, Nancy. That means we'll do it your way, doesn't it?"

"I have no way, Frank," Nancy said quietly. "I only know that Sallie's been a good girl till now, and I don't want to make a hasty decision that will ruin her life."

Frank sighed, looking at Sallie where she sat at the table, her head in her arms. Before he could say more, she flung herself out of the chair and ran from the room, sobbing.

"It's ruined already!" she cried from the doorway and then she was gone, and they heard her bedroom door slam.

Nancy was at last angry.

"Now see what you've done! You have no right to blame her so — to be so vindictive. We're all in this!"

"You are!" Frank flung back. "You pushed her all the way! Every inch you were there making it easy for her, always putting me off when I thought she was doing too much."

"That's not true!"

"I don't know how I've stood it all these years! Always trying to please you! Always giving in to your wishes!"

"What about me, Frank Victor? Haven't I given up a lot? Haven't I sacrificed trying to economize so we could have something in the end?"

Frank was in a rage. As usual, Nancy twisted everything he said to fit her ends, to make her look the martyr. He turned on his heel and went to the closet.

"I'm going for a walk," he said and slammed out of the house.

Nancy was left in the kitchen with egg-smeared dishes stacked on the sink, while her daughter, her pride and joy, sobbed in her room. There seemed to be no answer, no way to right things.

Nancy squared her shoulders and tackled the dishes. There would be a way! Thinking it over, the suggestion of an abortion made more sense. Why should Sallie go away to have a baby only to give it up? There was no way to live down an illegitimate child in the family. And as for marrying Cam — as Frank seemed to think she should — Well, Sallie had a future! College and a good marriage when she was ready.

Nancy scoured the frying pan, scrubbing vigorously. Why should her Sallie pay for a mistake for which they all had been responsible? Yes! They all had dreamed of matrimony, had let Cam and Sallie be alone too much. They had been as ignorant as Sallie, and there was no need to force the full burden on Sallie. She would arrange an abortion, she would make sure Sallie had learned her lesson, and then she would give her a second chance.

Nancy finished wiping the counters. She glanced at the clock. It was 8:30. Frank was late for work. She would call and say he was sick, give him some time. She felt better now that she had a plan. About that, for different reasons, Cam had been right. Cam probably couldn't accept responsibility for his part in it, but Nancy was out to save her daughter, her reason for struggling all these years.

At all costs she would do it. Neither Frank nor Sallie's misguided desire to bring an unwanted child into an already overcrowded world would prevent her. Sallie must be made to see that her life was most important now. If she could salvage that, then someday she could give some other baby a good home.

Nancy made the phone call to the office. Then she went down the hall to Sallie's room.

7

The next days were hard for them all. Frank had wandered back before lunch, seemingly having forgotten it was a work day. He was strangely quiet as if he had gone off into some private dream world. He didn't threaten to call the Harrises again and Sallie heard him and her mother arguing continually.

Nancy had come to Sallie's room and tried to point out the advisability of an abortion. At first, Sallie had been horrified at her mother's taking the idea seriously. She had sat in the little pink-flowered armchair in a state of shock. That her mother could so blithely advocate the ending of a life — or at least an almost-life!

Sallie had always been against abortion in any debate at school. She had led a discussion in sociology, taking the part of the unborn child.

Now her mother stood resolutely at the door, looking calm and serene as usual, painting a glowing picture of abortion. Sallie had always thought her mother an essentially sensitive person to whom the thought of any kind of destruction would be abhorrent. But Sallie was unaware of the depth of her mother's desire to make everything "normal" again.

After that first interview, which hadn't been an interview at all, but rather a presentation which Sallie resisted in silence, Sallie found her mind drifting along the direction toward which her mother had pointed. When Frank came home at night, she heard the two of them — her mother patiently, endlessly, pleading for him to see it her way, and her father loudly, incoherently refusing to listen. To Sallie, the whole thing seemed a useless waste of discussion. If she went quietly away — if only she had somewhere to go! —

46

she would have the baby, and by that time she'd have decided whether or not to keep it.

As her parents argued, Frank alternately slamming out of the house and slamming in again, Sallie tried to think of a way to get away. She would need money and a place to go. She had no money of her own, and her parents would never agree to help her in that course. Perhaps Cam had some money. As much as she hated the thought, she could call him and ask.

But when Sallie sneaked into her parents' bedroom and used the extension there, Cam's mother reported that Cam was working. Of course he was! Sallie cut off Mrs. Harris' questions as to why she hadn't been around lately and hung up.

That day her father came to her room — it had become a hideout for Sallie. He looked sadder than she'd ever seen him. His shoulders drooped in his business suit, his sparse hair was mussed, he spoke in a flat, dead voice that pierced Sallie's heart.

"Your mother says you should have an abortion," he said sitting on her bed, hands hanging between his knees, loosely clasped.

"I know."

Frank was sick of arguing. He could never win with Nancy, simply because she outlasted him. In the end he always gave in to her because he couldn't be right long enough. And now he wasn't sure he was right. Deep inside, he really didn't want the kind of marriage he knew it would be for Sallie. Deep down, he couldn't face such a grim end to all his dreams for Sallie. Nancy's "second chance" had sunk in, but what a way for a second chance!

"What do you think?" he asked.

"I don't want one."

Frank was becoming exasperated, "You don't want to marry him either! What *do* you want?"

Now was the time, Sallie thought. Ask him for money, now!

"Daddy! You want me to be decent. You can't think an abortion is decent. You must know that marrying Cam — even if he would, which he wouldn't — would be worse. Daddy, please! Give me some money, help me go away and have the baby!"

The thought of Sallie swelling, becoming fat with Cam's baby was too much for Frank. Yes, he had wanted her to be decent, to always choose the right path. But where had it gotten him? Nowhere! He saw now that marriage to such a boy who would kill his own child was impossible, and yet . . . Frank's stomach turned at the thought of a part of Cam being carried, in suffering, and at last agonizingly delivered, by his Sallie. Her purity had been besmirched enough!

"I won't help you do that, Sallie," he said quietly. "You don't know what hell the next months would be for us all! And in the end, you'd have to give away a baby who was part of you."

"Daddy, mom's made you come around to her way, hasn't she?"
Sallie felt sick. No one cared about the baby.

"No! Don't look at me like that, Sallie! I hate the thought of your
lying on a table while someone takes a life. But I hate even worse to see your
young life ruined by a folly you regret!"

Sallie swallowed bile; it seemed her stomach was always rebelling, sending up little spurts. She remembered how she had thought — was it
just last week? — that she would protect herself first from now on. She had
meant it in regard to boys — if she got involved, she'd be careful. But now, she
realized there was more to it than that. Secretly she had known all along that she
hadn't really wanted that kind of a relationship, a gradual disintegration of all
standards. She thought with horror of the things she had done with Cam, all for
fear of losing him. No, next time there would be no fear of losing, for it had
driven her beyond the limits of what she could stand. And the disgust, the
self-hate, had been bad enough even if there weren't a baby.

Sallie looked at her father. Frank sat on the bed desperately trying
to make some sense out of a senseless situation.

"You think I've learned my lesson, daddy, don't you? That
maybe, just this once, I should be given a reprieve, a new start, and that I
wouldn't be so foolish again?"

"I would hope you'd never let a boy near you in that way again,"
Frank said bitterly. "And yes, daughter. Just this once. I can see your mother is
thinking about you. To erase this mistake, to give you a clean slate." Frank
stood up. There was no easy way! But maybe this way would put things right
again. "Sallie, think about it. It makes me sick to tell you that! But I can't stand
your whole life being changed for this. I guess that's why I came in. No matter
how much I wish this hadn't happened, it did! And the best thing to do is to right
it, quickly."

Sallie remained in her chair as her father walked out quietly. There
were no more arguments to be heard now, just a funereal silence, as if they
already mourned the death of a child.

Sallie was defeated. She was too much like her father. She
couldn't hold out long enough. The same weak link that betrayed her with Cam
snapped again now. Perhaps after all, the best thing to do was to "erase" this
mistake. Then she could start over, sadder but wiser.

Once the decision was made, Nancy sprang into action. She had
heard some of her friends discussing a certain doctor of good reputation who
could arrange everything. Apparently, all she had to do was call him.

When she reached the doctor and mentioned her daughter's problem, he was immediately sympathetic. They set up an appointment for an
interview with Sallie in the next few days. He said that, with luck, they could
have the whole thing done within a week. There! All the worry would be over in
a week.

Now that the wheels were in motion, Sallie somehow felt the responsibility was no longer hers. After the days and nights of torment, it was a great relief to have the whole thing out of her hands. The shock had been great, but like most shocks once assimilated, her mind soon covered its existence. Even as the fetus grew within her, Sallie adjusted her mental outlook to the day all would be well again. She would go away to school. There would be no long-drawn-out torture. She was free!

And now Cam was a less hateful thought. Oh, there was no doubt he had misled her! But she had been in a state of cynical rage about him, unable to see any good in the whole event. Now she could see that, painful though it had been, she had experienced first love with him, and from this experience, she could glean some guidelines for future reference. For she saw that someday there would be another boy who would be important to her. If nothing else, she had seen the misery brought on by misguided sex.

Sallie went back to work at the bank. She worked in bookkeeping, and enjoyed the pleasant hours of chit-chat with the other girls. Mornings she shopped or cleaned with her mother, their old easy relationship restored, but with a new understanding. Sundays she taught Sunday school with another graduate. As she led the song, "If You're Happy and You Know It," she could join in with enthusiasm. The little faces of the kindergarteners shown with excitement at her stories read from the Children's Bible. Once again, Sallie felt in control. God must be smiling on her!

The day came and went for the interview with the doctor. Everything was proceeding smoothly. He would take her into City Hospital and release her the same day. If anyone saw her there, she was in for tests not uncommon for girls her age. There was nothing to fear — it would all be over in a few minutes.

Nevertheless, Nancy waited anxiously while Sallie was in the operating room. There were occasional hazards. Frank stayed home from work and found himself torn with guilt. Of them all, perhaps he felt it the most. He was sickened by the whole mess, and the removal of the baby only added to the sickness. He was nervous, unable to sit in his chair, yet he refused to go to the hospital. His sense of decency was outraged, but he simply had to accept it!

At last he mowed his already manicured lawn, finding some relief in physical exertion.

It was over quickly. Nancy went to see Sallie in her room again, lying pale and quiet on the hospital bed. She looked so innocent lying there, with her pale hair tumbled all about. It was as if the whole thing had been a dream, a terrible nightmare.

"Hello, darling," Nancy whispered. "How do you feel?"

"A little tired."

"Oh, well, it's been a great strain."

"Yes." Sallie turned her head to the wall. Her mother looked so pleased. Somehow, it seemed unreal.

"You must put the whole thing out of your mind, dear," Nancy was saying. "Forget that it ever happened."

"Yes." Sallie remembered the feel of Cam's hands on her, the sweetness of it. With a stirring of the old panic she thought. *Never again! I mustn't be carried away again!*

"You'll be home in a few hours. They just want to make sure your bleeding's under control." Nancy patted Sallie's hand. "I'll wait right here with you."

Tears slid beneath Sallie's tightly shut eyelids.

"Could they tell what it was?"

Nancy was shocked.

"Don't think about that," she said. "It's over."

The tears kept coming, unbidden. It was so silly! She should be happy! It was over. Why this feeling of loss, this missing of that knowledge of life? It seemed that every time she began to feel in control, she was jarred unexpectedly. She hadn't planned on missing a bit of life so unwanted.

Nancy sat, holding Sallie's hand, watching the silent tears slide down her cheeks. For a moment, she felt a twinge of apprehension. She had asked no advice on this, but merely pushed on till the end. Now the end was here. Surely, these tears would dry up, and in a few days all would be normal. Nancy quieted her fears. She had to! She couldn't let them get out of hand, or she would be no good to Sallie. In a few days, all would be well.

At last Frank saw the car coming down the road. He slid the mower to a stop on the blacktop of the drive, turning it off. He wearily got out of the saddle, wiping away the perspiration on his forehead with the back of his sleeve. It was hot! The July sun bore down from a cloudless expanse of blue, baking the earth, melting the freshly patched road. As Nancy turned into the drive, he saw little splatters of tar along the sides of the car. He'd have to clean that with kerosene.

Nancy got out, starting around to help Sallie. Frank watched mutely as Sallie got out, moving a little gingerly.

"Hi, daddy," she said with a watery smile.

Frank forced a smile. He went and opened the door to the breeze-way, and helped Sallie in.

At last she was settled on the couch.

"She should take it easy for a while," Nancy said.

Frank thought of the baby no longer there, threatening to spoil their dreams. It had to be right!

"Everything will be fine now, honey," he said, smiling again.

"I know, daddy."

Sallie relaxed on the pillows and allowed her mother and father to wait on her. They treated her as some delicate piece of porcelain that had to be protected from abrupt handling. Her mind drifted, without thought. There was nothing left to think about. It was done, and in time she would forget. But never again would she allow any boy to get her into this situation.

After a few days, Sallie felt better physically, and her mind began to let go of the horror. No longer was Sallie so quick to condemn abortion, to speak up for the unborn. Just as the intimacy with Cam had gone against some deeply hidden belief, so now she allowed her mind to consciously cover any misgivings. Once she had spoken out for life, each life on its own merits. She couldn't do that now, for she had chosen her life above another. There was no way to reconcile her old advocacy with her actions. When the chips were down, she had chosen herself.

There had been a day when Sallie could put herself last, and even if that had led her astray, she could at least bear thinking about it. But now it seemed her actions had led from one thing to another, and there was no going back. She could no longer be innocent and giving. She had deliberately chosen to stifle her conscience; she had entered the world of grown-ups where life is manipulated to protect self first. Now, she caught a glimmer of why her mother had been so adamant, so forceful, of why her father's shoulders drooped. They had both learned long ago what Sallie was learning now. Sometimes you had to ignore what you knew to be right in your heart in order to get ahead. There were times when conscience had to be locked away, so that life could be directed in the way you wanted.

To Sallie this was a bitter cup, but not bitter enough to force her to her knees before God. Instead, she rallied, accepting it as truth, as part of maturing. She began to develop a philosophy that allowed conscience to speak when convenient, that let her teach Sunday school, that kept her highly thought of by all who knew her. And when conscience threatened her security, threatened to expose a fault, or made a difficult choice seem right, she clamped her mind's door shut on it. The high ideals of Bill Dudley seemed irrelevant, and at last Sallie could see why her parents preferred Rev. Crumm. The brand of Christianity he dispensed was easy to put aside when necessary. And the more Sallie saw of life, the more she saw the need to let nothing interfere with the ends you sought. After all, by maintaining your good position, by not allowing a few mistakes to color what others thought of you, you could, when you reached your goal, do a lot of good.

Sallie's faith had always been an easy, accepted thing, not a thing to test her life by. Rather, by carefully keeping her life proper on the surface, she felt she would be a good example to all.

Of course, these past months had been eye-openers, and she knew caution was the thing to have. But, if you did get caught short, well, fix it up! What people didn't know wouldn't hurt them.

Sallie's concept of God fell short of someday being held to account. That was foolishness! So she hid a few things! Didn't everyone? Oh, sure, she guessed Jesus must have been fairly honest. But Sallie couldn't really believe God expected them to be like Him. It was better to act honest, to be honest when you could, but always to keep up appearances. Then, when and if they ever got to heaven, she would surely not be alone in having to own up to some subterfuge.

So Sallie covered the spot in her heart that ached for the child, and considered no possibility of having made another mistake. As the summer drifted on, drawing to a close, as college approached, as she spent hours in fun with Cara and on dates, she soon forgot those few days of questioning. She had all of life before her now! And it was going to be good!

8 Freshman orientation at Pleasant Valley College began one week before classes got under way. Sallie and her parents arrived on a Sunday afternoon in mid-September. They had risen early to make the six-hour drive to the small school in a neighboring state.

It was one of those glorious mornings in September, crisp, cool, and brilliantly sunny. As they left Hilltop Acres, their car shiny and loaded down with suitcases and garment bags, the sun glowed redly on the eastern horizon. As they wound through the hills and valleys of their midwestern state, the early dew sparkled, giving the whole landscape an appearance of freshness.

They were a subdued family. Sallie rode between Nancy and Frank, feeling rather lonesome already. Occasionally, Nancy blew her nose and remarked on her irritating late-summer cold. Frank whistled tonelessly until Nancy said, "Frank, please!" Then he sat silent, guiding the car through the deepening valleys. Every so often he told Nancy to stick her head out the window, since the back seat was packed so full he couldn't use the rear view mirror.

It was after two when they meandered around hairpin curves down into the last valley. From their vantage point they could see the college, a cluster of early American, early Depression, and striking modern buildings sprawled comfortably in the valley. A lazy-looking river wound through the grassy countryside, dividing the college from the town. The town was really too small to warrant that name; it was more of a waystop, consisting of a gas station, decrepit with age, an old-fashioned general store, a post-office-grocery-café called Joe's Come and Get It, and about a dozen houses, some of which were farms.

Sallie was enthralled with the view, even though by now the

promise of the red sun was fulfilled in a miserable drizzle. They had been here during the drab winter months to make the financial arrangements, but the appearance of the valley was completely changed now. The grass was startlingly green and abundant. For a city girl, the multitude of trees and bushes and annual flowers were a sight to behold. And now the river was still shallow from summer, displaying boulders and sandbars that invited habitation. On a sunny day it would be heaven!

They knew where Sallie's dorm was. They had seen it before. Frank eased the car to a stop in the parking area already swarming with girls and their parents. In spite of the rain, they were all running about, lugging piles of clothes and boxes containing items necessary for living away from home.

As Frank got out and stretched his cramped muscles, he was struck by the din.

"Where's my iron, ma?" one tall, homely girl shouted, throwing boxes and suitcases out onto the wet pavement.

"Sam, can't you be patient?" an equally tall, homely woman returned crossly.

Sallie looked around. She felt lost and afraid for a moment. Then the contagion of the havoc began to catch on. Before long she and her mother were shouting, too, as they ordered her father about.

They found her room on the second floor, threading their way through the crowded hallway, and tripping over other coeds' screaming little sisters and brothers. On the way up the stairs, loaded down with shoe boxes, one youngster collided with Frank, strewing lids, shoes, and papers all over the landing. Frank caught himself in time, while the child whizzed on down the stairs without a word.

Sallie's room was packed with assorted shapes and sizes of people. On one bed sat an old couple, fat and jolly-faced, obviously her roommate's grandparents. On the desk, dancing and jumping, were two identical seven-year-old girls with big, mischief-filled eyes, and long brown ringlets. In a corner, apparently trying to melt into the woodwork was a boy of about fourteen, standing like a sane man desperately holding out in a world gone mad.

As Sallie came in, closely followed by her mother, a short chubby girl with short brown curls fell off the chair she had been standing on to reach the top shelf of the closet. She landed in a heap at Sallie's feet.

"Hi," the girl said, with an engagingly impish grin.

Sallie suddenly knew she was going to like this girl very much.

"Hi," she returned.

The girl got up, smoothing her too-short, too-tight skirt over her too-big hips.

"I told mom I'd get one like you." The girl looked at Sallie's slim, cool blonde beauty and made a long face. "Hey, mom," she yelled. "Get a load of this!"

Miraculously, a short, incredibly round woman appeared from the depths of the closet. She turned around to greet Sallie.

"The roommate, eh?" she said and introductions were made all around.

Sallie's roommate's name was Clara Hoffmeyer. She had twin sisters, two older brothers married with children, the fourteen-year-old brother, the grandparents on the bed, the fat mother, and a tall, skinny, bald father, whose head nodded continuously. Sallie felt overwhelmed by family. Coming from such a small, quiet home, this large, rowdy group was quite a change.

At last Sallie's father struggled in with her trunk.

"That's it," he puffed.

Mr. Hoffmeyer sat down on the bed, which by now was sagging precariously.

"They sure got to have their junk," he said, nodding his head as if agreeing with this profundity.

Mrs. Hoffmeyer backed out of the closet, crushing her son against the wall.

"I don't think there's any more room in here" she shouted, pointing at the closet.

"No need to shout, mom," Clara yelled.

"You kids get off that desk!" Mrs. Hoffmeyer roared.

The twins grinned, and went on dancing.

Mr. Hoffmeyer stood up and nodded toward the twins. "They sure got their energy," he said, picking one up in each arm.

Nancy and Frank stood off to the side quietly watching. There was no sense in trying to unpack now.

Finally Mrs. Hoffmeyer declared Clara settled and maneuvered her bulk out of the room.

"Time to eat!" she shouted.

"See you later," Clara grinned at Sallie, as the clan left.

The twins, feet kicking, were carried out by their father who nodded to each Victor on the way out. The grandparents smiled jovially and shook Frank's hand. The brother peeled himself off the wall and slunk out at the rear, not looking at anyone.

When they had gone, the room was strangely silent, as if life had gone out with them. Quietly, Sallie and her mother unpacked her cases and bags, squeezing in where no room was left, until at last they sank down on Sallie's bed exhausted, looking at the cement-block walls painted dull green.

"Well," Frank said. "Guess we could eat, too."

Nancy looked with longing at the double-sided desk, the plain bureaus, the uncurtained window that viewed the river. Oh, how lucky Sallie was!

They ate at a little inn in the next town, which was crowded with parents and college-age offspring. Some students sat stoically enduring their mothers' last bits of advice, while others were silent and scared-looking, listening to the conversations at nearby tables.

Finally, Nancy and Frank left Sallie at her dorm in the early evening and began the long drive home.

Sallie sat in the quiet room, fighting back the tears, staring at the far-off hills, now drying in the late evening sun. It seemed that her whole past was over, all the years of closeness and love with her parents.

Soon Clara came in, her eyes swollen from crying.

"Well, the lovable monsters are gone," she sobbed.

The two girls held each other, mourned their lost childhood, and forged a friendship. They went to bed early, not bothering to venture out of their room.that night. They hugged the past to them. Tomorrow was time enough to begin.

And begin they did. Sallie was eighteen that week (she had celebrated early with her parents) and the girls on her floor soon found out.

"We've got a baby among us!" Clara yelled up and down the halls. "A seventeen-year-old, no less."

There were a few others still seventeen, but most of the girls were eighteen or nineteen by now. So they teased and arranged for a cake from the kitchen. It was an opportunity to break the ice, a common interest to be shared when all things were strange.

There were fifty girls on that floor and by the end of the first week they knew at least each other's first names. Days were filled with registering, counseling sessions, book-buying, and meetings. At night they showered in the large communal bathroom and dressed in studiedly casual clothes. There was something every night — mixers, dances, teas. The girls were kept so busy there was little time left for homesickness.

To Sallie's surprise, she wasn't homesick anyway. She was having the time of her life! She and Clara became inseparable, going everywhere together, pulling pranks on the other girls. During the first week, the girls roamed the campus in the September sun, exploring the hills and valleys, walking shady trails in the woods. Little cliques formed, dissolved, and re-formed. Sallie was asked for dates by the freshman boys, and even Clara, chubby and plain, but brimful with good-natured wit, had some invitations. It was a hectic time, filled with anticipation for the months and years ahead.

Sallie wrote home to Cara, who was getting married at Christmas, about all her activities, filling pages and pages with descriptions of the dormitory, the campus, and the feeling of peace and hope. Seldom did she think of those dark days last summer. All was new and bright now, the promised second chance seemingly, amazingly, fulfilled.

Sallie and Clara got a ride to the nearby town where the old inn was, and several nice stores. There were some upperclassmen on campus as guides and counselors, and one of these took them. A carload of chattering girls, they were deposited in front of one of the stores and told to be ready in an hour.

Clara found some curtains for their window with large melons, oranges, and bananas on them, which Sallie thought were horrible. Sallie bought some fluffy rugs to make comfortable flopping spots on the floor. They each got a dresser lamp and some throw pillows for their beds.

When they got back to their room and arranged their purchases, the dull green seemed to lose some of its dullness. Even Clara's curtains, ugly and loud though they were, gave a bright, warm touch reflective of Clara's cheerful personality. They were pleased with their joint efforts.

One day the two girls went to the kitchen and packed a picnic. It was a hot, dry September day, with no breeze. They put on their oldest cut-offs and tank tops and waded down the shallow river bed. Later in winter and spring the river would be deep and swift-flowing, but now it was low from heat and dryness.

The water felt delightfully cool on their hot feet, and every so often they stopped and cooled their perspiring faces, each taking a turn holding the lunch. They wandered far down the river, oblivious of time, feeling the sun and the water, and breathing the clear, fresh air.

They ate on a grassy bank, dangling their ankles in the water, talking about nothing and everything. After they had eaten, they lay back, side by side, listening to the gurgle of the water and soaking up the sun.

They got home late. By now the old dormitory was home, already loved and familiar. In a couple days classes would begin, and the girls would remember with longing the lazy happiness of that day. But now the two friends climbed the stairs, tired from a day in the open, enjoying only the moment. They showered and got into their pajamas and sat up talking far into the night. Other girls came in and out, sharing jokes and borrowing curlers and nail polish.

The whole week passed in a blur of new faces, new scenes, new things to learn. Sallie went with her dates to mixers and dances, but talked and danced with so many it was hard to remember who she had come with.

At last Sunday evening came. The campus was full now; it had been in tumult all day as the upperclassmen returned in full force. Chapel was packed with the eager students, glad to be there after a summer away. The choir sang for the first time, filling the high-arched ceiling with glorious sound.

Sallie was happy. She could hardly wait for her classes the next day. She felt an odd excitement when she saw the juniors and seniors, so mature-looking and sure of themselves. This was all hers! She was part of it! One day she would stand in a group of seniors and be envied by freshmen.

That first week for Nancy and Frank was far from happy. Nancy had cried all the way home, and even Frank had been moved to tears when he went into Sallie's empty room, now neat and lifeless. The two parents sat and talked until dawn, something they hadn't done for years. They remembered Sallie as a baby, sweet-tempered and so good! They laughed and cried over Sallie the toddler, who had painted their little white bungalow in great swaths of red paint (the paint can had been left open in the garage). They tenderly recalled Sallie's first years of school, her years of toothless grins and scabby knees. Conscientiously and mercifully, they skipped the past six months and stuck to the years and years of happy, nostalgic memories.

When morning came, Frank went off to work, exhausted but feeling closer to Nancy than he could remember. Nancy cleaned and washed and at last lay down on the bed and slept fitfully. Her mind was drugged with fatigue, but still she thought constantly, erratically of Sallie. In the half-world of dozing, her tired brain spun out the story of Sallie's life, reeling pictures in an unrelated jumble.

That night Nancy and Frank went out to dinner, unable to face the empty chair at the table. Now that their daughter was gone, off to that college where she would grow away from them, they wondered if all the years of loving and giving had been worth it. Now it seemed, they were the ones left with nothing more to do. All the sacrifice, planning, and desperate maneuvering had left them alone. Now they were just two, and a rather strange two, with little in common at that. The common bond, the transcending love of their child, began to dissolve that night, leaving them lonely and uncertain toward each other. The next months would be painful for Nancy and Frank, a painful search for themselves as a couple rather than a family.

Nancy was ill-prepared for such a search. She had always been the one who ran things, kept the house going, kept the meals interesting, and it was mostly for Sallie. It had all revolved around Sallie. Sallie liked meat loaf with bacon strips on top, Sallie liked homemade noodles, Sallie liked fluffy towels and crisp, outdoor-hung sheets. For Nancy, Sallie's exodus to college brought about total change, whereas Frank still spent the better part of his day at work. She had long ago switched her first allegiance to Sallie, leaving Frank a poor second. It seemed that now her life was without purpose, that driving purpose that had made her override all else in her effort to maintain her plan for her daughter's life. She was like a robot that someone had forgotten to program — aimless, empty, and useless.

Frank's feeling of closeness to Nancy soon diminished and their relationship became even less than it had been before. In the beginning, those first few aching days had caused them to talk and give comfort to each other, and he had felt a stirring of hope. But soon, as Nancy's melancholy grew deeper, as her sense of uselessness increased, Frank was cut off again. The little glimmer of hope went out, leaving a bigger heap of ashes in his heart. Now at night when he came home, Nancy put an unimaginative dinner before him and sat dully through the meal. It was as if he didn't exist. Frank, sensitive as always, was deeply hurt by the restatement of the already digested fact: He meant nothing to Nancy in comparison to Sallie. Frank retreated further into his job, accepted the chairmanship of the Christian Outreach committee at church, and avoided any more contact than absolutely necessary with Nancy.

This was the pattern of their days after Sallie was gone. More and more silence prevailed in an already silent house. Less and less communication took place between an already restrained couple. Each day brought more inwardness, more brooding. Nancy spent less time in outside activities, she withdrew from her circle at church, she shopped only when she absolutely had to, she spent more time sitting and knitting sweaters and hats and scarves for Sallie. Frank left earlier in the mornings, often eating breakfast out. At night he either went to a meeting or immersed himself in a book. Weekends brought dead coexistence, as each followed his own interests. For Frank, this meant he worked outside when he could or puttered about the garage. For Nancy, this meant nothing much, increasingly nothing held her interest for long. She even forgot meals sometimes, and Frank would go out and get them a sandwich. It was a dreadful way to live and couldn't go on forever. Something would have to give.

At times Frank raged at Nancy, desperately trying to arouse her old managing spirit, but to no avail. Finally, he gave up, waiting for something to happen. Maybe she would come out of it on her own.

Nancy lived for Sallie's letters and read them over and over. Often she forgot to tell Frank they had even come. He would ask and then she would vaguely tell him where she had put the most recent one. Nancy's mind was unable to function clearly, and she cried for no reason, sometimes for days at a time. It was not unusual for Frank to come home and find her lying on the couch, tears running down her cheeks, moist eyes staring at the ceiling. When a friend called, her answers were often unrelated to the question, bringing some friends to the house to check on her. After a dull visit, where the friends did all the talking, they went away shaking their heads.

Some of the women understood. They had already fought the battle of the empty nest themselves. They made sad faces and explained, "Nancy is just heartbroken over Sallie leaving home." "Yes," another said, "but you get over it in time. We'll just visit her and make her go out every so often." And they did, but Nancy was unaffected inside. In fact, she grew worse, for she soon learned that word spoken now and then, or a smile however false, would make her friends think she was coming along and they would hurry about their own business. Then she was left to her brooding, which was becoming more and more her real world. Her forays into reality became the rare practice she became good at, deceiving them all into thinking she was getting over the shock of Sallie's leaving for college. What her friends didn't know was that she hid more than that behind her facade. Only Frank and Sallie and a doctor knew there was more to hide. Of course, Cam must have figured out by now that something had happened, either Sallie hadn't been pregnant or something, but only they four knew that a baby was dead to preserve Sallie's future.

In Nancy's mind, twisted by the double shock of Sallie's pregnancy and subsequent abortion and the sudden departure of her daughter for school, she began to rationalize in an odd way. If the baby had been born, then Sallie would have had to put off college, maybe passing it up altogether. This would have kept Sallie home longer. Nancy had squashed any guilt feelings in July about the baby, but now, since Sallie was gone, they came back to haunt her. She was caught in a trap of her own making — she had so wanted to preserve the status quo before Sallie left she had taken a move that now could have prevented her all this agony. In her weakened state, perpetuated by her meager, irregular meals, she began to feel a burning guilt about the dead child, brought on more by wishing Sallie were home than any real concern for the baby.

Nancy had forged onward, saving her daughter's reputation, subduing all opposition in her drive to get Sallie to college. Now that drive had brought her misery, a confused mind, loss of goals, and, worst, a bitter guilt that, had she been her usual self, she would never have acknowledged.

That's why Nancy took the first drink while Frank was at work. It seemed to help. As the liquor burned down her throat, bringing a more pleasant fog than the one she was already in, she felt a peace, a forgetting. Her constant brooding led her more and more often to the kitchen cupboard where the whiskey was. Just for awhile, she needed peace. When she got used to things, she wouldn't keep it up. She would use the liquor to help her over a difficult time. Later, when she felt better, she wouldn't want it.

By the end of the first week Nancy and Frank had sunk into themselves. By the end of the first month, Nancy had begun to run from herself, to run to the comfort of liquor. Never having been a drinker — only at social functions — she hadn't realized how pleasant the euphoria of alcohol was. Her only problem was maintaining it. Increasingly, the fire of release required more fuel.

9 Pleasant Valley College was proving to be a pleasant place for Sallie. After the start of classes, Sallie became busier than she had ever been in her life. Her days were filled with classes, studying, library research, and inpromptu gatherings in the canteen. Her nights were filled with more study, dates, and football games, after which the girls would return to the dorm flushed with the crispness of the fall evenings and laughing with delight. Had Sallie been aware of things at home, she probably would have been concerned and subdued her enjoyment, but the letters she received were filled with cheerful trivia, carefully calculated to mask the real situation.

So Sallie was left free. Yes, free at last! She was so grateful to be a part of all this, to have been "saved" from judgment. And now she was older and much wiser. She was less self-conscious than she had been in high school, freer with her peers. But, at the same time, the wariness that came from her experience with Cam had grown into a strong guideline. It was true her motivation lay in self-preservation, but this strong sense of self-protection gave her a sort of reckless freedom. She could enjoy the fun and excitement of college, wrapping the boys around her finger and discarding them when they began to get serious. And they did get serious, some with high ideals of purity in connection with the fragility of her appearance, a few like Cam who were easy to scent out now, but most were in the large pool of mixed emotions that make up a boy in the throes of infatuation.

Sallie was ruthless. Once she had cared intensely for another and it had brought her trouble. Now she was free, with only herself to watch out for. She grabbed the adulation and attention, and dropped her admirers cold when she tired of the game.

She and Clara were the life of many parties on campus. Clara was the clown with a sharp, cutting sense of humor, yet saved by a genuine interest in those she teased. One seemed to sense a basic kindness in Clara. Sallie, on the other hand, was the focal point upon which the party revolved. Her cool, almost conceited, attitude of disinterest, of any real involvement, caused girls and boys alike to seek her favor. She could kill or raise a party to hilarity with the subtle influence of her attitude.

Clara had one boyfriend, then another. One at a time. Sallie, however, dated a string of freshmen and upperclassmen simultaneously. She began to get a reputation as hard-to-get, and therefore she was intriguing. She spent time with many boys, purposefully keeping the relationships light and undemanding. This was a careful, selfish method of getting along. But, after all, her past was still barely healed.

By mid-October, while Nancy was becoming infatuated with the bottle, Sallie was the talk of Pleasant Valley. She had five invitations to the

60

Homecoming dance; she argued logically and coolly in class, impressing the teachers with her knowledge and the students with her barely disguised disdain. In a word, she was a snob. And like so many snobs with the combination of looks, clothes, and manner, she swept the others off their feet.

Sallie never broke any rules. She went to chapel the required three days a week, she was in bed on time, she signed in and out for herself. Sallie was having enough fun within the structure. There was no need to risk her chances by flaunting the rules.

She and Clara and the other girls had long conversations about sex and marriage, and what Sallie said carried authority. If she didn't speak from personal experience, her manner bespoke knowledge, and many of the girls were still inexperienced. They developed a group philosophy, within which each girl lived, measuring her previous standards by the group's. They discussed all aspects of morality, with little remembrance of home training, at least consciously. Actually, they were extremely prudish, and when one brought a clipping from the state university paper advertising abortions, they were shocked. And when one in an excess of intimacy divulged that she had smoked marijuana, they were shocked. For these were girls from close homes, with careful upbringings. No matter how sophisticated they acted around each other, privately they were too glassed in not to be shocked by the actions of others their age.

Sallie and Clara had two classes together that year, French and English. They strolled across the campus on sunny days, relishing their freedom. They giggled and ran full speed on rainy days, which were increasing in number as fall deepened, getting soaked and knowing that their mothers would perish if they could see them sitting through hours of class in dripping jeans and shirts. It was a glorious chance at freedom for both girls — Sallie from the close-knit concern of her small family, Clara from the almost overpowering rowdiness of her large one.

As the leaves on the trees that carpeted the hills took on the aspect of varigated yarn, the freshmen began to feel that Pleasant Valley was their real home. They lived in a free and warm closeness that required no lasting commitment. They became members of the special, irrelevant section of society known as college students. Whether they were young radicals or conservative replicas of their parents, they were insulated, set apart, removed from the world. The river was their private canoeing spot, the hills their own hiking area, the college buildings their special home. Isolated from the rest of society, the college students developed their own values and their own system.

Sallie had long had trouble recognizing reality, confusing dreams with truth. College was for her the epitome of make-believe. Here in the peace of the country valley, she was a part of a large conspiracy to hold back the world. Even professors, away from the bustle of earning a living in the open society, perpetuated the idea that this life was the real life, that the calm, quiet, and largely irresponsible life was true living. Supported by their parents, these students of the small college, falsely sophisticated, set up their own society, their own guides and values. It was no wonder so many of them were ill-equipped four years later to face the onslaught of an unprotecting, heedless world. But now they were safe and secure, able to differentiate between good and bad, true and untrue, within their own little haven.

Actually, it was a good thing Sallie met Harvey Plimpton that first fall. For her, at least, he was a balance wheel. He was one of those steady, far-seeing types, a junior, unimpressed by college life. He was a great irritation to Sallie, a fly in the ointment, always pointing out with quiet, undeniable rightness the frivolity of it all. And he wouldn't let her alone; even though she tried her most cutting techniques, he was always back for more. It was unnerving. And worse, he was studying to be a missionary, a teacher in some far-off place.

Appropriately, Sallie met Harvey at chapel, rushing to get a seat before the bell caught her late. She stepped on Harvey's big foot and looked up into the skinny, homely, morosely humorous face and was speechless. She had never seen him before, and he wore an expression of such amusement — at her, it seemed! — that she bit off her instinctive, "I'm sorry."

"If you'll get off my foot, I'll let you by," he said.

Sallie squeezed by and sat down. Harvey folded his long legs like a collapsible chair and sat next to her.

"I've heard of you," he whispered while the bell rang, and then was silent, apparently involved in the short service, bellowing out the hymn in a bass voice.

Sallie was flustered from being late and embarrassed for looking foolish. She said nothing to Harvey that day, except "Excuse me" on the way out. She preferred to put him out of her mind.

One fine afternoon in late October, Sallie and Clara sat under a tree on the commons. The commons ran between the girls' and the boys' dormitories. It was grassy and shady, a good place to meet new friends. The girls sat enjoying the unusually warm sun, probably one of the last of such days. They leaned against the tree trunk, reading their English literature assignment.

"I'm bored," Clara said at last, wrinkling her nose.

"Yeah, me, too," Sallie answered. "It's no day for studying."

"I wish we could get into town."

"I sure could use some ice cream."

"Oh well," Clara slid down on her stomach. Then she rolled over on her side, propping her head on her hand.

"It's nice here, isn't it?" she asked, suddenly serious.

"You bet it is," Sallie agreed, looking at the colorful hillsides. "I had no idea I'd like it so much. I thought it would be awful."

"You, too? Boy, I was ready to stay home, I'll tell ya."

"It was scary those first few weeks."

"Yeah, we're lucky. Some girls got crummy roommates."

The girls laughed, thinking of some of the girls they could have been rooming with.

Just then an abnormally deep voice interrupted their laughter.

"You're not getting much studying done."

Sallie looked up with distaste. Harvey Plimpton stood there, gawking over them.

"Oh, go away, Harvey." Sallie couldn't seem to avoid this creep. Ever since they had met so ill-fatedly, he had a way of popping up. He had been consistently friendly, introducing himself politely, always trying to make friends with Sallie.

As usual, her cutting remark rolled off him without effect.

"Just wondering if I could help," he said.

"Go teach somebody else," Sallie giggled under her breath.

"Hey!" Clara shouted. "Hey, Harvey, you got a car?"

"Nope."

"Got a friend with one?" Clara persisted.

"Sure."

"Better yet!" Clara got lazily to her feet. "How about some ice cream in town?"

Sallie squashed her dislike for Harvey. "Hey, that sounds great!" she exclaimed.

Harvey stood uncertainly. "Guess I could see if he's busy."

"Sure you can, Harv," Clara yelled.

He wasn't busy. It turned out Clara knew him, so she sat in the front seat with him. At last Harvey said in a dry voice, "I guess you don't like me."

Sallie turned her head away from the window where she'd been watching the scenery. What a strange person this Harvey was!

"Whatever gave you that idea?"

Harvey ignored the sarcasm. "You're a nice girl, you know. You don't have to put on the little sophisticate act."

"I don't see that it concerns you."

"I'm worried about you."

Sallie stared in amazement. "You're what?"

"You're riding high, Miss Sallie, and you don't know how to ride very well."

"I don't see how you'd know — you don't ride at all!"

"I've watched. You've got the guys all jumping and you're playing it real cool. Won't be long before they're dropping you. I've seen it happen before. I don't want to see you hurt."

Sallie was furious. Underneath she thought she recognized a little wisdom there, something she suspected herself, but who was *he* to tell her?

"You really think you're smart, don't you?" she said. "A great big junior — a man, almost," she added cuttingly. "Well, you can just keep your mouth shut and leave me alone!"

Clara turned around. "Hey, Sal, keep calm, huh? Harv doesn't mean any harm."

Sallie squeezed into her corner of the car.

"Sorry," she said, feeling even angrier at having been tricked into a scene.

Harvey sat quietly, a dull flush on his homely face. He knows I can't stand him, Sallie thought, but yet he seems to be really concerned about me.

They rode on in silence, a damper on the gaiety of the excursion. They had ice cream at a drugstore and pretended that everything was fine.

On the way home, Sallie began feeling miserable. At last she couldn't stand it any longer.

"Look, Harvey," she said. "I appreciate your interest. I'm just not used to it. I'm sorry I got mad, okay?"

Harvey smiled, "Sure. Like I said, you're a nice girl if you'll cut the act. Some girls don't get hurt by it, but I don't think you're one."

Sallie fumed in silence. What act? So she was getting a rush. Maybe it would wear off. So she could enjoy it, couldn't she? Besides, Harvey Plimpton didn't know she had decided to put herself first in life.

"I can take care of myself," she said.

"That's when you're asking for trouble," Harvey said quietly.

Sallie remembered another time when she had been sure of herself. But she was naive then! Still, why was he so interested in her?

They got back in time for dinner in the dorms. By then Clara had a date with Tony, Harvey's friend.

"You know," Clara said as they washed up for dinner, "you're awful hard on Harvey. He's not as creepy as you think."

"Why?"

"Creeps don't have friends like Tony," Clara said, drying her hands.

"I know, but I just hate him!" Sallie brushed her hair into a halo. "He seems to expect something of me!"

"Well, he's right you know. You can't be queen-for-a-day forever. Maybe he's got it for you."

"Not him! He's concerned! He's worried! And I sure wouldn't pick *him* to get serious with."

"Well," Clara picked up her purse and started out of the bathroom for dinner, "I gotta say Tony's nice anyway."

Sallie felt a twinge of jealousy. Here she was pretty and popular being envious of her plump roommate! But Clara, under her wit, seemed to have a strong sense of direction, something her friend Cara had had, too. She didn't need the rush of lots of dates, the run of the chase. Maybe Clara trusted herself to get serious, but Sallie knew better. And with Harvey?

But it seemed that Harvey was determined to be a part of Sallie's life at Pleasant Valley. He'd run to catch up with her as she walked to and from classes, sometimes when she was alone and sometimes when she was not. It was embarrassing to have him seek her out of a group and soon, as she was afraid they would, the tongues began to wag.

"Harvey's got it bad for that little freshman."

"Yeah, he sure follows her around."

"I think she must like him, too. She's just the cool type."

Sallie was beginning to like Harvey in spite of herself. The thing she so detested about him was his knowing concern, as if he had been appointed her personal guardian angel. This frayed her nerves and at times made her angry with him, but she had a grudging respect for his ability to sort out the real from the false. He seemed to sense her problem in this area, and she suspected that was why he was so outspoken. And he was so unusual looking with his long, sad face, which completely rearranged itself when he smiled, and his tall, awkward build. He was no football hero, that's for sure, and Sallie felt safe with him. She didn't feel she had to be constantly on guard, so she began to trust him to feel that he was real friend, someone she could rely on. This was nice after all. She was so busy being popular that a real friend was a help. Of course, some of the dates started to slack off, and Harvey's inevitable presence may have been partly responsible. But also possible was that the rush *had* run its course.

Sallie accepted a date to the Homecoming dance with a burly football player. She was one of the few freshman girls with an upperclassman at the dance and she felt pleased with herself. Later she kept him in line and got through the evening with only a goodnight kiss. She felt she had finally learned how to handle boys.

The only sour spot in the evening was the uncomfortable encounter she had with Harvey. She had been sitting at the table waiting for her date to bring her something to drink. Harvey had been dancing with a girl nearly as tall and skinny as he was. Sallie recognized the girl as the same one who had yelled at her mother in the parking lot that first day. Harvey returned the girl to her group of friends and came over to Sallie.

"Care to dance?" he asked.

"I'm with someone," she replied.

"I know."

He waited, looking sadly at Sallie.

"Well, I better wait for him," she added lamely.

"Okay, mind if I sit a bit?"

Sallie felt uncomfortable.

"He'll be right back."

"There're four chairs, you know."

"Okay! So sit!"

Harvey folded himself into the chair.

"You're with a big hero, aren't you? Bet you're pleased with yourself!"

Sallie said nothing.

"I keep hoping you won't get taken in by all this," Harvey continued, waving his hand. "It's not real, you know. In four years all these kids will have forgotten what made them so sure of themselves."

Sallie thought, Here we go again. But she said, "I'm not taken in, Harvey, but what's the harm of making hay while the sun shines?"

"Plenty," Harvey said morosely, "you could be spending your time to more advantage."

"Oh? How's that?"

Harvey leaned across the table and talked rapidly as Sallie's date was approaching. "Someday you'll be on your own, like I am, and you'll see that the learning is most important while you're here — but it'll be too late. Then you'll understand what I mean. The discipline is better than the fun. Later you'll know."

Harvey stood up as Sallie's date returned.

"Hi, Marty," he said.

"Hi. Harv. Keeping Sallie company?"

"Just wanted to say hello. Thought she might dance with me."

"Guess she was waiting for me," Marty put Sallie's drink down. "Want to dance?"

As Sallie danced, watching Marty close his eyes and become absorbed by the beat, she kept trying to forget Harvey's long face. But always he was there, watching her sadly. Why can't he just have fun? she fumed inwardly, and let me enjoy myself, too!

Then she wondered what he had meant about being on his own. Didn't he have any family?

A few days later Sallie was sitting in the canteen, having a Coke. She was alone because Clara was at choir practice. She was going over her history notes when Harvey walked up.

"Hi," he said, "Mind if I join you?"

Sallie groaned inside. There was no use arguing. But secretly she was lonely and glad for the company.

"Sure," she said.

He sat down with his French fries and Coke.

"Dinner," he said.

"Don't you eat at the dorm?" She thought he couldn't possibly live on that.

"Nope." He munched a French fry.

"Why not?"

"I don't live there."

Sallie was dumbfounded.

"You don't?"

"Nope."

Sallie was silent for a while. Finally, she could remain quiet no longer.

"All right, where *do* you live?"

"Got a room over Joe's Come and Get It."

"Why not eat there?"

"Cheaper here. I eat there Sundays."

Sallie suddenly felt ashamed. "Well, you usually eat more than that, don't you?"

"Every other day." Harvey swallowed his last gulp of Coke. "Ah, good," he said.

Sallie was really intrigued now. "How do you pay for school?"

"I don't. Got a scholarship to be a missionary. Good field for teachers — especially if you believe in Jesus."

Ordinarily, Sallie's rather stiff religious background balked at just bandying Jesus' name around in public. But she was fascinated by Harvey now.

"You mean you really want to be a missionary?"

Harvey leaned back and regarded Sallie's earnest, surprised face with amused eyes.

"I guess you wouldn't understand, would you?"

Sallie flushed. She *was* a Christian, after all.

"I'm going to be a teacher, too," she said softly.

"I'm first a missionary, then a teacher. I'll go to the Philippines probably. They'll send me out there when I graduate."

"Who? Your folks?"

Harvey smiled broadly for a moment, redistributing his face.

"No, Miss Sallie." He sobered, again sad. "I was raised in an orphanage. Don't look so sympathetic. It was great. It was run by the mission group that's educating me now."

"You mean you never knew your parents?" Sallie felt like crying. She'd been so nasty!

"Not personally."

"Not personally?"

"They were killed by natives in South America."

Sallie was awe-struck. "You mean they were missionaries, too!"

"Runs in the family."

"But after they were killed!"

Harvey studied Sallie. She was so pretty, and so sweet underneath that armor, he thought. I wonder what she's running from? He sighed and stood up.

"Got to go back to work."

"You work, too?" Sallie was confused by his calm acceptance of his parents' deaths.

"I tutor."

"Oh."

"Take care, Sallie. Remember what I told you at the dance."

Sallie would have made a smart remark like "Yes, father," had she not been totally amazed at the things she had just heard. Instead she said, "I don't know what you meant. I *do* study hard."

Harvey sighed again, looking sadder than ever, "Someday, little girl, you'll see that there's more to learning than books and more to life than fun."

Sallie felt suddenly that she had to defend herself, make him see she wasn't that way. "Harvey, wait. In high school I only had one boyfriend. Now do you see?"

Harvey was surprised to hear that, with her looks and personality.

"You're putting me on."

"No, I was shy and scared. Then — then I . . . Something happened and I made up my mind to have fun like the other kids. Why don't you?"

"I told you. There's more to life than fun."

"Well, why can't I for awhile anyway? I can grow up soon enough. Besides everyone should have some fun."

"There are different ways to have fun."

"Yes, I know. I like to read, too."

Harvey smiled and started to go.

"Harvey, wait!" Sallie put her hand on his arm. "Why are you always worrying about me?"

Harvey looked at her upturned face, eager and unsophisticated. If only she were always this way, he thought. And then, if I told her I believed God had asked me to help her . . .

"Because you need somebody to," he said. He took her hand away and laid it on the table next to her other one.

"But why should you bother?"

"That's the way I am."

With that he went away, leaving Sallie with some strange new emotions. It seemed that no matter how she acted, he was interested in her. Now she was glad. Even her muddled head could see he was no ordinary young man. She had written him off as a creep, then as an irritating, but dependable, fixture. The more she saw of him, the less sure she was of herself and the more he intruded into her thoughts.

A missionary! She shuddered, thinking of his parents. Where did he get his courage?

10

The first snow began falling on October 30. Frank was sitting at his desk in his office, staring out the window, when he noticed the flakes drifting aimlessly. They were big fat flakes with defined shapes, melting the minute they hit the window pane.

Frank had been thinking. He was supposed to be finishing up the check on the day's transactions, but suddenly he was unable to concentrate any longer.

Nancy was becoming more of a problem every day. More and more she was in his thoughts, waking and sleeping. Oh, she had resumed some of her activities sporadically, and they had fallen into a quiet coexistence that was not unbearable for Frank. In fact, after his initial disappointment at having been rejected again, he had come to see that, for the first time in their married life, he was in the driver's seat. Nancy was too dazed and preoccupied to continue her strong control over the both of them. Now he was master of the house — at long last.

Yes, actually Frank felt to be more of a man, more in control than he could ever remember. But Nancy was definitely a problem.

Frank stood up from his desk and stretched. He was tired. He would finish in the morning. He went to his window and looked out over the landscape, bearing now a tinge of white. The traffic chugged along on the wet street carrying tired, homeward-bound people. The neon signs on the stores glowed dimly in the twilight, highlighting white patches of drifting flakes. Everywhere people hurried on foot, trying to get in out of the weather. One little girl in a shabby dress and no shoes stood on an apartment porch, face uptilted to catch the snow, until her mother yanked her inside. A newsboy wheeled down the sidewalk flinging papers and shouting, "Paper!" his head bent into the wind. It was a typical late fall night, with people going about their business as usual.

Frank shrugged and reached for his coat and hat. He put them on and cleared his desk of the financial papers, stuffing them into his drawer and

69

locking it. He left his office, went through the bank lobby, luxuriously carpeted and papered to give an impression of security, and let himself out into the cold, wet snow. Turning up his collar, he hurried to his car, which was parked in the slot reserved for the branch manager. Even in his most dejected moments, his heart never failed to lift at the sight of that sign: Branch Manager, meant only for him.

As he drove, Frank continued to think. He knew Nancy was drinking, and he was appalled. This was totally incomprehensible, completely unrelated to his understanding of Nancy. After all, she had always been the near teetotaler, having an occasional glass of wine, a rare cocktail. Now, when he got home tonight, if things ran true to form, Nancy would be half-drunk, struggling to cook a dinner, mixed up by her muddled brain. One night last week she had served rice in great quantities and peaches — and that was all! Frank said nothing about this strange combination, but how he longed for a decent meal! At least at lunch he was eating more, but at the end of a long day he did not need more problems.

Perhaps he had taken Nancy's calm serenity all these years for granted. She had always been efficient — running a clean, smooth house, serving deliciously appetizing meals. All for Sallie, true. But even a dog eats the crumbs from his master's table. Now, Frank came home to a house thick with clutter and dust, slept in a bed unchanged for weeks, ate from questionably clean dishes. And Nancy sat silent, disappearing periodically to the bathroom, coming back looking sly and a little more relaxed, a little more inebriated.

It had taken him a few weeks to catch on. Don't forget, he comforted himself, she had begun acting strangely as soon as Sallie was gone. But at last he had gone to the bathroom and found, hidden awkwardly behind the sheets and towels in the linen cupboard, the bottles. Always, Nancy smelled of spearmint, and hidden there, too, were some little spray mouth fresheners, ready for use.

This was ridiculous! Frank turned into Hilltop Acres, now smoothly paved, golf course completed. Nancy, a secret drinker! Secret? He knew, and that's what worried him. How many others? The milkman? The dry cleaner? She had gone to circle at church last week. Madge Brunner had insisted. When Frank got home that evening, Nancy was drunk once again, laughing about her marvelous day with the girls. How much had she drunk before Madge came for her? What had she said that had caused eyebrows to shoot up at the meeting?

Frank parked the car in the garage and put the door down. Resolutely, he went in through the breezeway into the kitchen. The kitchen was dark with no sign of a meal cooking. Wearily he took off his coat and hat, laying them on a chair. He went on into the dining room, still dark, and then into the living room.

A dim light burned, the lamp on the television, which played softly an afternoon talk show about to go off the air. Immediately Frank saw Nancy, lying loosely on the couch, arms dangling, legs spread, hair unkempt, stringy with oil. At first he thought she was dead and his heart lurched. But as he leaned over her, he saw she was in a stupor, sleeping it off. Her breath came in little whistling snores, somehow pathetic in a woman once so strong.

Frank lowered himself beside her, suddenly overcome by emotion. What had happened? Where had this started? With the abortion? With Sallie's going away? Or long ago when they had stopped being honest, stopped facing life? The sobs came dry at first, long, racking gasps for breath. But soon he was dotting Nancy's face with tears, moaning in misery. •

Nancy slept, blissfully unaware, as Frank cried. At last he got up, somehow purged, somehow more sure of himself. He saw now that Nancy must have always had some weak link beyond which she could not endure. Also, he saw that it was up to him to somehow save his marriage, to preserve his daughter's home. He was the one in charge now, by default, but in charge, nevertheless.

Frank hadn't really prayed for years, except in church where, when he was an elder assisting in the service, he read pretty words. He had never been so alone. Always before, Nancy had been there to guide him, to run things, sometimes against his will, but always safely as far as he was concerned. Not for years had he been required to make it by himself. Not since he was a young man. And now he recalled how then he had relied on God, calling on Him to see him through his youthful troubles. Sometime, somewhere, Frank had unknowingly switched his allegiance to Nancy. In the end, she had been his god.

Now Frank stood in the dim living room, seeing the white ground through the picture window, and he was aware of God. Perhaps even now it wasn't too late. Perhaps he could ask God's forgiveness and ask for Him to take the situation. Maybe there was yet an answer.

"Oh, God, I'm sorry," Frank whispered into the room, empty except for his sleeping wife. "I knew we were all mixed up; we've been going all wrong. But it was so easy, Lord. Life is so confusing, and I just don't know what's right. Somehow, God, please help us! I'm so sorry. Please, won't you help us?"

Frank would have felt foolish a while back praying like this. But a man standing in the shambles of his life is not easily embarrassed. Besides, he knew God was there in that room with him. He could feel His presence, and somehow that feeling had changed him.

He would be in charge now! And God wanted it that way. It was for him to give God the lead — that was his job now.

It was several days later that Frank began worrying about

Thanksgiving. Surely Sallie would notice the difference in her mother. In fact, he was afraid Sallie would be so shocked she would refuse to go back to college.

One dark, rainy night in early November — the snow of the previous week washed away — he broached the subject offhandedly to Nancy. They were sitting silently in the living room; he was reading; Nancy was trying to knit. Increasingly her needles would not move the way they should.

"Won't be long till Thanksgiving," Frank mused.

Nancy had been thinking hard, trying to remember how to bind off.

"What?" she asked.

"Soon be Thanksgiving. Sallie will be home."

"Oh." That was right. Sallie would be home. Then Nancy thought hard.

"Isn't she dead after all?"

Frank was astonished. He had had no idea she had deteriorated to this degree.

"Of course not," he said. "She's away at college. Haven't you written her all these weeks?"

Nancy remembered then.

"Oh yes! Of course, I wrote her yesterday — told her about this knitting. Guess I got confused."

The baby was dead, that was it. Not Sallie. It seemed harder to keep the two straight. Sallie and the baby. Poor baby.

Nancy felt a wet spot on her work, and realized she was crying. Why had the baby died? Maybe Frank knew.

"Why did the baby die, Frank?"

Frank was sitting in a cold sweat now. He couldn't handle this! He didn't ask what baby.

"It was too little to live," he lied.

"Oh, yes. But Sallie's coming in a few weeks, then?"

"Probably."

"Well, I'll make some extra rice, then."

Rice! What was this rice thing? They'd had rice again tonight. Rice and chicken — better anyway.

"No," he said patiently. "I'll help you fix a turkey and dressing."

Nancy was angry. He'd never helped before. She could cook for her own daughter!

"Now listen here!" she screamed. "I'm the mother around here! I know what's best for Sallie. We'll have rice and plenty of it!"

Frank stared at Nancy, appalled. Her lip was trembling and tears were running down her face, streaking the old powder caked on too heavily. She was painfully thin, her hair filthy. He knew then it was useless to try to hide the truth. Nancy was obviously sick. He must try to get her help.

Nancy fiddled with her yarn. "Now I've forgotten what I was

knitting!'' she stormed. What was it? Oh yes! Baby booties. No, they were finished. It must be a sweater. She looked at the shapeless mass in her lap. Yes, it was a sweater. She began to knit again. The idea of Frank telling her what to fix! She knew the value of rice! Why, they threw it at weddings and fed it in cereal to babies! If Sallie ate enough rice everything would be fine. She couldn't remember what was wrong, but rice would fix it up.

"Would you like some more rice, Frank? There's some in the pot."

Father, Frank prayed. You've got to help me!

Just then the phone rang, trilling cheerfully into the madness of the moment.

"I'll get it," he said jumping up and running to beat Nancy.

It was Sallie.

"Hi, daddy!"

Frank felt a warm feeling steal over him at the sound of her sweet, young voice.

"Hi, sweetie. What's up?"

"Oh nothing much. I'm getting along fine. Say, daddy, is mom there?"

Frank lowered his voice. "She's resting just now. What do you need to know ?"

"Well, I don't want to hurt mommy's feelings, but I've been invited to Clara's for Thanksgiving and I sure would love to go. They're such a scream, you know." She spoke in a rush, a timid hope in her voice. "Would mommy be hurt?"

Frank was being swallowed by relief. Maybe by Christmas Nancy would be better. He'd get her help, a good psychiatrist. Once she stopped drinking, she'd soon be herself.

"Well, we were looking forward to seeing you," he said. "Your mother was just planning dinner tonight."

"Oh."

"But I suppose you would enjoy that big family."

"Well, if you've already got things planned."

Mustn't let her suspect, Frank thought. She may never need to know.

"Not anything done yet, sweetie. But we're always planning for you. We will be disappointed, but I think you should have some experiences like this."

"Then I can go!"

Frank glanced at Nancy, now busily knitting, humming to herself.

"I'm sure you can. I'll write you after I've talked to your mom, but I think she'll agree."

"Oh, thanks, daddy! I'll be home for Christmas, of course. I want to see you, too; but they are such a big bunch, I guess I want to see what it's like.''

"I know, honey. Well, we'll write. We love you, sweetie.''

"Me, too! I mean, I love you, too, daddy. And thanks again!''

Frank hung up and looked at Nancy. He would find a doctor first — a good one. Later, if she was better, he would tell her about Sallie. Now, he would let Nancy go on thinking Sallie would be home.

As for himself, he was immensely relieved. Perhaps God was helping. Two things he had learned tonight: He must get help for Nancy, and Sallie wasn't coming home. The latter would aid the former.

11

At Pleasant Valley, November was an exciting month. The trees had gone bare, making the evergreens and pines on the hills the only source of green. The valley lay in a snow belt and often from early November on, the ground was covered with snow, never completely thawing before the next storm. Football was at its peak, and busloads of young men and women went to away games when possible. Otherwise, if they knew someone in a city or town too far for buses, they descended by carload on that family, eating their food and staying the night, strewn all over the house. The first quarter was nearing completion, and finals were in the air. Last minute rushing for papers due by Thanksgiving kept the librarians busy. There was a smell of excitement in the air; you could feel it.

Sallie was especially excited. She was looking forward to her visit at Clara's home. She could hardly wait to experience a clan dinner and to live for three days in a house filled with loud and vigorous people. Perhaps she felt the vitality would rub off and replace the quiet and somewhat dull heritage of her own.

But into this anticipation, increasingly there came a doubt. Her mother's letters were so strange lately. And her father was writing more. Neither of these became more than a vague feeling. She hadn't been away long enough to really know how to gauge her mother's letters, and she felt rather proud to receive letters from her father. Hardly anyone did. So the doubt was unformed and shapeless, but there nevertheless.

And the last few weeks had added a disturbing form of excitement to the general anticipation. She found herself thinking more and more about Harvey, unable to categorize him any more, to file him neatly in a corner of her mind. He confused her. Sometimes he was serious, sometimes dryly humorous. Sometimes he sought her out at gatherings, sometimes he seemed to deliberately ignore her, as if watching to see if she would be good without him. Often now, she found the false rush of boyfriends distasteful. Oh, at first it had been the bread of life, but Harvey had changed all that. Combined with his perceptive, searing attitude about college and life in general, his conviction and dedication, not to mention his background, had worked to forever remove him from the lowest category in her estimation. Sallie seldom spoke of Harvey to anyone, instead almost savoring the disturbing feeling he gave her. She couldn't say she really liked him — not like the silly, yet sophisticated boys she dated. But the thought of him stirred her somewhere she had never before even known about.

Harvey had seen Sallie at one of the first freshman mixers. He had been there a week early working in records for a few extra dollars. Standing on the sidelines of the gym, he assessed the newcomers. He had done this the previous year, too. For he believed God had a mission for him at college, too, and he was always seeking chances to perform it. The sight of Sallie had been like recognizing the piece to a puzzle you had thought was lost. He knew that she was to be a part of his mission. But how? Her glowing hair hanging down her back, her fragility, and her pseudo-sophistication were all things that would never withstand hardship. She would need taking in hand.

After that, he had watched her. He had found out her name and everything he could from the records office. She had an admirable scholastic ability, a stable home. And when the inevitable meeting came, he was ready. Harvey had with prayer and praise set about to complete the mission. He knew this was irritating to a girl so popular and willful, but that was not important. Harvey was not a quitter and he had faith that God was directing him.

He did not suspect that he was to fall in love with this girl. She was too unlike the image of the stern, strong, stolid, and skinny missionary wife he had pictured. For one thing she was beautiful, and beauty had left him cold. For another, she was silly and frivolous, loving pretty things and lacking any real goals. No, Harvey would have laughed at the thought of falling in love with Sallie as he perceived her. But she was his mission for here and now, and he supposed that the ultimate end in God's mind was to get her on the right track, keep her there awhile, and let her find an area to serve, probably unrelated to him. That's why it was shocking, unnerving for Harvey to discover a sneaking feeling in his heart and an uplifting of spirit when Sallie was around.

This was the situation when Harvey and Sallie sat together on a bus to an away game. The town was two-and-a-half hours away, and it was a snowy, blowy November day when the bus, only half-full of the staunchest supporters, pulled out. The roads weren't bad, and if they got stranded at the other college, they could stay the night. But Clara, basically a sun worshiper, refused to go. Besides finals were coming up, and she needed to do some studying. Sallie, however, was determined to go. She loved the snow and the danger. And she wanted to have the fun of the bus ride and game. She didn't have to study as hard as Clara, either. So, Sallie, all bundled in plaid wool slacks, camel's hair coat, hand knit muffler, cap, gloves, and sweater, braved the wind and biting cold.

When she got on the bus, Harvey was already there, sitting near the back, ears red from the cold, an old hunting cap on his head. Sallie was glad to see him. She didn't feel like being silly in the cold. Maybe after awhile she would.

Harvey looked up as she approached, his long face solemn.

"What are you doing here?" he asked.

"I might ask you the same."

"But I asked first."

Sallie loosened her scarf.

"Can I sit with you?"

"You mean you want to subject yourself to me?" He waved a hand to indicate the other seats and other kids.

"I want to relax a while. At least you won't mind if I'm quiet."

"You mean I'm good enough to fill in when you don't feel like putting on a show, huh?"

Sallie was becoming angry.

"Well, for heaven's sake! I don't have to sit here. I'll go sit with Jim in the back."

Jim was smiling at her from his seat in the rear of the bus.

Harvey slid over. He didn't want her sitting with Jim.

Sallie hesitated a minute, then waved at Jim and sat down.

"What are you doing here?" Harvey asked again.

"I always go."

"On days like this?"

"Why not? You are."

Harvey didn't tell her he was there because Clara had told him Sallie was going.

"I've got nothing better to do."

"What?" Sallie feigned surprise. "No tutoring? No studies?"

Harvey grinned, his lovely grin that somehow shortened his too-long face.

"It just so happens I'm free today," he said.

"This is nice and comfortable," she said.

"Not bad."

"You don't usually go to away games. Why this one on such a lousy day?"

"I told you, I'm free today."

He had changed two tutoring appointments to Monday evening. Actually he had a feeling. He knew Sallie was going and he felt he should too.

He glanced sideways at her. She was taking off her gloves, bright red ones that matched her hat and scarf. As she unbuttoned her coat he saw her sweater matched, too. As usual, she looked beautiful.

"You ready for finals?" he asked.

"I've got two weeks yet."

"Don't wait till the last minute."

Sallie looked at him. "You *are* a little busybody, aren't you?"

Harvey burst out laughing. "I may be skinny, but I'm sure not little!"

Sallie had never seen him laugh before, and now he was laughing at her. She liked his laugh, but not at her expense.

"You know what I mean!"

Harvey sobered.

"So do you," he countered.

"Look, Harvey — "

"Look, Harvey, what?" he interrupted. "I know, Miss Sallie, you are at the top of your classes — a smashing student. Well, don't get too cocky."

"You are really just a bully, Harvey! And I don't know what made me think I'd want to sit with you for three whole hours!"

"Two and one half," Harvey said conversationally.

Sallie was gathering up her things in confusion.

"Oh, shut up!" she said.

"You're always right, aren't you?"

She started to get up.

"Oh, come on." Harvey put his big hand on her shoulder and pushed her down in her seat. "You take me too seriously."

Sallie glared at him.

"Last time we talked, I actually thought you might be nice."

"I am."

"You're not! You're so self-righteous and always interfering."

Sallie struggled to get up, but his vicelike grip held her down.

"Will you please let go?" she whispered fiercely.

"If you'll sit still," he answered reasonably.

"I don't want to sit with you any more. You're worse than I thought."

Sallie felt like crying as she looked around for a seat. Jim's was taken, but there were some empty ones at the front. If Harvey would just let go!

She looked at him and saw that he was regarding her with amusement, his lips twitching. Suddenly, she was no longer upset, wanting to escape from him. She felt a smile spread slowly across her face.

"We *could* have fun together," she said plaintively.

"You always think of that," he answered in his amused voice.

She would not let him beat her! She relaxed in the seat, putting her purse back down. She smiled sweetly.

"You can let go now."

"Maybe I like your shoulder."

Sallie felt a funny feeling in the pit of her stomach.

"Well, it's kind of an awkward way to hold me, don't you think?"

"I wouldn't know. I've never held you any other way."

Harvey's long face almost broke into a grin, but he managed to maintain his serious expression.

"Okay, Harvey," Sallie said. "I get it. For some strange, unknown reason you love to tease me. Well! I will *not* be upset. I will be calm and collected and stick to you like glue no matter what nasty, rotten, interfering thing you say!" She shoved her face next to his, eyeball to eyeball. "Do you hear me, Harvey?"

Harvey blinked. His hand still squeezed her shoulder, no longer awkwardly since she was turned toward him. He could feel her warm breath on his nose, see her mouth smiling sarcastically, temptingly. It would be so easy . . .

The bus started with a lurch, and Harvey was aware of where they were; the ruckus of students on holiday, especially a snowy, wild holiday, filled the air. The lurch threw Sallie back and his hand kept her from falling on the floor.

She squealed.

He pulled her back into her seat, the moment past. But Harvey was aware of her in a new way, and as they rode around the sharp curves, and their shoulders touched, he was stirred by her nearness. They began to relax and he stopped teasing her, and for much of the ride they were silent, each soaking up the other's closeness. Her hand lay on the arm of their connecting seats, small and white, and occasionally she would grab his arm as the bus swung and swayed. Harvey was glad he had put off the tutoring.

When the bus arrived at the football game, the sun was trying to break through the clouds. In sudden bursts it would succeed, illuminating the scene like fairyland. They were in a small city, where the opposing college was located. As Harvey and Sallie walked up the bleachers, they could see the clean white field and smell the crisp air. Now, only a few flakes drifted down at random and the wind had died down.

It was a good game, but Pleasant Valley lost. The little cheering section in the visitors' stands jumped up and down, shouting encouragement, all to no avail — except to keep their feet warm. The game was over by 4:30, and by the time the bus was loaded, it was beginning to get dark. The kids who had come as dates snuggled together, anticipating the best part of their excursion. No one seemed to mind that they had lost, rather it was a good excuse to be subdued and quiet.

Sallie sat next to the window on the way home, looking out at the city, where lights were being turned on. With the dark came more snow, and the wind began to pick up, drifting the snow across the road.

Harvey took off his cap and settled into the aisle seat, feeling very content. Both he and Sallie were quiet, as was the whole bus. It was a romantic atmosphere, the cover of darkness only occasionally interrupted by the lights of passing trucks.

During the day, Harvey and Sallie had held hands once in awhile as they became involved with the excitement of the game. But now they were shy. Harvey was not the kind for casual kissing on a homebound bus; Sallie, who had learned to be casual as an expert, somehow did not feel casual with Harvey.

So as the landscape darkened, leaving only a haze of dim white against a black velvet backdrop, and as the bus left the city and began the tortuous trip in the hills, Harvey and Sallie sat silent and afraid. Neither wanted the day to end, but they were at a loss as to how to prolong it.

At last, Sallie shifted in her seat, feeling somewhat ridiculous.

"We could talk," she whispered.

Harvey turned in his seat to look at her. He could dimly see her face, halved by her helter-skelter hair.

"Why are you whispering?" he whispered back.

Sallie glanced around at the other passengers, all quiet and absorbed in one another.

"It seems sacrilegious not to," she smiled.

Harvey grunted. "They don't know what they're doing. Later *she'll* wonder what made *him* think he could go so far."

Sallie felt a little stirring of apprehension. "Why must you always disapprove? It's just a little harmless . . ."

"Harmless? I'm sorry, Miss Sallie, but when you've seen the babies dumped on our home! *You* raise them, they say. *You* find them a good home!" Harvey paused and Sallie's heart froze. He went on, "It's better than abortion. We do place a lot of them, at least in foster homes."

Sallie felt stifled, as if there weren't enough air. "What makes you think that necessarily follows this?" she managed in a dry whisper.

Harvey tried to see her face. She was such an innocent! Of course, she could play around a little and not get burned, because she was basically decent. He grunted again. "You'd be surprised how many babies are made more casually that this. Don't get me wrong, Miss Sallie, I'm all for sex — but coming from where I did, seeing all those kids, hearing all the excuses. . . . " He took a deep breath. "Do you realize how many people are hungry, or have never heard of Jesus? Oh, yes, you *know* about it, but these people rot while nice kids get pregnant and have abortions or otherwise take up the time of those who could be doing something of value for someone who really needs it!"

This conversation couldn't be happening, Sallie thought. If he knew! "You're so bitter, Harvey! How can you call yourself a Christian and have no compassion for the people involved? What do you know of loneliness? Of longing to be loved?"

"Plenty," Harvey said quietly. "But there's a right way and a wrong way — and the wrong way wrecks lives."

Sallie was silent. What did she know of loneliness, after all? She had parents and a home.

"I'm sorry, Harvey. I forgot. You've probably been lonelier than I or most of these kids can imagine. But, Harvey, they may not have the inner strength that you do! And, besides, do you really think babies are going to result from tonight?"

Harvey, too, was silent a moment. No, he thought, those who found a quiet corner to make love later would most likely be prepared. They'd be on the pill if they were girls, and the boys would have planned for such an eventuality. But then, why all the babies — dead before they were born, or tossed aside for someone else to care for? Oh, sure, there were those who raised the child now, but to what? A fatherless home? More illegitimate brothers and sisters? A philosophy that taught "play now and pray never"?

Harvey shifted again in his seat. What should he answer? What did God think? Sometimes he wished there were rules written down for everything.

"You don't think that," came Sallie's whisper. "You know it is mostly harmless."

"No!" Harvey turned to her, grabbing her by the shoulders. "I find kissing pleasurable, too. And yes, most of it is 'harmless' as you say— meaning it's not as drastic as I say. But, even so, how many boys have kissed you, Miss Sallie, or touched you . . . ?"

"Stop it!" Their whispers were full of emotion. "You're hurting my shoulders. Please."

But Harvey went on, holding her, searching her face. "How many, Miss Sallie? And when does it lose all meaning? When do you stop being 'harmless'; when is a little casual kissing not enough?"

He released her and sank back in his seat. His insides were in turmoil. He knew now! There was no denying it. He was jealous. After a minute he heard a soft whimper, a sharp little gasp for breath, and he realized he'd made her cry. She spoke so low he could hardly hear her.

"Oh, Harvey, why do you do this to me? Why can't you leave me alone? You're always making me think further than I want to! Why can't I just stay away from you?" She began to cry harder, tears staining her face. "And we had such fun today!"

Harvey reached for her and pulled her head down on his shoulder, wrapping both arms around her. "Can't you see I care about you?" he whispered. "I don't want you to be ruined! That's why I hate it and tease you when you act so sophisticated! Oh, Sallie, at first, I believed God wanted me to heckle you into thinking beyond the end of your nose — just as a mission. But now," he patted her head awkwardly, "now, I guess you're more than that to me."

Sallie lay in his arms, the sobs silently going away, her shaking bosom quieting. It felt so good to lie there, even across the arm of the seat. To feel his arms holding her, to hear his words. From that moment, she had an inkling of why she must think further. She had known Harvey was no casual friend, no passing romance to be played with. But she still didn't understand why he had to be so — so stiff!

Then she felt his lips on her face, softly kissing her wet cheeks.

"Oh, Sallie, Sallie," he murmured.

"You're kissing me," she said.

He laughed a little. "But not casually," and he lifted her chin so he could kiss her lips.

When at last he raised his head, she felt an excitement she had never felt before.

"Harvey, I've never been kissed like that." Cam had been demanding, hungry, her dates light and titillating. But this was deep and involved the heart more than the body, a kind of flowing together of spirits.

Harvey held her tighter and kissed her again, feeling a happiness unbounded growing within him.

"I've never kissed like this before," he said, breathing deeply. He ran his fingers over her face, wiping away the last traces of tears. "I guess I've never felt like this before."

"Me either. And Harvey?"

"What?"

"I don't want any more — I mean — well — do you know what I mean?"

"I think so. It's too special to take any chances."

"Yes, and it's all I can take anyway."

They rode the rest of the way in a companionable quiet, Sallie's head on Harvey's shoulder. There was no need for words now, they both knew.

Harvey left her at her dorm, kissing her lightly on the nose.

"I'll see you," he said, and meant always.

"Yes," she said, and answered for always.

"Harvey?"

"You *are* nice."

"I told you I was."

"Well, good night."

"Good night, Miss Sallie."

And he was gone, disappearing quickly into the snowy night. She stood in the shelter of the doorway for a minute, thinking, remembering.

Unbidden, the doubts came. If he knew! What would he think of her if he knew what she had done? She bit back a sob. Oh, how could she have been so foolish? To risk losing such a guy as Harvey for Cam?

At last, she began to feel the cold, and she went inside. She would have to pray that he never found out. She couldn't bear it if he did.

The time flew. It was Wednesday afternoon, and Clara and Sallie were waiting with their suitcases in the living room of the dorm for Clara's folks. It didn't seem possible, but only last Saturday had been the beginning of Sallie's initiation into selfless love. She had seen Harvey only a few times since, in the ensuing five days, but the encounters had been heavy with meaning. A casual walk on sunlit snow up the hill, a tender embrace in dappled woods, a touching of hands under a library table. It was enough and more than enough, so that Sallie sat dreamily wishing now that the visit to Clara's was over, that she was back, near Harvey.

Clara sat silently, too. She knew Sallie was in love, and she wasn't surprised to find out it was Harvey. She'd just had a feeling. You don't resist something so hard unless you know its power. Clara knew herself what it was like to be overcome by unexpected love. Nobody knew, least of all the professor involved, that she worshiped from afar. She knew it was hopeless, but hopeless is a word that hearts tend to disown.

So the two girls sat silently in a living room furnished with big, old, comfortable chairs and couches in ugly shades of green and brown, waiting for an anticipated visit no longer desired.

It was like a storm breaking over a calm sea, a placid place of rest, when the door burst open and Mrs. Hoffmeyer waddled in, closely followed by the twins and Mr. Hoffmeyer, forever agreeing with his head.

"Clara! Baby!" Mrs. Hoffmeyer screamed, tears of happiness starting. "You've gotten so skinny, dearie. Don't they feed you right here?"

Clara groaning almost audibly, got up from the couch where she had been dreaming next to Sallie.

"Ma! I'm fine." She hugged her mother.

"You're thin! So thin!"

Sallie was amazed. Clara *wasn't* so plump any more.

Mr. Hoffmeyer came over to Sallie.

"Look's like you're all ready," he nodded.

Sallie smiled, "Yes."

"That's good." Mr. Hoffmeyer bent his skinny frame and picked up her case, head bobbing all the while. Sallie bit her lip.

"I can carry it," she said. "It's not heavy."

Mr. Hoffmeyer straightened. "I got it," he agreed with himself.

Before Sallie could protest, she was enveloped by Mrs. Hoffmeyer. "Sallie! You look like an angel! But so skinny! Ain't she painful, pa?"

Mr. Hoffmeyer nodded.

Sallie was released to sink back on the couch, limp.

"We'll fatten you up!" Mrs. Hoffmeyer screamed. "Well, what are we waiting for? Let's go! We'll be home in a few hours and I got a great meal for you girls."

The twins latched onto either side of Sallie, barraging her with questions.

At last they were in the Hoffmeyer's station wagon. Sallie and Clara sat in back with Sherrie, one of the twins. Clara whispered to Sallie, while her mother was rambling on about the wonderful feast they would have tomorrow.

"Can you stand it?"

Sallie giggled. "Better than you can."

"Boy, I'll say. I'd forgotten how loud ma was."

"She's great!"

Clara beamed. "Well, her heart's as big as she is."

"I know. She doesn't even know me, really, and she seems so glad to have me come."

"She's that way. What do you think of pa?"

Sallie could see the back of Mr. Hoffmeyer's head in the dimming light as they drove along. It was still keeping its perfect rhythm, as if sometime long ago he had discovered that if he appeared to agree, Mrs. Hoffmeyer wouldn't pester him.

"He's fantastic," she said.

Clara peered at Sallie for a moment. Then both girls broke into smothered giggles. Sherrie sat between them straining to catch their whispers over her head. Suddenly, she jumped up, knocking Sallie's chin painfully with her hard little head.

"Hey, ma! Hey, ma!" she shouted, making Mr. Hoffmeyer break his rhythm for a minute like a syncopated clock. "Tell them to stop whispering about you. That ain't polite!"

But Mrs. Hoffmeyer didn't hear over her own voice. She pushed Sherrie back in her seat absently and yelled, "And you bet, I got fresh cranberries. And ten pies! — three mince, and three pumpkin . . . ."

Sallie and Clara, worried for a minute, resumed their whispers, this time with Sherrie shoved in a corner.

It was to be a wild weekend. Sallie couldn't remember when she'd had so much fun, unless it was before things had fallen apart with Cam, at some of those pajama parties. But this was even better! She and Clara talked and giggled and stuffed themselves on turkey and pie, only to restuff themselves later on ham and cake, bit, thick pieces of rich chocolate, with frosting an inch thick. Clara's older brothers came with their wives and children, filling the big farmhouse with noise and confusion and love. Clyde, the fourteen-year-old, spoke to Sallie once, but mostly he slunk about, looking trapped and miserable, the only one unable to enjoy the rowdiness. Sallie felt sorry for him briefly, and then bundled up and joined the gang for a sleigh ride.

Whey they got back to Pleasant Valley, the girls were exhausted, but happy. They felt warm and close and loved. They screamed good-bys to Clara's family, and Salled thanked them again and again. At last they had greeted all their friends and exchanged hilarious stories of their various vacations, and Clara and Sallie got ready for bed.

It was good to be back in their own room, dull yet bright with their own handiwork. It was good to have homes to visit but better to have to return to their new life of dreams and expectations.

Sallie thought of Harvey as she went to sleep that Sunday night. She would see him tomorrow. He had gone to the orphanage to help give a family feeling to the younger ones there at Thanksgiving. But he must be back now in his room over Joe's Come and Get It. Thinking of her!

She sighed with happiness and went to sleep.

Nancy Victor lay on the bed trying to remember where she was. The room didn't look at all familiar. Perhaps someone had redecorated it while she was away. Away where? She couldn't recall.

The walls were a dull greenish beige, and the plaster was rather rough and looked old. Now, she knew her bedroom was blue and white — a gorgeous shade, the color of bachelor buttons for the carpet, paled for the tweedy, textured wallpaper, combined with navy for the window pane plaid curtains. These windows had old olive drapes, and no sheer, frilly liners. This was not her bedroom.

She lay thinking, feeling a little stir of fear. It really was awful not to know where you were or how you came to be there.

Suddenly, she had it. This was her bedroom in the old bungalow they had lived in for so many years. Somehow, she had gotten back there. Of course, she would have to change the paint, but she had done that before and it had worked wonders.

Nancy relaxed a little. It was all right once you recognized the place. Although, it still bothered her about that other bedroom — the new blue one.

All at once, she had an idea. Of course! Why had she been so surprised to be here? It had all been a dream — a long, horrible dream. That beautiful new house — oh, how she longed for a beautiful new house like that — was just a dream. It had never happened — none of it.

Nancy stretched her thin arms and legs, enjoying the tingling motion. She must have been sick, delirious for some time. She wondered where Sallie was, probably out playing on her swing. And who had been taking care of Frank and Sallie? Well, she was better now. She would soon be on her feet and taking over her job again.

Thank goodness that was a dream — the lovely house notwithstanding! Why Sallie had been grown up and had gotten into trouble. And then she, Nancy — a mother! — had forced her into having an abortion. Of course, now that she was awake, she knew it was ridiculous! But dreams could surely be realistic.

She lay back against the pillow, waiting for someone to come. They must have someone watching over her. They probably kept Sallie out, too, so she wouldn't get sick. She heard a noise at the door and lifted her head. A man in a white jacket was standing there, a youngish man with thinning hair and a wide, friendly smile, that crinkled his eyes. She'd never seen him before, but he must be her doctor, dressed like that. Where was old Dr. Baird?

"Hello," the doctor said cheerfully. "Are you feeling better today?"

"Oh, yes!" Nancy exclaimed, forgetting Dr. Baird. This man seemed so nice. "I've been sick, haven't I?"

The doctor's smile widened. Incredibly it didn't break his face. "Yes," he said. "You've been delirious for quite a while."

"That long!" Nancy was amazed. "It's been terrible, I can tell you."

"Yes," the doctor said, seating himself next to her bed in a straight chair. He crossed his legs and looked at her earnestly. "Now tell me. What do you remember?"

"Well, I had this horrible dream. Sallie — she's my daughter."
The doctor nodded.

"Well — I don't know how to say this — I'm still rather confused."

The doctor smiled. "That's normal."

"I can't remember how old she really is, but in my dream she was grown up — in high school, a senior — and she got pregnant . . ." Nancy covered her face with her hands, "It's too terrible, doctor. I don't want to talk about it. And the house was so lovely!"

The doctor shifted his weight, uncrossing his legs. He leaned forward and pulled her hands gently away from her face.

"Tell me," he said quietly. Somehow she couldn't resist.

"I made her have an abortion! Isn't that awful? Then I started drinking. Oh, she went away — to college, I think — it's all fuzzy. But so terrible!"

The doctor sat back.

"You did talk a lot about the baby. You kept saying you killed the baby."

"I was out of my head!" Nancy was becoming upset. To change the subject she said, "Where's my daughter? And my husband?"

"Your husband's downstairs."

"But this is downstairs!"

The doctor smiled gently. "No, you're on the third floor."

Nancy was becoming agitated. "What do you mean? We don't have more than a story and a half! And where's Sallie? What have you done with her?"

The doctor stood up, patting her shoulder. "Don't worry about Sallie, she's fine."

Nancy looked wildly at the walls, the dull curtains, the tile floor. Where had the tile come from?

"What's going on here?" she screamed. "You're hiding her from me! And you've changed my house! Get out right now! Get out!"

The doctor held her struggling form firmly, while she beat on him with her fists, screaming all the while.

A nurse came running in.

"She needs sedation," the doctor said quietly. "Quick!"

The nurse ran out. In a moment she was back with a hypodermic. The doctor held Nancy in a steel grip, while the nurse gave the shot. After a minute, Nancy subsided, relaxed.

The doctor stood looking down at her. Face it, he thought. She's getting worse. They would have to transfer her to a better facility. This hospital wasn't for cases like this.

Wearily, he took the elevator down to the lobby, where Frank stood, staring out at the snow. He touched Frank on the shoulder.

"Let's sit over here," he said.

Frank went with him to the secluded corner indicated. He had been praying, hoping he could see her. Now that she was pathetic and weak, he loved her more than when she was strong and in control.

"How is she?"

The doctor looked grim.

"Oh, no! Can't you do something?"

Frank sat. Christmas vacation was a week away.

"Have you told your daughter yet?"

Frank shook his head.

"You must! I'm going to have her transferred to . . ."

"You mean a mental hospital?" Frank looked shocked.

The doctor sighed. "Look, you're going to have to face facts. Your wife is very sick. She has almost completely retreated from reality. She now thinks all these things that have happened were a dream. She becomes hysterical when I suggest that they're not."

Frank leaned his head on hands, supporting his elbows on his knees. "If I had said no! If I had been stronger . . . ."

"Don't blame yourself, Mr. Victor. She's got a problem that goes beyond recent events. True, the guilt has triggered this, together with the alcohol. But she's got a deep emotional inability to accept reality. It would have come eventually."

Frank sat up.

"What should I do?" he asked.

"Tell your daughter, for goodness' sake! She may need help, too. People just can't mess with life thinking they can control everything without regard for rules. I don't mean laws! I mean cause and effect. You commit a crime against life — and you pay one way or the other." The doctor paused. He remembered the mother's screaming. "Your daughter must know; she'll be home soon. You must try to prepare her. And," he paused again, "I can't stress this enough, tell the psychiatrist at her college about this. All the facts! Sallie may go to pieces."

Frank sat still. God, help me to do this. I can't bear it unless You do.

"All right," he said.

"Good." The doctor rose, holding out his hand. Standing himself, Frank took it and they shook hands.

"I'll make the arrangements to have your wife moved to Sunshine Acres — it's the best around," the doctor said.

"Yes."

"And, Mr. Victor?"

Frank stood watching a woman trying to fix her wilting hair. "Yes?"

"There is hope, you know. Once we start intensive therapy, she may improve rapidly. The important thing is to quit skirting issues."

"Yes," Frank said. "Thank you, doctor."

The doctor nodded. "I'll call you," he said, "when she's moved."

Frank stood on, as the doctor walked briskly away, watching the woman give up, and clamp her hat on angrily. A little boy of about three ran back and forth between two couches as the man who appeared to be his father told him periodically to sit down. An empty table, ready to carry a patient somewhere, was rolled by an orderly into an elevator.

At last, Frank buttoned his overcoat and put on his hat. He went to the revolving doors, through them, and out into the pale winter sun. The snow looked sloppy underfoot; there were piles of dirty cindered slush lying about. The car was surrounded by a large puddle.

As Frank drove home through the melting snow, he realized there was no use going back to work. He would have to miss tomorrow, too. It was Thursday, and he would drive down to Pleasant Valley.

He thought of the last three weeks, of waiting and hoping that Sallie wouldn't have to know. Of lying to Nancy's friends — saying she had just gotten exhausted, maybe had a rather severe case of mononucleosis. All for nothing.

Well, he'd have to tell the truth now. Deep within he had known this would come. It was almost a relief. He had tried to protect them all, but now they would have to get at the truth. What was the truth? What had gone wrong?

Frank knew that God was somehow behind this. They had tried to fight the rules, like the doctor said, tried to make their own laws. Frank knew it was wrong, had known it all along. Well, he'd asked God for help. He'd finally come to Him. And he'd hoped that God would solve it without his having to tell the truth. But they'd gone too far; they'd twisted their lives too much. Frank believed God was behind this because He knew that only digging out the truth, all of it, would save them now.

And of course Sallie had to be told. She must be made to see that only an honest admission of failure — on all their parts — would clear the slate and prepare her for a better life — a real life.

Now that it was forced on him, Frank was glad. God was working!

Sallie was in her room ironing when one of the girls came to her with the news her father was downstairs. She couldn't believe it. Perhaps he was in the area on some kind of bank business.

She unplugged the iron, ran the brush through her hair, and went down to the living room. Frank was standing awkwardly near the door, sending anxious looks toward the stairway. When he saw her, he came over and met her at the foot of the stairs.

"Hi, daddy," Sallie said cheerfully. "What a pleasant surprise! What brings you way down here a week before quarter's over?"

Frank studied her shining face devoid of makeup, even lipstick. Her hair looked freshly combed, and her eyes sparkled her delight at seeing him.

"You look good, honey," he smiled taking her hand. "Where can we go for lunch — or do you have a class?'' After all, it was Thursday.

"Not till three and it's only noon now. You sure must have left early.''

"About seven this morning.'' He didn't say, I waited as long as I could stand it. "Where can we eat, toots?''

"Well, there's Joe's Come and Get It here, or the Inn at Watertown where we ate before, remember?''

"I'll treat you to the Inn. You must get tired of Joe's.''

Sallie laughed. "I do!''

On the way to Watertown Sallie asked why her mother hadn't come. Frank waved it aside with, "She's under the weather a little.'' Sallie was becoming disturbed by this strange visit, and she couldn't believe her mother was too sick to visit her.

At last they were settled at a cozy table near the fireplace in the old Inn. They ordered the specialty — country fried chicken and vegetables served family style. Frank asked about classes and finals. Sallie told him she was doing well. They talked gingerly around any real subject. Frank didn't mention the truth about Nancy. Sallie didn't talk about Harvey — during the meal. By the time they were finished, the Inn was nearly empty, except for an elderly couple across the room.

Finally Frank put down his coffee cup.

"There's no use beating around the bush, Sallie,'' he began. "You must know this is unusual for me to come a week before I have to come get you for Christmas.''

"I was wondering,'' Sallie said in a low voice. Here goes, she thought.

"Well,'' Frank took out his handkerchief and wiped his brow. "Your mother is sick. There's no easy way to say it . . . .''

"She's dying!''

Frank hadn't realized that naturally Sallie would think her mother to be physically sick.

"No, no,'' he said. "Nothing like that.''

Sallie felt the panic clutches loosen a little. "Then what?''

Frank took a deep breath. Lord, give me strength!

"It's her mind, Sallie. She's broken down. It's a long story, and I prayed we could fix it before you knew.''

Sallie felt a new kind of fear grab her. Her mind! Mental illness!

"Why?'' she whispered. "What caused it?''

"A lot of things, honey,'' Frank reached for her hand lying on the table between them, fingers tensely curled.

"It was me, wasn't it?'' Sallie's face was pale, frightened. "I caused it! All the trouble . . .''

"Stop that kind of thinking right now!'' The elderly couple

glanced over at his raised voice. "You are only a small part," he lowered his voice, squeezing her hand. "She's been getting sick a long time, the doctor says. I may as well admit that, yes, the combination of your — uh — troubles — and don't forget her strong insistence — and your going away have been too much. She became very despondent right away, and I — I just couldn't accept it. I thought she'd get better by herself if I just gave her some time."

Sallie sat still, frozen. She couldn't imagine her mother incompetent, confused.

"How bad is she?" she asked.

Frank released her hand and mopped his forehead again.

"Well, that's why I had to tell you. The doctor's moving her from General Hospital, to Sunshine — "

"But that's an insane asylum! I've seen it! In school we went there! She's not like that!"

Sallie's heart was shrinking, her ears roaring.

Frank prayed. Can't I lie? Just a little? But there was some glimmer. Remember?

"The doctor says, that once she's there, she can receive intensive therapy. She may improve rapidly."

Sallie remembered her mother. Helping her sew her first dress. Showing her the right way to make a bed. Encouraging her to bring her friends home. Cheering her when she had no date. Fixing everything, no matter how badly broken, even . . . . Now, her mother was paying the price! All those years of sacrifice! The shock of the events of the summer!

Sallie began to cry.

"It is my fault, daddy! Oh, you must know it!"

"No, I don't blame you or me or your mother. Except for our blind inability to accept our mistakes. Not just you, Sallie! Look how I could feel! Why, we left you free — I didn't like all the time you spent with that boy — but I gave in! Always I gave in! And your mother! She always was manipulating — first me — then you. "Look at the . . ." Frank took a deep breath. "Look at the abortion! You didn't want it! But she wore you down."

Frank stopped abruptly. Sallie sat wiping her eyes with her napkin, trying to stop the tears.

"Oh, daddy," she said. "I was so selfish — I just wanted love. To think I thought I loved him! Mommy loved me so much that she went against herself to save me. I think I knew it then! It wasn't just me that was against the abortion at first. She always said it was wrong . . . ."

"Until it struck home," Frank said bitterly. "But this is useless. We could argue and discuss and theorize all day. What I tried to point out to you was this: It happened. The summer happened. We were all wrong. We all tried to avoid the truth. Well, maybe it's a good thing your mother broke down. Now maybe God can get at the root of the problem — at least in her."

"God!" Sallie was angry. "Where was He when I needed Him? Why didn't He tell me — why didn't He help? He doesn't really care, daddy. Grow up!"

Frank's hand stung, and he looked at Sallie's face, the cheek turning bright pink against the pallor. Why, he'd slapped her! He'd never touched her before in any way but love. But he wasn't sorry. There came a time when you stood your ground, when you stopped abdicating.

Sallie was shocked. It didn't really hurt so much, just a sharp sting. She saw the elderly couple getting up to leave, looking embarrassed. Suddenly, she felt very small again. Like the time her mother had punished her in front of a friend for being sassy. When she was in first grade.

Frank spoke, slowly and with authority. "I've taught you wrong. I've been wrong myself. There's plenty of excuses to give — that's the way life is: Save the surface, let the real truth go, but they are all false. The truth is that we — your mother and I — taught you wrong. We aren't alone either. There are many more like us. We bent over backwards for you. We gave up things for you. We went against our conscience — or I did anyway — for you! Well, no more. I've finally realized how very real God is! We've ignored His system of things, His code of values. We've gone to church, we've perpetuated our own piety, and we've told Him how it'll be. When was the last time you told God to take your life? When you were thirteen? Or did you then? When did you start thinking God wasn't real if He couldn't do as you said?"

"Daddy, please."

"No, listen, daughter. You're interrupting! I'm at fault! I knew we weren't honest Christians, because I have been honest and I know the difference. If any one person is to blame for all of this, it's Frank Victor! I slowly and eventually totally stopped being truthful with God. At long last, I was only a shell, a surface expression of a false god. My own god! And you learned, not only from me, but even at church, that God was to be used, that He supported your viewpoint!"

"Daddy, I'm sorry. I was upset. Please!" Sallie didn't understand him. He seemed so different. She felt somehow condemned by his very insistence that she wasn't the only one to blame.

"Well, it's not that way," Frank went on. "I've finally seen the truth. We should have admitted our mistakes when you got pregnant and stopped trying to make our own laws. Now, we have only to face up to our failure and go on. There's no use blaming or hurling threats or feeling sorry for ourselves. Let's just face it. And let's let God take over now, before we even forget He's there."

"I've got to go, daddy. I have a class."

Frank stood up.

"Have you listened at all?"

Sallie's cheek no longer hurt. But her pride did.

"Yes," she said, not adding, But I don't understand you.

"I'm going to tell the school psychiatrist about this, so he can help you if you need it."

"Oh, honestly, daddy! Can't you just leave it alone now? Do you have to be so all-fired honest?"

Frank looked at his daughter. She was angry and stubborn looking.

"Don't you think you might want to talk to someone?"

Sallie sighed. If you knew how badly, she thought. And you don't even know about Harvey! But to a shrink! She wasn't sick — at least not yet.

"Please, daddy. I'll be home in a week. In fact I meant to call you. I've got a ride, so you won't have to come. Give me a little time before you spill the beans." She felt as if she were hanging onto the last shreds of her respectability.

"He won't tell anybody."

"I know. But I won't talk to him, so why tell him? I want to think. Can't you allow me a week? How long have you known and not told anybody? Please! Give me a little time!"

Frank thought of the doctor's advice and thought of his own reluctance to bring the situation into the open. Perhaps a week would be a good thing. Then Sallie could see her mother's doctor who already knew everything. He would be better able to make her accept the truth. He had helped Frank.

"All right. If you will see mother's doctor, so he can try to help us all."

"Of course, daddy! I want to help all I can to make mommy well."

Frank left Sallie at the dorm and she rushed to her class. A test! No time to worry about things now. She would think about it later.

Frank drove home, the long six hours going quickly with his thoughts chasing around in his head. He knew he should have heeded the doctor's advice even without telling Sallie. Just as a precaution. But somehow he believed God was even now working out an answer. Perhaps he was foolish, but he couldn't shake the feeling that God's answer was coming and in a way that would help Sallie far more than talk.

13

The test was difficult. And Sallie wasn't in the best of shape. Somehow she got through it, and wondered if there were any chance that she'd passed it. If only her father had come this evening!

She wandered out into the late afternoon light oblivious of the raw wind. As she made her way across campus to the canteen to meet Harvey, she thought of her mother, locked away, lost in her own private hell. All the anxieties, the secret doubts, the suspected inuendos of the past months assaulted Sallie now. There had been those strange letters. And the time she called to ask about Thanksgiving and her mother had been resting. Then the last few weeks her father's increasingly general letters and the total stop of mail from her mother. Yes, there had been doubts and worries and a growing awareness of fear. Sallie had a fatalistic view. She was going to get hers now.

What a thought to have on the way to meet your boyfriend, no, your own true love, Sallie reflected. Sallie's heart chugged painfully in her chest and her stomach churned. Oh, wow! First, she'd been scared Harvey would find out about her. Sallie smiled ironically. What a laugh! Harvey! The world's number one puritan on sex! The award-winning advocate against abortion — or, as he said, for life. Oh, sure. There was good reason to want to hide the truth. Oh, daddy, if only you knew! I love Harvey! I can't bear losing again!

"Harvey, I want you to meet my father. Where's mom? Well, she's not well right now. You see, we had a few problems. What problems? Well, look, you may love me, but you'll just have to take me the way I am."

And how! Beautiful, aren't I? Mother's nuts, because of her daughter — oh sure, she would have cracked anyway, but it's always super to be the one who dropped the egg — and daughter's a little liar who acts sweet and innocent! Wow!

Sallie stopped at the door to the canteen. She looked around. There were a few kids running for the dining hall of the boys' dorm. She was suddenly aware of the icy wind. She looked up and saw thick, black clouds ready to burst, it seemed. Across the campus, down by the village ran the swift flowing, bloated river, carrying chunks of ice with it. How nice to ride one of those chunks away, far away.

She opened the door. The warm air felt good as she looked around. Harvey was eating French fries at a corner booth. Her heart constricted at the sight of him, skinny, serious, homely, and kind. She took a deep breath. How kind would he be when he found out?

Well, she couldn't tell him. Not yet.

She went over to him. They touched hands and for a moment she forgot, lost in the beauty of the look he gave her.

She sat down across from him, smiling, feeling like a hypocrite.

"Hi."

"How'd it go?"

What? she wondered in a panic. Surely he doesn't know dad was here. Oh, the test.

"Terrible."

Harvey smiled easily. "Aw, come on, brain."

"Don't tease! Not now."

Harvey gave her a searching look, shoved the last French fry in his mouth, and leaned back.

"You serious?" he asked.

"Yes — I mean I don't know. It was awful and I — I was up-tight."

"You pass? I mean, it's a final."

"For heaven's sake, Harvey! Don't you think I know?"

Harvey reached for her hand. "Hey, come on. I feel like that lots of times. You did okay."

She felt his hand squeezing her own, gently massaging her fingers.

Oh, Harvey! she wanted to cry out. Oh, Harvey!

"You didn't ask about mine."

"Oh, I'm sorry. How was it?"

He smiled impishly, pleased with himself. "I aced it right out."

Sallie had to laugh. "You big shot," she said. "You're finished now, aren't you?"

"Yup. And no more chemistry at all, ever!"

"Well, that's nice. Wish I were done, too."

"Next week, my sweet." Harvey turned her hand over examining each finger. "And then three weeks apart. You want to rush that?"

Sallie felt the tears stinging her eyes. She couldn't answer for a minute. At last she said, "I could stay, too. There must be something I could do."

"Nope, you go home. Check in like a good kid and get me invited for the last week." He fixed her with a steady look. "You've got to lay the groundwork."

"I could call. You could talk to daddy."

"Nope again."

"Why not?"

"I got records work to do and I'll be running quick-like down to the Home for Christmas. Then where'd you be? All alone." He picked up her hand and brushed it with his lips. "Besides, we need chaperones. Not a nice, big, empty campus."

Sallie turned her hand in his and laid it on his cheek. She gave him a watery smile.

"You're right as usual," she said.

"Yup! That's what I'm always telling you."

She laughed. "Oh, Harvey."

He smiled and kissed her hand again and put it down on the table. He stretched and stood up. "You want to go to the library for awhile?"

She nodded, trying to keep the tears back. Oh, I really can't take this. He's so sweet.

They left hand in hand and went to the library, where they could talk quietly and alone. They discussed their plans, Sallie trying to act as if nothing were changed. He would finish school, taking his special language courses in the summer. She would take the language courses, too, and continue on for his final year, completing her liberal arts credits. Later, when they were back in the States, she could get her degree.

Sallie felt small and lost and mixed up. He thought she was wonderful, clean, good. She knew he was. There was no hope. When the day came that he knew, it was all over. And the suspense was killing her anyway.

She pictured the situation, as if by some miracle he remained ignorant for that long. They would have been married for, say, ten years. There were children and they had a life together. Someone told him. Who knows? Maybe Cam — out of meanness. "Oh yeah, I had her when she was a kid." He wouldn't need the rest. Or maybe her mother — even if she got well. Or her father: "We must face the truth."

But she couldn't wait that long, or even a year, or a month. Not any more. Not now that it was there, full-blown, ugly, obsessive in her mind. Not now that all the fears had taken root. Not now that it had already gotten to her mother.

She shivered and Harvey saw it, stopped talking, watching her. There was something wrong. Very wrong. She didn't even notice that he'd paused.

At last they walked to her dorm, and she knew what she had to do. She looked at Harvey's dear face and thought: You'll find out probably, but at least I won't have to watch your love for me go out. They stood in the shadowy doorway, the snow hurling around them, swirling, and biting at their cheeks. Harvey wrapped her in his arms and held her close, feeling her melt against him.

"What's wrong?"

Sallie caught her breath.

"Nothing. Just the test."

"Sure?"

She nodded and lifted her face for his kiss. Oh, kiss me, kiss me, Harvey!

They stood together for a long moment, locked in an embrace to last forever. Harvey felt her tension, sensed the terrible fear that made her cling as if for life. More than his body, stirred by her warmth, he felt sucked in, drawn to her from his mind. They had never kissed this way before.

"See you tomorrow," he whispered at last in her ear.

She squeezed her arms about his neck. "Just one more kiss. For the road."

Finally, Sallie was inside, drained, no longer afraid. There was an answer. But only one. There was just so much you could take.

Harvey went home. He had a tutoring appointment at seven o'clock. Poor kid. If he passed freshman English, it would be a miracle. Well, Harvey did believe in miracles. He'd seen some. And Sallie. She worried him. He heated some water on his hot plate, made instant coffee. He heard laughter downstairs as the nightly gathering of card players at Joe's prepared for a serious game. Sallie was a problem. She'd been so strange. He had one of his feelings about her. Watch her! Better stick around. He went to his window and looked up the hill to her dorm. Watch her.

And out his rear window, below him, swift and dark, the river flowed on, carrying its ice and sand and secrets of other years.

It really is easy once you've decided. Making the choice is always the hardest part. You think and think. You ask yourself if, after all, you can go on. You try to find just one reason to keep going. But if you are aware of all the facts, and they point to nothing but fear and defeat, you are forced to try to save yourself. What is suicide but a desperate attempt to save oneself from an intolerable situation?

Sallie skipped dinner. She wasn't hungry anyway. She sat in her room, planning, while Clara and the other girls ate. There were several ways to do it, but one seemed obviously much better. She had no pills or knife, and slipping into the kitchen to get one was only half the problem. After you had one, you had to decide where to be for the end. She certainly didn't want to shock the other girls any more than she had to. Of course, she could jump, but that was really a shocker. Splattered all over the parking lot, or, worse, not dead at all.

No, the river was the obvious, cleanest, and surest. It was a dark, snowy, cold night. No one would be out walking the river path. The water was half ice and swift, as surely her end would be. She would tell Clara she was going to study in the library. Clara would not be surprised, since she often did that. Sallie felt a clutch of fear. What if Clara wanted to come along? Why not go now? Leave a note saying she'd gone to the library and hope Clara didn't check too soon. Besides, all she needed was a few minutes.

Sallie got off her bed where she had been lying. Quickly she put on her coat and red muffler and cap. No use freezing before she had to. She pulled on her fur-lined boots and picked up a pencil to scribble a hasty note. No suicide note for her. What could she say? It would take volumes.

At last she let herself out the deserted side door of the dorm. It was really blowing out. Skiffs of snow bit her face, the wind whipped her hair into her mouth. She could see fairly well. It was a black night, but the contrast of the snow made clear her way. She slipped and slid down the icy sidewalk into the village. Vaguely she could see a light in Harvey's window, and for a moment she thought she saw him looking out. Her heart ached for Harvey and an accusing voice asked why she didn't give him a chance. Because she couldn't

96

bear the possibility of life without him, that's why. And she couldn't, most of all, stand to watch that face register the meaning of her tale. To see him become aware of the real Sallie.

She gave the window a wave. Well, good-by, Harvey. Good-by, love. The Miss Sallie you knew was a myth, and soon, Miss Sallie shall be no more. Soon no more sweet innocence to fool you. She approached the river path, dimly seen as an outline in the snow, a slight depression. She picked her way along it until she came to a spot where she knew the water was swifter and very, very deep. She could swim, but she wouldn't.

Suddenly, she remembered her father's words: " . . . we weren't honest Christians . . . God was to be used . . . ." Where was God in all this blackness and misery? Was He out there in the big, ugly, turbulent clouds? No, she saw that now. He wasn't any particular place, unless you asked Him to come. But how did you know when you were being "an honest Christian"? She was adept at twisting the truth to fit the need of the moment. Yes, she had made God her own way and thus, in the end, when she ran out of resources, so did her God.

Sallie stood next to the river. Now's when I should be afraid, she thought, but her heart was quiet, her mind at rest. Somehow, it seemed the right thing to do. But maybe that's what all suicides felt like at the end.

The water was cold. In fact, at first Sallie was only aware of the current, the pull of her heavy clothes. Then, she felt a stinging, tingling on her skin. But soon she was numb, and she drifted, head bobbing, thoughts dulling into oblivion. Her last thought was very pleasant. She was riding an ice floe to a far-off land where the truth was known and accepted. No more hiding for Sallie.

Harvey had decided to cancel his tutoring appointment. The weather was too lousy for the poor guy to come over. He went downstairs to Joe's and called the student's dorm. He changed the time to first thing in the morning. The fellow sounded relieved.

After he hung up, Harvey ordered some eggs and toast and home fries and sat down at the bar to wait. Joe's wife, Prissy, made small talk as she expertly turned the eggs.

"Where's your girl friend?"

"Studying."

"Me, I'm glad I was too dumb for college."

Harvey laughed. "You're too smart, you mean."

Prissy set the plate of steaming food before him.

"Could be," she grinned, her plain round face showing approval.

"You've got it good, Prissy, and you know it. A steady clientele, plenty of friends, and a job working beside your husband. How many of those college girls will end up with that?"

Prissy shrugged her plump shoulders. "They'll marry some rich little college boy and go away from here. Me, I'm stuck."

"Hey, Prissy! They're the ones who are stuck. They've got to keep up appearances and they work so hard at it that they don't even know what they're keeping up."

Prissy laughed. "How about you? You gonna marry that little blondie? She's just like the rest of them. Wants a soft life."

"Nope," Harvey grinned. "She's not the same. She used to be, but I changed all that. Now she's ready to soil her pretty hands and get old doing something worthwhile. Like you."

"Me? What do you call worthwhile? I fry hamburgers and serve a bunch of kids."

"True, true," Harvey said wiping egg yolk off his chin. "But you're an example, too. A cheerful servant. A happy wife." Harvey smiled his sad smile and shook his head. "How many of those little girls will grow up to be as content with their lot as you? Maybe they watch you, and the guys, too."

Prissy blushed. "You just want them eggs for free."

Harvey let out a yelp of laughter. The men playing cards looked over at him and smiled.

"Put it on my bill," Harvey said and got up.

When he got to his room, he went to his window. It was wicked out there. He looked up the hill toward Sallie's dorm, but it was obscured by the snow.

All at once, he felt a Presence surrounding him, unbidden. "You think you love my daughter, Sallie," a Voice said. "But you don't know the meaning of love. Do you love her as much as I do?"

Harvey looked around.

"Watch her!"

"So, where is she?" Harvey asked aloud.

He looked out the window, and for an instant the snow stopped swirling, revealing a familiar red cap atop streaming blond hair. Sallie! What was she doing out on a night like this?

The Presence was gone, the feeling of being engulfed absent. And with the absence, a curious emptiness. Harvey had no doubt that it had been God.

But now he felt an urgency to be outside, to get to Sallie. Without putting on his coat, he ran down the back stairway out into the howling weather. Vaguely, he could see Sallie far down the path that ran along the river.

He shouted.

"Sallie! Sallie! Wait!"

But the wind carried his words away, melting them before they'd gone a few feet.

He began to run. Where was she going? She seemed unaware of

the wind and snow, and stopped at last on a bluff overlooking the water.

Oh, no! Harvey thought. I can't get there in time. If she . . .

The next moment Harvey saw her head bobbing in the water, being carried quickly away from him.

"Oh, Father," he shouted. "If You love her, help me! I can't reach her!"

Harvey ran harder, slipping and almost falling into the icy depths himself. Sallie was floating, miraculously, her coat had formed a sort of balloon, buoying her up. She lay relaxed in the water, her face occasionally going under.

He was gaining a little! The river slowed here, for a corner. If he ran — come on, God! — he could get to the curve and on the other side of it before Sallie floated around.

With a last burst of energy, Harvey pushed his long legs faster, leaping to reach a tree that hung out over the water. Precariously he hung on with his ankles and dangled one arm as far as he could.

Sallie rounded the bend. The coat was losing its air pocket, and she was lower in the water. Harvey strained to reach. She was beneath him. Just a few more inches! Please, God! Just a little more!

He felt the soggy fake fur of her coat. He had her! She wasn't drifting on! The pull was mighty, though, and he had to get a better grip. He let go his other arm from the tree trunk, relying solely on his strong legs to hold them both.

Somehow, he was able to lift her, to pull her limp form to the tree with him. Once she was out of the water, he supported her with one hand, getting a grip on the tree with his other. Then, he gave a heave, and Sallie flopped across the trunk, dangling from either side.

For a minute Harvey let her dangle. He couldn't believe it! Surely it had been impossible! But here she was out of the water. But maybe it was too late!

He roused himself and dragged her onto the river bank. He laid his face near hers. No, she was breathing, had taken in little water because of her coat. She was unconscious from the cold, and had just floated.

A miracle!

Harvey picked her up and began to carry her wet form minus the entangling scarf and heavy coat back to the college. Thank God they had a decent infirmary and a doctor nearby! Yes, thank God.

He thought of the Presence that had come to warn him to watch her. Why? How? Was he weird? He had had feelings, intuitions, before, but nothing so graphic. It had been so real. He had believed that Voice implicitly. Thank God!

And then Harvey gave a little laugh, on the edge of tears, as he hurried towards the lighted infirmary. Thank God for the tree, too, and the curve! He swallowed in amazement. That really was fantastic! For Harvey couldn't swim. Not one stroke.

14

They finally reached Frank at the office. He was busy working on some mortgage papers for tax purposes. Keeping busy was important lately, and, ironically, he had come to respect his job. In fact, Frank had, in the last few weeks, discovered, or rediscovered, his own self-respect. He realized that he enjoyed his work and the pressures weren't as great as the high-powered executives faced in the main office downtown. All the trouble had at last pointed out to him his blessings.

He was thinking about these things as he worked, when the buzzer on his desk phone went off. He picked up the receiver and his secretary said there was a long distance call from a place called Pleasant Valley.

"I'll take it," Frank said, and in a moment he was surprised to hear a male voice inquire if he was speaking to Sallie Victor's father.

"Yes." Frank felt a flutter of apprehension.

"Mr. Victor, before I say anything else, I want you to know your daughter is all right."

Frank felt panic growing.

"What's happened?" he croaked.

"This is Dr. Behmer — the on-call physician at the college," the male voice went on. "Your daughter appears to have wandered into the river — "

"Oh, no!" Frank exploded.

"Calm down, Mr. Victor. I told you she's all right. Luckily, she was seen by — as fate would have it — her boyfriend and he fished her out."

Boyfriend? No wonder Sallie had been so reluctant to allow the truth to come to light. No wonder she had requested time. Why hadn't she told him?

"Are you there, Mr. Victor?"

"Yes." Of course, she had seen no way of facing it. Where were You, God? Frank felt bitterly let down. What a fool he had been!

"How is she?" he asked.

"She's in shock a little yet, but coming out of it. It was pretty cold. Luckily, she didn't swallow much water. She should be coming around by the time you get here."

"Yes," Frank thought, another day gone. When would it end? "I'll leave immediately."

100

The doctor repeated that Sallie was all right, and hung up, leaving Frank in a void. He wasn't aware how long he sat in his chair staring at the phone. Finally, he rang for his secretary. When she appeared he told her he'd have to be gone the rest of the day, to cancel his luncheon appointment with the realtors. The trim young woman gave him a questioning look and retreated. This was the third day this week her boss had canceled appointments.

As Frank left the bank, walking out into the overcast day, portending still more snow, he realized things were going to have to straighten up, or he'd lose his job. Right now, it seemed that would be par for the course.

He had tried to trust God. Well, face it. He'd been scared when Nancy broke down. He'd needed an anchor, however nebulous. And oh, how much better he felt, giving the responsibility to God.

Frank didn't bother going home. It was 9:30, traffic was thinning out from the rush hour, and soon he was headed out of the city toward Pleasant Valley. Yesterday he'd made this trip determined to face Sallie with the truth and to save her from the same hidden consequences Nancy had suffered. What had he done, though? Told her. Sermonized. Then gone off without really asking how she felt — without warning anyone. And why? Because he believed in God! God would handle it! God was even then working it out!

His daughter's words came back to rebuke him.

"Grow up, daddy!"

Yes, all his life he'd been relying on someone else to support him. First God — oh, probably first his parents — then God, then Nancy, then God again. When was he going to grow up and rely on himself?

Then he thought of Sallie's going into that river. That had been no accident. And the boyfriend? How had he been there at the right moment? Sallie's self-reliance had led her to attempt suicide. Was it possible the existence or active presence of God was not the vital thing? If Sallie's belief had been strong enough to relieve her of guilt, would she have found the courage to go on? Frank couldn't answer that now. Life was such a mess! Even the existence of God seemed doubtful in the light of the continuing chain of tragedy.

But ignorance was bliss. Believing in a nonexistent God was still much more pleasant, especially when you were relieved of responsibility. Perhaps though, just perhaps, God had been there, not only existing but helping.

Frank thought of the river. He had noticed it yesterday — its swiftness, its churning depth. How could anyone have gone in after Sallie — in the night — and come out alive? Even a champion swimmer would have had difficulty with that one, especially carrying a dead weight. And the coincidence of the boyfriend being there. Unless they'd been together all along.

The miles rolled by with Frank's questioning, conjecturing, demanding answers. Where would it all end? When would they have peace?

His newly found faith in God seemed dormant now, if not dead. When he stood off from himself and coolly surveyed the wreckage of his life, he was appalled he hadn't joined Nancy.

But still, one thing he had learned, or was learning. If he had spoken soon enough! In all his troubles he could see that his failure to speak out had allowed these things to develop. Even yesterday he had spoken out some, but not all.

In that instant Frank had an insight: *God was there*. Prodding, trying to get Frank to notice Him and give over his will. And even though Frank had asked for God's guidance, he was still unwilling to go full-throttle, to stop holding back.

By the time Frank was half-way to Pleasant Valley, he was no longer panicky or confused. Hard to accept as it was, in view of all the mindless destruction in the world, God had protected Sallie; He was giving Frank yet another chance to really level with her. It was indeed a miracle she wasn't dead. God had some purpose for all this — deeper than he had first thought, more than merely dredging up the truth. But Frank must be willing to accept his part, his job, and not hide behind God. These were strange thoughts for a banker on the way to the bedside of his suicidal daughter, but, whatever the reason, Frank was relying on God. He simply couldn't totally reject the idea of Him, or His concern, no matter what happened. With a growing awareness, Frank sympathized with the early Christians. Once God had you, He wouldn't let you go, and even death became only a passing irritation. Through crisis came strength.

Harvey got up early Friday morning, finally giving up on sleep. His night had been short and restless, filled with strange dreams. They were like those dreams where the bad guys are after you and your legs are two pillars of lead you can barely lift. He kept reaching that tree a moment too late, and Sallie would drift by in slow motion as he vainly grabbed thin air. He would wake up in a cold sweat, remembering with relief that Sallie was in the infirmary, sleeping.

As Harvey dressed and fixed coffee and a soft-boiled egg, he thought again of bringing Sallie to the infirmary. The lights had been on — it was early after all and the college nurse was watching TV. He had battered in the door, carrying Sallie, who looked like a giant log of ice. In the bitter cold, they had frozen together and nurse had to pour hot water on them to pry Sallie free. Then, between the two of them, they had melted the rest of her clothes and got her undressed and into the bathtub. Harvey had phoned the doctor, while the nurse gently sponged the girl with cool water, working up to lukewarm.

When the doctor got there (in his tuxedo since he'd been at a formal dinner), he had taken over, recording the nurse's findings in his mind and prescribing medicine to offset shock. He was amazed she wasn't more badly frostbitten, only patches of her extremities appeared affected. At last Sallie was settled in bed, still unconscious, but sedated now and with vital signs holding steady. Then the doctor had questioned Harvey, never blinking an eyelash at his fantastic story. The nurse had given him coffee and lent him a coat, left by a boy in quarantine with mumps, so he could get home. By then, it was midnight.

Now, as Harvey finished his last bite of bread and apple butter, he had a chance to reflect on the events of the previous night. In a few hours he would be tutoring the freshman who didn't know a noun from a pronoun — how did he get out of high school? Harvey cleaned up, washing his dishes in the bathroom sink, making sure the hot plate was off. Then he took his coffee cup to his old rickety armchair near the rear window. He sank back into its sagging springs and looked out the window. The sun sparkled on the freshly fallen snow, glinted on the river, deceiving the eye into thinking it was calm and slow. Harvey was astounded.

There was no way to categorize what had happened last night, and the sight of the river, which he knew to be churning and fast, caused an awe to settle over him.

He had run against that powerhouse and won! He had been there at the right minute! Harvey thought of the Voice — it was capitalized in his mind — directing him. If it hadn't happened to him, he would never have believed it. He could picture the disbelief if he were to repeat the story.

But without the Voice, he would not have been there.

And the tree. Well, if the story got around, the kids could go see the tree for themselves. Later, upon second viewing, Harvey was to wonder how he had hung on. But stranger things had happened, like a man lifting a car off a child. When crisis hit, one didn't question whether one could do it. Questioning came later. Like now.

Harvey sipped his coffee, relishing the feeling of awe. Sallie would be okay! Of course, there was the question of why. Harvey shook his head and looked at his unmade bed. Getting up, he proceeded to straighten the room still asking himself why. They were in love. They were happy. What could be lurking in her mind to override all that?

Harvey tugged his sheets smooth, kicked his pajamas under the bed. The fellow would be here soon, and after that he could go see Sallie. His heart beat hard in his chest. He looked up at the peeling ceiling.

"Thanks, God," he said simply. "I don't know how You swung this, but I'm just glad You did."

The young man came. Randy was a football "scholar" and he had a great respect for Harvey's brain, one which could actually decipher this madness called English. Harvey, in turn, was amazed and awed at the size of Randy's arms and his bull neck. Next to Harvey's skinny physique, Randy made a striking contrast.

They worked for two hours. In class Randy would have to write an essay graded not only for content, but for grammar. Randy lacked in both areas.

When the session was over, Harvey was exhausted. Randy was a nice guy — not cocky like some of them. He really wanted to learn, but it was a tough grind. Harvey always told them they'd be great, figuring that confidence could cover a lot of ignorance, but poor Randy had a lot to cover.

Harvey put on his coat and, picking up the borrowed one, started for the infirmary. He waved to Joe, who was mopping the floor, cigar smoke curling from the butt left over from last night's game. What a character! The butt probably wasn't even Joe's!

It felt good outside. The snow was about eighteen inches deep. Even Harvey's long legs had to strain to get clear of it, and how they ached! He must have pulled every muscle he had.

He saw kids he knew. A few asked him if it were true he'd swum for a half a mile against the current trying to reach Sallie. Harvey just stared. The grapevine was working, defectively as usual.

When he reached the infirmary, Dr. Behmer was talking quietly with Sallie. He glanced up when Harvey came in.

"Hey, look who's here. The boy wonder!" The doctor stood up from the edge of the bed and went over to Harvey, who waited at the door to the room.

"She's very depressed," the doctor said. He was a short man with a disarming grin and mischief-filled eyes. "I've been trying to find out her problem. I gather she's a good student, so it's not that."

Harvey could see Sallie, stretched out beneath the covers, looking away from him, at the wall.

"You got problems?" Dr. Behmer asked. "Like a baby, maybe?"

Harvey looked down at the little doctor, who was smiling conspiratorily. He was too tired to be angry. Besides, you couldn't blame the guy. He must see a lot of coeds in trouble.

"No," he said.

"Got any ideas?"

"Not now. Can I talk to her?"

The doctor looked at the pretty girl lying on the bed. Despite the chapped, red skin, he could see she was a real beauty. She was smart, too. He shrugged his shoulders. "You can try. So far, I haven't gotten anything out of her, but the bitter knowledge that she failed. I'm afraid to let her go home at this rate."

"Is she going home?" Harvey felt a pain in his chest. How could he watch her there?

"Well," the doctor said, "I called her dad. Had to, you know, with classes almost over for the quarter. He'll want to take her home now, I'm sure. Besides, she's no less safe there than here. If she wants to do it bad

104

enough, she'll try again." Dr. Behmer shifted his weight from one foot to the other. "You talk to her. You're close to her. Maybe you can find out something."

Harvey nodded and went over to the bed. Sallie looked very tired, her skin red and chapped from exposure, and her face a mask of dejection. She wouldn't look at him. For awhile he stood there, trying to perceive what lay inside that head, trying to think of a key phrase to unlock the tight, mean look clamped on her lips.

"Hi," he said and wondered if they'd told her who had rescued her.

But she lay still, unmoving, appearing not to hear.

Harvey sat down and prepared to wait. He crossed his legs and leaned back in his chair.

"Well, Miss Sallie," he said. "Any time you care to talk, I'm ready to listen."

Being dead isn't really much different from being alive, Sallie thought. There is still pain. She had thought that there would be no after-effects from freezing to death. Maybe just a memory of what if felt like to pass from one world to the next — if one really did pass on. But she must have frozen to death before she drowned, for her skin burned terribly.

Sallie opened her eyes and looked around. She was vaguely surprised to see she was in a room that looked very much like one she'd known on earth. No heavenly harps here, or fiery dungeons — just a plain bureau, a table that rolled over the bed she was lying on, a bedstand with a pitcher and glass on it, and a middle-aged-looking woman sitting in the only chair near the wall. Everything looked very familiar, even the woman. Where had she seen her before?

Sallie lay still. Her skin stung, her head ached. She felt awful. Then suddenly she knew.

She wasn't dead after all.

With a lurching feeling in her stomach, Sallie realized who the woman was. The college nurse! This was the infirmary of Pleasant Valley College. She moaned and turned her head painfully away from the woman.

A moment later she heard the nurse in the outer room speaking, presumably on the phone.

"You wanted to know when she began to come around, doctor. Well, she's begun to moan and move her head."

There was a pause.

"Yes, I'll wait with her and make sure she doesn't disturb the I.V."

Sallie opened her eyes again and looked at her arm laid out flat on the bed. A thin tube ran into it, dripping a colorless liquid into her vein. Then she noticed her skin, red and chapped-looking, glistening with some kind of medication.

I failed, she thought, and began to cry.

Oh, God, why do I have to live? Please, please, I'd rather be dead.

Sallie lay in a mud-brown limbo while the doctor came and took her vital signs, prescribed more salve and antibiotic. She kept her eyes closed, but she could hear him conversing with the nurse. At last all was quiet.

She opened her eyes and there was the doctor, in a white coat, smiling down at her. Hastily, she reshut her lids.

"Ah-ha!" the doctor said, with a grin in his voice. "I caught you now, young lady."

Sallie lay silent.

"Oh, come now, Miss Victor. I know you're coming along nicely. You may as well face up to the fact that you are still very much a part of this world."

Involuntarily, Sallie's thoughts boiled over.

"Not for long!" she spat.

"Suppose we talk about that," the doctor said.

But Sallie lay silent, cursing the doctor, the nurse, the I.V. that fed her, and most of all God.

"I know you tried to end it all," the doctor went on in a conversational tone. "But apparently your boyfriend didn't agree with your diagnosis of the hopeless situation."

Sallie's eyes flew open. The doctor was staring down at her, compelling her to answer. My boyfriend! She moaned again and turned away from the doctor. How had Harvey worked that one? Had he been there at the window after all? Why can't he *ever* leave me alone? The doctor was talking, but Sallie turned him off. Go home, she shouted in her mind. Go home and let me die!

For a long time then, Sallie lay still, feeling the soothing relief of the salve, and ignoring the doctor's questions and gentle probes. Suddenly, the bed shook as the doctor stood up and she heard him say, "Well, look who's here! The boy-wonder!"

Harvey! Sallie clamped her eyelids tight, grinding her mouth closed. She didn't hear them talking. She was too upset. How could he come here and see her like this? The next thing she was aware of was a chair being slid over near her bed and the creak of it as someone sat down. She heard Harvey's voice say "Hi," but she lay still, heart hammering. Oh, why won't he go away!

"Well, Miss Sallie, any time you care to talk, I'm ready to listen."

I can't, Harvey, she thought, madly searching for some way to go on ignoring. I can't, or I'll tell it all! Please, go away! I'm so tired of pretending! Please go away and leave me alone.

The seconds passed, piling up into minutes, and still Sallie lay still, outwardly calm and unmoving. Inside she waged war with herself.

Open your eyes, you idiot! Tell him! Quit running!

No! I can't. Please, I just want to die. It's too long and too much. Why can't I die?

Because, you fool, it doesn't solve anything! You'll just hurt more people. Think of your father! Of Harvey. Quit hiding!

Sallie realized she was shaking her head, and stopped it. Too late.

"I won't go away, Sallie," Harvey said quietly. "There is nothing more important than you."

I hate you, Harvey Plimpton! her mind screamed. You are always, always there! Please let me die!

With a shuddering sigh, Sallie opened her eyes and looked at Harvey sitting in the chair, legs crossed, looking as though he would wait forever.

"Good morning," he said, giving her his heartrending grin. "You sort of gave me a work-out last night."

It was morning then. Only one night gone and nothing gained. You won't like this, Harvey.

"Well, are you just going to stare at me, or are you going to say something? Like hi, maybe. Or thanks."

Sallie began to feel the old irritation, closely followed by the knowledge of his unshakeable love. Oh, Harvey!

She looked away from the infuriating grin, toward the wall again.

"Go away," she said softly. Turning her face to him again, she added, "Just go away, now, Harvey! Before it's too late! Please!"

Her voice shook and she tried to cover her face with her hands, but the one arm was strapped securely down to the bed. So, giving up, she lay, her face exposed as she sobbed.

She felt Harvey's hands on her face, wiping the tears, trying to hold her still.

"Hey, stop this," he said low. "You'll shake the tube loose."

"I don't care! I don't care!"

"Sure you do."

"Oh, Harvey, go away! Please let me alone, you'll just hate me when you know!"

"Shsh! I'll have to get the nurse if you don't stop," he said kissing her forehead. "Please, Sallie! I can't bear it to see you like this! Please tell me!" His kisses covered her face, and then, abruptly, he sat up, taking away his hands. She heard him sigh long and hard. "Sallie, I love you. How could you do this to me?"

His voice was plaintive, yearning, and Sallie's heart broke. The dam gave way, the last retainer, "Oh, Harvey," she sobbed. "I love you, too. Can't you see that's why I did it?"

Through her tears she could see him sitting dejected, unhappy, his arms hanging between his knees in an attitude of defeat.

She took a deep breath. "You'll have to know now. I didn't want to be the one to tell you all the ugly truth about myself. Surely you must see I didn't want to be the instrument of my own torment?"

Harvey looked at her sadly. "What do you mean?" he asked.

Sallie reached for his hand, all at once unafraid. At least, when it was over, she would be free, free of it all and free of Harvey. Free to die, with no one to stop her. No more Harvey to protect her.

"Harvey," she said simply, "I had an abortion." Of course, there was more to it than that. There was Cam, there was loneliness and pride and self-preservation. And there was her mother, sick, and her father burdened by them both. But for the moment, she lay back, feeling his hand go stiff, seeing his face change from sadness to horror.

"You!" he said unbelieving.

"Yes." She felt the calm slipping away. "You will never understand, I know."

Harvey stared at her, as if he were seeing her for the first time. He pulled his hand away, leaving her with the feeling of loss she knew was inevitable.

"Now you see, Harvey!" she said in a ragged tone.

"My gosh!" he shouted, getting up. "I thought you were pure!"

"I know," she moaned pitifully, but Harvey was unaware of her voice.

"You looked so sweet! And I felt God meant you for me!"

Harvey wrung his hands, and Sallie watched, with one corner of her mind a disinterested observer. He's so shocked, she thought. His puritanical mind is so offended that he can't believe he could have been so taken in. She felt a wave of nausea, both for his reaction and her causing it.

"Don't you want to know why, Harvey?" she asked quietly. "Don't you even care why?"

"Why?" he repeated. "You know how I feel. Who cares why! You got pregnant — for whatever reason. One boy or a thousand! Who cares? You killed a baby to save yourself. You really are just like the others. You really don't care about any other human life!" he shouted, and the nurse came in, staring at his flailing arms. "I spend hours and days loving children without parents, trying to give meaning to their lives, started by some careless girl like you!" He stopped, and suddenly seemed to see the nurse.

Sallie lay still tears raining down her cheeks. It was worse than she had imagined. He hated her all right! And soon she would hate him, too!

"You must stop that," the nurse said, looking Harvey in the eye.

"Shut up!" he said and went to Sallie. "I broke my back for you and you lied all along!"

"No!" Sallie found her voice. "Can't you see what you're doing? Where's your Jesus now? Your loving, forgiving Jesus? You don't care about my human life — just some baby's. Look at me, Harvey! What would your Jesus say to me? My Jesus must not know yours!"

Harvey looked down on her, his face registering a deep sorrow.

"Maybe neither one of us know Him," he said. "But I saved your life last night! So don't say I don't care about your human life. What's your excuse?"

Sallie looked deep into Harvey's eyes, seeing the hurt and disappointment, seeing the faint hope that he was dreaming.

The nurse touched Harvey's arm. "You really must go."

Harvey ignored her, shaking off her hand.

At last Sallie's eyes slid away from his, unable to meet his challenge.

"Now you see," she moaned. "I have no excuse. I did it. That's all."

Harvey stood looking at her a few moments longer, and then, turning on his heel, he walked out.

The nurse smoothed Sallie's sheets, nervously. "There, there," she soothed in a confused tone of voice.

But Sallie didn't listen. Death was preferable to this, surely. Condemned and alive must be the worse thing to have happen.

15

It wasn't yet noon when Harvey left the infirmary. Just a few hours before he had been exulting about the marvelous, if unexplained, intervention and direction of God in regard to Sallie. It was a far different mood that possessed Harvey now, as he made his way back across the sunlit snow to his room over Joe's Come and Get It.

When Harvey arrived, he took off his old duffel coat and flung it on the bed, throwing his hunting cap down on top of it. Then he went to the rear window, where the river still flowed unfeelingly, inexorably, constantly.

Unbelievable! Unthinkable! That he would be directed to save Sallie knowing what he did now. Surely, it would have been better for them all if Sallie had drowned. That grief couldn't have been as devastatingly final as this. At least he would have had good memories! Now he had only the sickening knowledge that Sallie had been right after all.

Harvey felt a sense of failure. He knew a bigger person would forgive — all right, he believed Jesus would forgive. But, after all, he was only a man and a young one at that. He had no special strength to see him through this kind of disappointment.

Harvey flopped down into his armchair, flinging his head back against the frayed cushions. All right! So he had listened, and he had been there when God called. Sallie was supposed to be just a mission after all! So, he had gotten personally involved. And how! It wrenched his heart, broke it into tiny fragments, and ground it to dust, to think of how deeply involved he was. And even now! Yes, even now he loved her — surely, it would fade someday!

Harvey bowed his head in his arms, his shoulders shaking with dry sobs. This was surely hell.

Frank arrived at the infirmary at a little after 3:30 that afternoon. It was very quiet there, except for the soft music from the nurse's radio. The nurse herself sat in an easy chair near the radio, reading. She looked tired, her gray hair a little disheveled and her eyes heavy.

"Hello," Frank said tentatively. "I'm Frank Victor."

"Oh, yes!" The nurse stood up, smoothing her white dress. "Dr. Behmer said he had called you."

Frank stood awkwardly for a moment, twirling his hat in his hands. "She's still here, I suppose."

"Oh, yes," the nurse said again. "Right in here." She led the way down a short hall into a dimly lit room, very institutional.

Sallie lay on the bed. Her skin looked dreadful to Frank, but already it had been helped by the salve, and had lost some of its sore, angry look. When Frank came over to the bed, Sallie opened her eyes.

"Oh, daddy," she whispered, and the tears flowed again.

Frank stood and looked down at her, so miserable and alone. Why had they allowed this to come about? Why hadn't they been firmer, more sure in their own values and aims, when the opportunity had been theirs? Now he must pray that God would speak through him. Really give his will to God's ultimate goal, no strings attached.

"Oh, daddy," Sallie repeated tearfully. "I'm so glad you're here. I want to go home. Please let me go home!"

"You will, sweetie," Frank said, and lowered himself into the chair left there by Harvey.

"I'll phone the doctor at his office and tell him you're here, Mr. Victor," the nurse said, and left them.

Sallie's eyes clung to Frank's face. "I just couldn't take any more, daddy. Everything was so good! I had really forgotten — or at least put it out of my mind. But mommy — " She couldn't go on.

"I know, honey," Frank said, and then he breathed his prayer and took the first, unexpected plunge. "You've been very alone and misguided.

110

Your mother and I long ago decided you were more important than anything else. That was wrong."

Sallie nodded her head painfully, through her tears.

Frank went on, a little surprised at what he was saying and that she should agree.

"You see, sweetie, we tried to change the rules — God's rules — to make the game a sure thing. But you can't do that. Even if everything doesn't tumble down, you become so confused and lost that even the new rules you made no longer help. Soon there is nothing to hold onto. No foundation, no place of knowledge. We did that — not just when you went with Cam, not just with the abortion. No, those were the results of many long years of slow erosion."

Sallie shook her head, crying steadily. "Oh, daddy, I know that now! Oh, I knew something was wrong with us. We always listened to the platitudes at church. I did all that was expected of me. But there was nothing to back it up. And I was so cocky! I was so sure I could handle anything! Alone!" Sallie reached out with both hands, now that she was no longer tied to the I.V. She grabbed Frank's hand convulsively, as if searching for some sure ground.

"Now, I'm so scared, daddy! I don't even know where God is, if He is. And I can't go on alone. Not any more."

Frank held her hands tenderly. "Where's your boyfriend?" he asked gently.

Sallie stopped rolling her head on the pillow, the tears slowing. "How did you know about him?"

Frank smiled a little. "He fished you out, they say."

"Oh." Sallie looked hard at her father, and drew in a big breath. "Well — uh — well, I told him and he — " She started to cry harder again.

Frank felt a slow rage spread through him. He put his arms around her as she went on.

"He demanded I tell him. He said he loved me, needed to know what could be so horrible as to override all our — happiness." She ended on a sob.

Frank squeezed her slender body to him. "He must be awfully old-fashioned to allow your past to influence his feeling for you."

Sallie shook her head. "He's very religious, daddy. I mean, really. His folks were killed as missionaries. He lives and works at an orphanage — where he was raised — trying to teach those kids about God's love. Unfortunately, he's seen too many deserted, unloved kids to have much tolerance for my weakness." Sallie realized she was defending him. Oh, Harvey, why must I defend you?

Frank was very angry now. "Religious?" he said. "He sounds like an old-fashioned fanatic! Most boys would not be too concerned about your previous life in this day and age." Frank paused, getting hold of himself. "Of course, I'm concerned and you are, because we see now that unthinking freedom is disastrous — or can be! But, if he's so religious, where's his forgiveness? Where are his Christian tolerance and love?"

Sallie shook her head. "Daddy, you don't understand. He is human, after all." How much she herself had grown in understanding, now that she was finally down and out! "He had circumstances and influences to make my particular situation unbearable for him. And, oh, daddy, he idolized me!" She smiled, a little shaky smile. "You know that's not a good idea." She bit her lip, remembering her own idolization of Cam.

Frank sat still trying to comprehend. For once, he must really try to understand. He must control his temper, not use it as an excuse to avoid working out an answer. And he must pray for God's answer. What was it, anyway?

"Do you love him?" he asked her quietly. "Even now?"

"It's more than that, daddy. For awhile, when he was raving, I thought I would hate him — like I did Cam. For rejecting me — the real me, with no shams. But, I've laid here for hours since he walked out, thinking and praying, and I can't! I just can't take the easy way out any more, daddy!" Sallie felt as though a weight were lifted off her shoulders, for just admitting she no longer wanted to hide in hate or fear. And, surprisingly, she didn't.

"Daddy," she went on as Frank sat trying to take it all in and understand it. "When you came, I was so scared, so alone. I still am alone. But not so scared. I really did pray to God. I really did ask Him to help me — any way He wanted. I didn't really even know if I still had any belief left — after everything. But I see, after talking to you, and after all the thinking, that I do. In fact, I feel like I've really begun to look for God, and I know that hating Harvey is a terrible waste." Sallie paused rather self-consciously. "Especially since I love him. Even his high morals. Maybe partly because of them. Is it confused, daddy? Can you see at all?"

"The Lord is working on you," Frank said, and was amazed that he no longer hesitated to bring God into it.

Sallie nodded, her tears dried up, her heart strangely at peace. "I guess all I needed was to know Jesus loves me — like the kids' song. But it's hard to know that, when you are lost and lonely and trying to work out your own answers. It isn't easy to let Jesus be enough — even when you know about Him, and believed in Him at one point. I guess I got off the track when I put other things first, and the only way to get back on is to put Him first." Sallie shook her head again. "I never really understood how important it was. I thought I could use God when I needed Him."

"Well," Frank said, feeling rather as if he were speaking lines in an unrehearsed play. "Where do we go from here? You think he'll cool off?"

"I don't know," Sallie said, and then she clasped her father's hand between her own. "He lives over Joe's Come and Get It. Why don't you talk to him? You helped me. It wouldn't hurt to try, daddy." She sighed a little. "Anyway, whatever he does, I'm not running. It's too painful. I feel like whatever happens, I've got to live my life. I've got to let God call the shots."

Frank smiled at her. "We've made a big move, you and I. Maybe we can help mommy, too. But you're right, honey. The only way we can help is by giving it to God, and using our best efforts for Him. We must leave the outcome to Him."

Frank stood up as he saw the nurse come into the room.

"Dr. Behmer says he'll check her tomorrow morning and if she's still progressing, you can take her home."

The nurse smiled at them. They looked very happy. What had happened?

"I'll need a bed, then," Frank remarked. "I'd better call that inn."

"I'm sorry, daddy," Sallie said releasing her father's hand and leaning back against the pillow, suddenly tired. "I seem to have caused a lot of problems. I hope they are about over."

Frank patted her head, smoothing the golden hair, now rather dull and lifeless.

"Don't worry about it," he said. "I'll see you tonight, after you've rested some more. Try to sleep now." He started to go.

"Daddy?"

"Yes, honey?"

"Will you try?"

"Try — hey, what's his name?"

Sallie laughed. "Harvey. Harvey Plimpton."

Frank laughed, too.

"Yes, I'll try Harvey," he said. "But don't worry. Remember what you said."

Sallie nodded, and Frank went out of the room into the hall and out to where the nurse sat reading again.

"I'll be back later if it's all right," he said.

"Of course, Mr. Victor. Dr. Behmer says she needs to talk."

Frank smiled and, buttoning his coat, went out feeling somehow lighter.

Sallie lay quiet in the twilight world of pre-sleep, at last relaxing enough to sleep. Tomorrow she would go home. Then she could really begin to think. Vaguely, she thought of Harvey.

I do love you, she thought drowsily. But this time God's will be done. I mean it, Harvey. Even if I lose you! It's too horrible any other way. She drifted off into sleep where only her dreams reminded her of the realities of her life. And they were distorted, obviously false. For the first time in many months, Sallie slept the sleep of the purged. No longer did she hide in sleep, but she gave herself up to it in total trust.

In the past, Sallie had almost desperately sought her own happiness. She recalled now how sometime last summer she had decided to look after herself first — the first rule of survival. At the time that decision had seemed permanent, and the only way to avert serious danger in her personal life. Before that there had been the all-out, if foolish, devotion to Cam, controlling every thought and action. Easily, that emotion had loosened the mediocre ties to religion and idealistic goals. Somewhere, all along, there had been a deep need for self-gratification, and even her days of dreamy, pure goals had been oriented toward gratifying her own self. She remembered that day — years ago in events, but only last spring — that she had stepped from the school bus and thought of her pleasing excuses for why she was not the most popular girl in her class. Always she had excuses to explain away her behavior. Always there were ways to twist the facts to fit her needs.

Now Sallie lay in the dark room, barely able to make out the outlines of the furniture. She felt much better after her late nap and her light supper of soup and toasted cheese sandwiches. The nurse had offered to bring her a magazine and to lift her bed a little so she could read a while, but Sallie had refused the offer, grateful for the dark, restful room. Soon her father would return. He must have eaten and gotten a room in Watertown. And maybe he had seen Harvey. Maybe Harvey would understand.

Thinking back, Sallie could see that each new mood had seemed lasting, the ultimate answer to self-preservation. Then they had been eroded by events and fears and the lack of a strong foundation.

After Harvey had walked out, shocked and hurt, as she had known he would be, she had gone through the worst torment of her life. Oh, before the abortion, she had been miserable with fear and failure. But with the problem of being found out removed, she had pushed those fears and feelings of defeat away from her and stubbornly continued on her way. Then there had been Harvey, and he had forced her to develop a conscience, a conscience that had finally brought her to the brink of death when confronted with the harsh reality of her mother's collapse. That, then, was the final admittance of defeat — at age eighteen, she was unable to cope with life as she had made it. And seeing Harvey leave this morning had been the turn of the knife blade, the last raw recognition that she couldn't go on alone. She didn't even have the courage left to run.

Lying there in that void, in that great empty hole of knowing how badly she had blown it, of finally seeing that her own willful and, oh, so ignorant nature had destroyed everything of value — her mother, her former purity, her own true love — she just had to accept the blame, there was no diluting any longer. Even contributing factors and people could no longer excuse her, for she had made the final decision to go along, no, to lead the way into self-deception.

No, she couldn't hate Harvey for walking out. Oh, she tried. How she tried! But there was no longer any escape. Harvey may be straitlaced, but so had she been until her drive for self had lessened the hold of values. Harvey had condemned her actions without hearing the full story, but previously she would have done the same thing. Black was black no matter how you tried to say it wasn't. Convicted by her own guilty feelings, there was nowhere left to turn. No longer did she seek her own answers — she couldn't any more. She had no energy, even if she had had an idea.

That was when, in the darkest moment of her life — and it really was heartbreaking to be eighteen and utterly lost — she had turned to God. Oh, again in self-preservation. Let's face it: She had tried to kill herself and couldn't even be a success at that. She had nowhere left to turn, and in the laxity of the past years, the ruin of a strong faith through neglect, she wasn't even sure if God were there. She no longer had the simple faith that had explained creation in eighth grade. Now she was a searcher, a desperate seeker. But if God weren't there, then life was oblivion and even death would not remove the awful disappointment.

Sallie remembered the strange conversation with her father, who had arrived about the time she had been most scared that God wasn't there and couldn't save her. Her father seemed different. Who wouldn't be? But the tragedy that had torn her mother's life to bits had served to reorient and strengthen her father. And he had, miraculously it seemed to Sallie, spoken of God in a way that made Him real. To outsiders, they would have seemed weird, fanatics no doubt, and a little silly. But when it's your own life at stake, you don't stop to ask if you're a little foolish looking.

After her father had gone, Sallie had slept, knowing that at last she was forgiven. Finally, she had come before God, so desperate she had chanced begging a reprieve from a nonexistent Deity, and her father's unashamed faith had shown her that her begging was not without reward. "Ask and ye shall receive" had come to her from Bible-reading days. A genuine desire for salvation, for a life-changing renewal of a dead faith, had indeed given her the only true reprieve.

But now, after the exhaustion was assuaged some, awaiting her father and possibly, just possibly, Harvey, she realized that each time in the past, she had sought her own answers, she had been convinced they would last forever. She was a little afraid that her mind was tricking her again. For she no longer felt the guilt or the driving need to run. She felt almost an eagerness to face reality, to live life, to turn her failure into God's success. But this feeling was new and untested and she was scared, with that gnawing feeling in her stomach. She knew if it didn't last, if this too passed away, she was really lost. Her entire life hung in the balance, her whole hope for the future, for a return to decency.

Sallie lay on the bed, her skin still a little sore, wondering if she could do it. And then, with a little shock, she remembered. She had given her life to God, not as a child who feels no responsibility, but as a convicted sinner, an adult made aware of God's grace. From now on, she need no longer consider if she could do it. She no longer had to solve life's riddles with her brain or her own will. She had a pattern to follow in the life of Jesus, and a guide to call on in the form of the Holy Spirit from God. Her years of Sunday school training came back now, and the only thing she need do was to take each step at a time, letting the strength and direction come from God.

It all seemed somewhat unreal, yet so much more vital. Sallie waited, hoping and praying that God would use her life for His plans on earth in some way. She was now glad she had failed, for through her failure she had discovered the reality of God. It seemed unreal only because it was new and different. Even living under God's command took some getting used to. Her only prayer was that she could be of value to God, and it was stupid to worry if it would last. As drained as she was after all the trouble she'd brought on herself, she had no leftover energy to waste on doubts. It was full-steam, all the feeble strength she had left, to cling to God. She would hold on and see where He led her.

16

When Frank left Sallie, he drove into Watertown to the Inn. The Inn was a pleasant century-old building, a rambling white-frame structure with many windows and old brick chimneys. This was where, just three months ago, Frank, Nancy, and Sallie had hopefully and sadly eaten that first day at Pleasant Valley. This was where Frank had told Sallie the truth about Nancy and given his ideas for how Sallie should handle her future. As Frank parked the car and stepped out onto the pink- and gold-looking snow, he was struck by the beauty of the place — the old Inn, glowing in the fading light, the tall evergreens guarding it, the smooth, deep, and quiet snow giving the overall picture a look of unreality in the sunset.

It was beautiful, and Frank felt that the Inn in all its years must have seen many tragic events. It gave Frank a sense of continuity, a feeling of life-goes-on, and at the same time the poignant memories of a whole Nancy and eagerly, blindly hopeful Sallie swept over him, making him wish somehow it all hadn't happened. Yet Frank knew without a doubt now that the turn of

116

events that had brought him to this moment were for the best. Before, he had been a bitter, defeated man, miserable in his plenty, the typical middle-class American searching for meaning. Now he was a serenely joyful man, content with his lot, even though that lot was harder than ever before.

Frank went on into the brick-floored foyer, with the giant fireplace in the right wall and the reception desk on the left. He could hear the clatter of dishes and smell the mingled odors of dinner. He went up to the desk and got a room. He would need to buy a few essentials before the stores closed. That done, he ate, for it was after five and he wanted time to think before he saw Harvey.

Who was this Harvey anyway? Frank was wary of the strongly outspoken religious, not because he didn't approve, but because so often a strong "faith" was really a cover for a narrow mind. Frank, in his new interpretation of God's way, was sure that God's mind was very broad indeed. He judged from the foundation of a pure and loving heart, and forgave and forgot the worst of sins, when sought. Frank wondered if Harvey could possibly find the strength to do that.

As he ate the lusciously seasoned fried chicken and the creamy mashed potatoes smothered in milk gravy, Frank prayed. He didn't actually ask for any specific favor, but for God's guidance. He knew that his mission tonight was important, not only to Sallie and thus to him, but to the young man, Harvey. Frank felt strongly the weight of his forty years and their accompanying experience. What if Nancy had become involved with some other boy before he'd met her? What if she'd had an abortion? Of course, they were rarer then, but still he'd heard of some girls he knew having it done. Thinking of Nancy now, being electrically shocked, being filled with drugs, in order to regain some semblance of her former self, it was hard to remember the serenely quiet, and sometimes joyful girl he had courted. And it was certainly impossible to imagine Nancy sleeping with another man. She had been so modest when they first married that it had taken months before she could fully relax with him. No, Frank could not put himself in Harvey's shoes. Assuming that Harvey really was in love with Sallie, with the kind of blind adoration Frank had felt for Nancy, then the blow must have been great.

Frank finished his dessert and looked at his watch. 6:15. He could go now. Harvey would most likely be at home.

Frank went to his room and got his hat and coat, briefly thinking how restfully furnished and quaint the rough-walled and wide-board floored room was. Later, he would sit in that chair by the plain white-curtained window and read the Gideon Bible laying on the nightstand. Later, he would need a chance to unwind, to read the soothing words of the Psalms or hear again Jesus' words of hope on the mountain. Now he prayed only that his mouth would speak words from God, words unhindered by his own feeling of protection toward his daughter, words filled with persuasion and truth, honest words and

117

kind, so that Harvey might find the strength to overcome his disappointment. For Frank was not deluding himself. How much nicer and better it would be if Harvey and Sallie could grow in love together, overlooking each of their failings. For Harvey had failed Sallie in the wavering of his love, just as surely as she had failed him by testing his love.

Frank knew, from twenty years of marriage, that the high ideals and expectations of youth gave way to the forgiving acceptance of time — if you were to succeed, that is. In a way, Frank envied Harvey and Sallie, for they were forced to test their powers of forgiveness before they married, and if it proved too great a test, they would know before they stepped into the intricate, multileveled structure that was modern marriage. If they could live with their mistakes now, then perhaps they would not drift away from each other as he and Nancy had from an inability to be open and concerned, and from being too busy to care.

Frank went out of the room, locking the door behind him. Slowly, he went down the carpeted stairs, into the foyer, giving his key to the desk clerk.

Outside it was dark and cold — at least zero. The air stung Frank's nose as he breathed and made him aware of his own frailty. He could not allow himself to really think of the outcome, because, down deep, he knew he would have rejected Nancy all those years ago. Now he was less critical, more tolerant, but then he had been idealistic and pure. Frank could only pray that God was truly a part of Harvey's life and not a protective fetish. And as he spoke with Harvey, that they would both be open to God's will.

Frank was reaching out now, groping in the dark for God. In his groping he cared not what the outcome was, but only that it was of God. For by now, Frank could see that there was no other way to live in peace.

He had hope. Who doesn't hope for the happy ending?

For how long he sat in that decrepit old chair, first crying like a small boy, and finally just staring at the floor, seeing all the little and big cracks in the linoleum, for how many hours had passed before he was aware of where he was or what he was doing, Harvey didn't know. One minute ago, in the late morning, he had sat down. Now it was dark, or nearly so, and still Harvey sat. He seemed to have lost all desire to do anything; he had no wish ever to have to move or eat or live again.

Finally, the total darkness of his room drove Harvey to turn on a light, and the motion of reaching for the switch of the old floor lamp beside him made him aware once again of his physical existence. It seemed funny that, despite the misery of dying inside, his stomach churned from lack of any lunch. It seemed unfitting that his physical drives ignored the state of his spiritual self. But that first motion, having made him aware, led him to the next and Harvey was on his feet.

He decided he'd better eat — just anything to stop the churning. But when he had finished two peanut butter sandwiches and a cup of lukewarm coffee, it still churned. Then he realized it was his misery and anxiety causing his discomfort.

He couldn't believe it! How stupid he had been! Like a sixth grader with a crush. He had worshiped Sallie. Oh, of course, he hadn't known it. He was completely against that kind of all-consuming love that detracted from the priority of God. He knew that was what got so many people off the track. But, he, Harvey Plimpton, number one dope, had done it. And without even knowing!

Harvey went back to his chair after he had put the peanut butter in the little cupboard near his table. When he looked out, he could see the river, a dark snake crawling on a white bed.

Oh, Sallie! Why do I love you so? Why can't I walk out in hate and contempt and keep on hating? What has happened to me that it is not even a question of forgiveness any more?

Harvey wrung his hands, a habit left over from his lonely and anxious childhood. Maybe she hated him now! His love would never fail! But he had walked out in anger.

Harvey's strong conscience beat himself for his rashness. Why hadn't he waited to hear the rest? Why hadn't he tried to understand?

As he leaned his head against the cold windowpane, staring out at the quiet landscape, he thought of all his ideals, all those beliefs he had guarded so closely. Now they were like sawdust.

Careless girls cause homeless babies. True.

Heartless girls kill their babies. True.

Silly girls don't think about their actions. True.

God meant for all people to respect and carry out His plans. True.

All true! And he still believed it. Knew it. If girls weren't so careless, or heartless, or silly, then they would pay attention to God's laws. They would think!

But this was Sallie. Sallie! Sallie of the sweet face, the spun-gold hair, the soft lips. Sallie of the quick, sarcastic tongue, of the gentle heart, of the promising future. Sallie!

The pane was no longer even cool. Harvey's face ran perspiration like tiny replicas of the river down the glass.

There was no getting around it. When you loved someone, you just didn't walk out and forget. And Harvey was very unpracticed at hating. He'd never needed it before. He didn't hate anyone. And having never loved before like this, so suddenly, so completely, he couldn't understand why finding out that his view of Sallie was warped, misshapen, and distorted didn't strangle the love. Strange! Why did his heart, still miraculously intact after breaking into a thousand pieces, ache for her so? Why did he feel a kind of relief to be able to let go of his image?

"Thou shalt worship no graven images." God didn't like it, and it wasn't healthy either!

"And forgive us our sins, as we forgive those who sin against us." Oh, now I see. Who sinned first? Who's in position to play God but God? Again it's not healthy. Unforgiveness leads to hardness, mercilessness, and soon no particle is left of love or kindness. Hate destroys the hater, condemned by his own attitude, requiring no more judgment from God.

Harvey's face was dry. The sweat of his thoughts formed a smeary, blurry window.

There was a knock at the door. No tutoring now. School was almost over. Who could be there? His heart leaped a little at the possibility of Sallie. He got up and went across the cracked floor to the door.

When Frank saw the skinny stalklike young man standing there, looking red-eyed and very unappealing in his rumpled clothes, he wondered what Sallie saw in him. He was no Cam, certainly.

"Hello," he said, nervously twirling his hat.

Harvey blinked, trying to remember if he'd met this man before. A rather overweight, fortyish man, with gray, wiry hair and dreamy-looking eyes.

"Hello?" he said with a question in his voice.

"I'm Frank Victor. Sallie's father."

Oh, that's why he looked a little familiar. Those dream-laden eyes.

"Come in," Harvey said, feeling nervous about his shabby room. "Won't you sit down?" He indicated one of his two straight chairs, and when Frank had lowered himself gingerly onto the edge of one, Harvey sat in the other.

Frank cleared his throat. *Well, Lord, what now?*

Harvey sat awkwardly, spindly legs sprawled, not really caring if they spoke. There must be hope then! He was here for Sallie!

Finally Frank said, "I guess you're Harvey."

"Yes."

"I don't know you. Never heard of you before today."

She hadn't written then. That hurt a little. But it was nothing really, considering the most recent events.

Harvey pulled a grotesque version of his face-changing smile.

"Well, I've heard of you. Sallie thinks a lot of you." He cleared his throat. *Look, why don't we get it out in the open?* He cleared his throat again.

"I . . . ," Frank began.

"Why . . . ?" Harvey did, too.

120

They looked at each other and suddenly there was no need to ask or to probe. Frank knew this boy still loved his daughter. It was all there in his eyes. He was struggling, trying to understand, but loving nevertheless.

"You love my daughter."

Harvey felt tears stinging his eyes.

"Yes," he whispered. And then, "I walked out on her. She'll never forget that. I was so hurt, so mad. I couldn't see any other way!"

"No," Frank said. "She doesn't hate you. I don't know why, but she doesn't."

Harvey was writhing in misery.

"*You* must though."

"No, at first I was angry — like you. But you don't know all that's behind this — I see that. And once," Frank paused, sighing a little. "And once, I put all my hopes on a girl. Her mother."

Harvey took another look at the man across from him. He was sad, infinitely sad, but seemed to be at peace with his sadness.

"No, I didn't bother to stay to hear the rest. I was too hurt."

"She's a good girl, Harvey. What happened to her may have come from thoughtlessness, and lack of understanding, but her mother and I didn't help her. We weren't there when we should have been. And when we were, I was weak and her mother was out of her mind with grief. We all went a little crazy. We thought we could fix things." Frank shrugged his shoulders and spread his hands.

"You believe in God?" he asked.

"Yes." Sallie told him that.

"And in Jesus?"

"Yes." Harvey looked hard at Frank. "But even if I didn't, or maybe because the belief is so internal, I love her. And I feel I need forgiveness from her more than she does from me. I thought I could condemn her, Mr. Victor, but I can't. Even if I wanted to, I can't."

Frank and Harvey sat silently, each in his own thoughts. The boy was more sincere than he had been at that age, Frank thought. Less prone to dreams which only keep out reality and which can be dealt with more effectively than wavery wishes. Perhaps God had sent this man to Sallie. Harvey liked Frank, his quiet manner, his gentle approach. That was where Sallie had gotten it. That serenity that made you feel she was always thinking nice thoughts. What was her mother like?

But he need not have wondered, for Frank was talking, and as Harvey listened, he began to understand. The two men — one worn by years of defeatism, and now, after many false starts, learning that truth and honesty were part of God's salvation; the other, shocked by harsh reality, and supported by the training and love he had received and given in a short idealistic life — sat, talked, questioned, and answered for the next few hours, lost in a private world, unlike Nancy's of fear and delusion, of trust and commitment sent by God. For as surely as the two sat at the table in that shabby, somewhat dirty room, so also God sat with them answering their spoken and unspoken need for guidance. For the first time in either of their lives, they laid aside their petty prides, their small hurts, and even their larger pains, and allowed God's love to communicate with them, through them, for them, and for Sallie.

And as Frank told Harvey about Nancy, about their past devotion to Sallie and their subsequent downfall, he felt that if only this kind of communing had come sooner, Nancy would be well.

And when Harvey heard the sad tale of Sunshine Acres and the shock treatments, of Frank's not being able to see his wife, he saw how Frank's disappointment must be even greater than his own. His heart went out to Frank, and he prayed for Nancy. And suddenly Harvey knew that God's love never quit no matter what, and that because of this fact, if one could call upon God, one could and would love through anything. Therefore, hate was obsolete for the Christian, he who is guided to love. All this business of Jesus' loving His church like a bride became clearer now. For if one really loved his bride, nothing, no event past or present, could destroy that love, but only deepen its ability to rejuvenate itself. True love didn't die with trouble, it only found deeper expression.

17

It was Sunday morning and Sallie lay in her own bed in her own pink-and-white room. There was something wonderful about being back in that room, a safe, protected feeling. At the same time, it was sad to realize that the one who had spent so much of her life taking care of Sallie, and carefully choosing the colors and fabrics and papers for this long-awaited new house, was not here. It gave Sallie a strange mixed feeling — she had never grown used to her new room, always remembering her old, pine-paneled, sloping-ceilinged room in their little bungalow. Now she welcomed her sweetly feminine room as a haven, a place to rest for awhile, and yet deplored the fact that her mind was too wounded by her life to ever again strictly and luxuriously enjoy a room.

Sallie looked out her window, seeing snowflakes, little hard icy ones, pinging against the panes. How often she had lain there, looking out that window! In the past year-and-a-half it had become a habit, an aid to thinking.

Today there would be no church, of which Sallie was glad. She was still a sorry sight, her skin stiff now and flaking in places. And the drive home yesterday had been exhausting. So she was to rest yet a few more days. At least, until the soft new skin was not so painful. But she was glad there was no church for her today for another reason. This new commitment, this new depth of purpose, needed hardening before it was bombarded by Rev. Crumm.

Sallie thought about Rev. Crumm for a minute. He was so lifeless, not solemn, but just not caring enough to laugh or joke. He had spoken the words of the Bible, had given Jesus' message, in such a pedantic, scholarly fashion, that all the life-changing qualities were drained out of it. It would not be easy to maintain a living faith with him as a mentor. And Rev. Dudley (Bill, as they all called him) was young, friendly, and knew how to joke. He was supposed to "relate" to the young people so their parents didn't have to. Well, maybe that wasn't true exactly, but he gave you the feeling that you were just a job. Had Jesus made Mary Magdalene feel that way, or the blind people, or the little children? No, and even now, the thing that had dragged her back into living was knowing that Jesus cared; she was not just a job. He cared all the time.

But she couldn't blame Rev. Crumm or Bill for their lack of real involvement. They were products of their age, and the same influences that worked on others worked on them.

Sallie glanced at her clock. 8:15. She could hear her father rattling pots and dishes in the kitchen. She breathed a fervent prayer that God would somehow make her faith live and work, and got up.

She ached today from the effort of coming home yesterday. As she combed her hair and found her robe, she thought of Friday night, when, unexpectedly, ahead of her father, Harvey had come into the infirmary. They hadn't said much. There had been no need. The look they exchanged had erased all the hurt and disappointment, and accepted the other as each one was. It was a relief. No more secrets now. Harvey knew it all, and she knew that, painful for him though it was, Harvey loved her more than any test could quench. They had held each other, not kissing but like two lost children, reunited with their parents. After a while, her father had come in, and they had talked until Sallie's eyelids began to droop. They had said that Harvey would visit them between Christmas and New Year's Day, after he had played Santa Claus at the orphanage. It seemed as if they were already a family. Frank and Harvey had a sympathy for each other that was rare, and Sallie felt almost jealous, except she knew that their mutual love for her had helped create that sympathy. Their love for her and for God. She had no doubt that God had worked a miracle in their lives.

As Sallie stepped into her fluffy yellow slippers, she sighed a little. The only bad thing at college was that she had to take an incomplete in two courses, until she could take her tests. Well, she would be concerned about that later. When she had jumped into the river she had never dreamed she would be around to worry about it. She could make them up early next quarter. Still, in her new frame of mind, held only for three days, it bothered her that there were hangovers from her terrible time of despair.

Sallie went gingerly along the hall into the dining room. The aroma of cooking bacon wafted out to meet her.

"Hi," she said as she went into the kitchen.

Her father was standing at the stove, frying the bacon. His face creased into a smile.

"Feel a little more rested now?"

"Yes, but I hurt. Take it from me, a six-hour drive after being beat up by a current is no cure for sore muscles."

Frank didn't laugh and Sallie realized it really wasn't funny. She just felt as if the whole experience was crazy, and laughing helped dim it in her mind. She changed the subject.

"Can I fix the toast?"

"Sure, but sit down. You make me nervous."

Sallie gratefully sank into a chair at the table. Frank brought her the bread and she popped four pieces into the toaster on the table.

Frank drained the bacon and cracked four large eggs into the sizzling fat.

"Be a hearty breakfast for a sick girl," he smiled.

Sallie smiled back, watching the toaster. They seemed so strained. Oh, well, what could you expect? She buttered the golden toast just as Frank brought their plates of eggs and bacon.

Frank asked the blessing, mentioning Nancy. Sallie's heart ached for him. It must be worse for him, she thought. He has the responsibility for all of us now, and he must be lonely for her. Sallie had never paid much attention to her parents' life together, but now she saw that it must be very painful for her father to have his wife so ill.

"How's mommy?" she asked.

"When I talked to the new doctor he said she seemed to be talking a little more coherently. He thinks you can see her next week — if you want to."

"Oh, yes!" But Sallie was scared. What would she look like after so much mental turmoil? "Are you going to see her, too?"

Frank wiped his mouth with his napkin.

"She becomes very agitated when the doctor mentions me. He thinks I should wait a bit. She's always referring to her daughter, but thinks you're about ten. Doctor Haynes says this is part of her retreat pattern. He hopes that by having you visit, she may gradually return to the present."

Sallie felt terrible for her father. And more frightened for herself.

"But why would you upset her?"

Frank looked infinitely sad.

"I don't know. Unless she associates me as the villain." He smiled humorlessly.

Sallie finished her breakfast in silence. She would need all the help she could get to carry this off. How naive she had been last spring! Thinking she could control life! The only thing she could hope for was that God would give her the strength to see her through.

The next few days were spent in gradually getting up more, in just allowing her body to recover from its ordeal. While her father was at work Monday and Tuesday, Sallie tottered around from bed to couch, keeping her skin well-lubricated with the salve the doctor had given her. She didn't spend much time in deep thought. It was sufficient to be alive and able to face that fact. This in itself was a basic change in her personality, a totally new concept. Her past life had been apparently devoted to avoiding life's realities, to forming her own. Now, as she lay around recuperating physically, she began to see herself in a new light, as God might see her. No longer was her own individual life of primary importance, rather, she was only a cog in the giant wheel of the universe. It was a humbling thought, and one that was helpful to her in the face of the earth-shaking changes in her life.

On Tuesday she decided to call Cara. She hadn't written the last weeks of school, and the two friends hadn't talked for months — not since Sallie went off to college.

When Cara answered the phone, Sallie bubbled, "Hi! It's me."

"Sallie! I thought you weren't due home till tomorrow."

"I wasn't. I had a few problems so I came home a little early."

Cara was silent a moment.

"Oh, your mother," she said at last.

Sallie played with the cord to the phone.

"Well, partly. I just found out last Thursday. It's pretty shattering."

"Just last week?" Cara was obviously surprised.

"Guess I was kept pretty much in the dark."

"Well," Cara paused uncertainly.

"I know," Sallie interrupted. "She must have acted kind of strange for a while. I suppose your mom noticed."

"Well, we all thought she missed you — you know, your being the only child and all. But it — well, she did get strange. Boy, Sallie, I'm awful sorry for you."

Sallie took a deep breath. Actually it was easier being the last to know — no explanations necessary. "Well, say, that's not why I called," she said in a cheery voice. "But I appreciate your concern. I wanted to know what's doing with you. Is the big event still on?"

Cara laughed. "Oh sure! December 31st, 7:00 P.M. I can't believe it's so close."

"Yeah, boy! Just two weeks. Time flies."

"Sal?"

"Yeah?"

"You do understand, don't you? About not being in the wedding?"

That was the least of her worries now! Had she been a little hurt when Cara had said she was having her cousin? A small wedding, inexpensive, with mostly family and a few friends? No, not really hurt, just surprised.

"Of course, silly! I'm glad I'm going — that's partly why I called. Mind if I bring a guest?"

"Cam!" Cara was breathless.

Sallie felt a little shock. Why on earth would she think of Cam?

"Heavens, no!" Sallie said a little snappishly.

"I thought — "

"Thinking is dangerous," Sallie said lightly, and before Cara could say more, "I have a friend visiting after Christmas — from school."

"Friend?"

Why did Cara's natural curiosity perturb her?

"A boy, dear, yes."

"Well!" Cara sounded a little exasperated, too. "I *am* interested, you know."

"I guess so," Sallie giggled. "It's your wedding, after all. Can I bring him?"

"You're my friend, too — I thought, anyway." Cara was hurt.

Sallie sighed. How silly! Becoming upset over something so small. "His name is Harvey Plimpton. Yes, you heard right. Harvey Plimpton and furthermore he's kinda funny looking, and very satirical and . . . ."

"Sallie!" Cara laughed. "You're impossible! You make him sound like a creep."

"He is — to some."

"But not to you?"

Was he to her? Well, once he had been. Until she saw beyond the surface.

"No, not to me — any more."

"Ah-ha!" Cara had the smug sound of the about-to-be-married, hoping that soon her friend would be, too.

"We've got years, dear. If ever." Why had she said that? She didn't want to be tied down yet — not formally anyway.

"Anyhow, can he come?"

"Sure. It's just cake and ice cream."

"Great! How's your dress?"

"Beautiful!"

Cara went on to describe her gown and veil, all the little details of the coming event. To Sallie, she sounded so young and eager, and a little shallow. Oh, well, people change. And much had happened to her. Cara was still essentially a girl, untried, hopeful for perfection.

When they had said good-by, promising to meet for lunch, Sallie decided to get dressed, something she hadn't yet done.

She selected an old skirt and loose blouse so the salve wouldn't ruin anything good. In a few days, she could stop using the goop — her tender skin was improving quickly now. It would be nice to put on something pretty again.

That night she cooked dinner for her father, and he seemed grateful to have someone care for him. Again, she wished for her mother's return to health — not for her sake, but for his.

They discussed Nancy. Frank had talked to Dr. Haynes. He chewed his steak thoughtfully, relishing a meal cooked by some hand other than his own.

"Dr. Haynes wants to see me tomorrow," he said. "He seems to think there is some missing point. Something in her past that triggered this."

"You mean not — not all the trouble?" Sallie munched on a piece of garlic bread. How calmly they spoke of "her."

"Well, not entirely. Dr. Haynes suspects — from your mother's rambling stage — that there is more behind it."

"But, what, daddy? Mommy has always been so calm and I always thought she was content."

"It could be deeply hidden. Anyway," Frank reached for more green beans and mushrooms, "I'll know tomorrow. Maybe, if we can find out what could be hidden, she'll get better. We have to believe in that for now anyway." Frank put down his fork. "You know, if anyone had told me my wife would break down, I wouldn't have believed it."

Sallie felt young and useless, unable to really offer help to her father. What could she do? She sat still fighting the tears. What did her mother have to run from, if not the problems of the past nine months?

"Oh, well," Frank shrugged. "God must have a purpose." He looked at Sallie. "You believe that, don't you?"

Did she? Why must her mother suffer? Was she suffering?

"I think He knows why she's sick," Sallie said. "Maybe if we ask Him, He'll show us why, and we can help."

Frank looked surprised.

"It wouldn't hurt to try," he said. So, they joined hands, and first Frank, then Sallie prayed for insight into the problem. Sallie even asked God to let them know what was bothering Nancy through some outside source. Why she had said those words, she didn't know. But somehow she believed the prayer would be answered.

It wasn't Thursday that Sallie first visited her mother, but Friday. The talk with the doctor on Wednesday made it clear it would be a difficult thing for Sallie, and Frank set it up for a day later to give Sallie a little more time. It definitely appeared that Nancy was now dragging things up from some unknown source, but still her daughter was a continuing thread.

When Dr. Haynes met with Frank, he warned him to be sure Sallie was really agreeable to seeing her mother. It would be upsetting, and in view of Sallie's own instability, maybe dangerous. However, Dr. Haynes felt that one way to develop internal strength was to devote energy to helping loved ones. Dr Haynes was willing to risk the visits if Sallie were willing as well.

When her father asked her again at supper that night if she were really prepared to do this thing, Sallie said she was. She no longer felt the need for self-protection, for her life was out of her hands. She felt that if she could help, just possibly, then she must. This, too, was part of the new Sallie. She had a little understanding of Dr. Haynes' philosophy. Grasping hands came up empty — well she knew! Giving hands were at least not worried about what they received, and thus, any reward, or return, was a gift.

Sallie was scared, though, as she maneuvered the family car into the parking lot of Sunshine Acres. She believed, with the devoutness of the only lately desperate, that her own salvation lay in forgetting herself in a higher goal, but she was wary, too. For higher goals could include all kinds of evil and wickedness, too, thus making the final ruin worse than the first. That's why she needed a guide. Whereas before she had been her own protector, now she would not be simply unprotected in selflessness, but praying for God's direction.

Sunshine Acres was a beautiful place. Sallie could imagine the rolling lawns and shady trees in summer, dotted with bright zinnias and marigolds. Now the smooth blanket of snow gave an air of secrecy to the place, a shut-in look.

Sallie parked the car and locked it, pocketing the keys. The drive was plowed, but slippery, so she trod carefully as she made her way to the salted sidewalk. The building was brick, a splotch of rosy color against the white background, edged by carefully shaped evergreens, with stalklike trees scattered about. The many windows caught the morning sun and threw it back at Sallie as she walked up the path.

She knocked at the big, white double doors, letting the heavy brass knocker bang loudly in the stillness. How quiet it was! Was it always this way?

A uniformed maid let her into a tiled hall, bare and utilitarian, with only a bench along one wall. Sallie sat quietly on the bench looking at the calendar prints high on the walls, wondering if they were hung so as to prevent the patients from reaching them.

Dr. Haynes saw Sallie before she saw him. He was impressed by her serene appearance, her neat hair and carefully coordinated lavender sweater and plaid skirt. Beside her lay her scarlet coat and some hand-knit white gloves. He was halfway into the hall before she saw him, and then quickly, with a natural politeness, she got up and came to meet him.

Sallie was equally impressed with Dr. Haynes. He reminded her of Santa Claus, now seen everywhere in the city. He was late middle-aged, with white fringe around a bald dome, a large stomach protruding over his belt, twinkling eyes, and a jolly manner.

"Well, well!" he said gustily. "You must be Sallie!"

"Yes." Sallie felt slightly overwhelmed.

"Are you sure you're up to this? From what your father says — "

"Oh, yes, doctor. I was pretty depressed last week — "

"I should say so! I thought perhaps we might talk a little about that first."

It was not a suggestion, but a gentle command, and Sallie felt herself being propelled down the hall and into a large, homey-looking room with a desk, several easy chairs, and a couch, all in muted shades of gold and orange, softly lighted by table lamps. Of course, the doctor would want to talk. Why had she done it? Was she sure she could stand the strain so soon after? But, strangely, Sallie was not upset by the prospect of discussing her previous fears. She only hoped that Dr. Haynes would accept her new peace as genuine, and not turn her away. She must convince him, a scientist no doubt, of her complete renewal through faith in God. Perhaps this experience was not unknown to him.

Dr. Haynes waved Sallie into one of the plaid easy chairs, and settled himself behind the desk, rocking back on his orange-padded swivel chair.

"Well," he said, looking intently at the young girl before him, "where shall we begin?"

Sallie hadn't given any thought to what she should say to her mother's psychiatrist. Somehow she had thought that, without preamble, she would be ushered, up or down or wherever her mother was, into the room and left to visit. She was so accustomed to referring to her mother under normal terms that she hadn't expected this talk.

"My father says mother talks about me a lot — that that was why you wanted me to see her."

"Yes," Dr. Haynes looked over his gold-rimmed spectacles at her. "She is apparently associating you in her more lucid minutes — though at different ages. She seems to move around in time, and each memory, or illusion, is real at the moment. Yes, I do think your visiting her may help to stabilize her, to make her aware of the difference between reality and past memory again. Already we have reached points when she seems to be more aware. But," the doctor paused and leaned forward on his polished desk. Sallie felt the sympathetic probing of his gaze. "What about you, young lady?"

"Well," she began, "I was pretty upset when my father came down to school last week. I had no inkling that my mother was — ah — sick. Oh, well, her letters stopped, but who thinks of mental illness? I thought she was busy or something. When I heard, I just suddenly couldn't go on. I blamed myself, I guess." She sat and waited. Perhaps that was enough.

Dr. Haynes regarded her silently a few moments more, then leaned back in his chair again, fingers lightly tapping his desk.

"Of course, your father has told me everything. You do understand that?"

Sallie blushed. "Yes."

"Then let us not beat around the bush. Surely not just blame alone drove you to attempt suicide." It could, though, he added silently to himself. But let us see.

Sallie squirmed in the comfortable chair, pulling her skirt down. It was not easy to tell a stranger all her inner thoughts. But then she had told herself that this time was for real. She must be willing to subject her own sense of privacy to a little scrutiny.

"Well, you mean my — my baby," she stumbled.

It still hurt, Dr. Haynes could see.

"Specifically, yes. And the abortion. Why didn't you seek help? There are plenty of organizations to guide girls in your situation. We no longer live in the Stone Age, you know."

Why hadn't they sought help? "I guess we really couldn't accept the fact that we were in trouble — or I couldn't. When mother suggested the abortion — oh, I'd thought of it — it seemed like it would take away the whole problem. And then, afterwards, it was such a relief to be free that we — none of us, I think — didn't expect more trouble from it." It sounded silly, immature, and confused.

Dr. Haynes pursed his lips and ran a hand over his bald dome. "It's not that easy," he said. "There are feelings you aren't even consciously aware of. Studies have shown that many girls suffer trauma after an abortion. Psychiatric care is important." He waved his hand at her. "You shouldn't be expected to have known this then. But I never cease to be amazed at the way parents blithely manipulate their children's lives without regard for possible results. I told your father that I believe this is part of your mother's sickness. But only a part. There is more, something we haven't been able to reach yet. But this manipulation has taken its toll on her. But, what about you? When you walked into that river — what were you thinking?"

Oh, God, help! How do I say it? Surely he must be wondering why I attempted suicide but now sit here outwardly calm, apparently never suicidal. It was shocking. She had been suicidal. Well, there was Harvey.

"I have a boyfriend, Dr. Haynes. A very decent boy. When daddy told me about mommy, I knew my boyfriend would find out — about me, I mean. Or, anyway, I couldn't bare the deceit any more. It just seemed the answer then. Mommy was sick, and I felt guilty. I had tried to forget my past but I couldn't. And I hated myself. It seemed better to remove myself." Sallie flipped her long golden tresses back with her hands in a nervous gesture. "Do people always know why they're doing it?"

Dr. Haynes smiled. "Not really. I've had cases where the root of the depression was nothing more than a small insult, months before. Or it can be a huge change in the life of the individual. Almost anything can be the reason for suicide under the right — or perhaps I should say, wrong — circumstances. And, no, often at the time the person is not aware of why he's doing it." Dr. Haynes spread his hands on his desk and pushed his bulk out of the chair. "And many times one attempt makes the person aware of his problems — if he's lucky enough to fail. I believe you are fairly intelligent and can see another avenue now?" It was a question.

"Oh, yes," Sallie was eager. "I was very angry when I found I'd failed. You see, that just proved how useless I was. But then two things happened. First, I began to see my life in perspective — I was so depressed that, suddenly, I no longer mattered; and then I saw myself as a small part of things and I realized I'd been taking myself too seriously — I'd made myself primary. And, at the same time, I met Jesus. I'd been raised on the theory of sin and repentance and removal of guilt, but never comprehended it." She turned a little in her seat, embarrassed. "It was real then — and is now. You see, doctor, I'd never admitted doing anything wrong."

Dr. Haynes saw that she classified her sexual experience and subsequent abortion as sin. She seemed to have little knowledge of motivation, of the causes for her involvement and the choice of abortion rather than, say, adoption. But he also saw that, whatever her degree of understanding, this religious explanation would probably accomplish two things: She would no longer feel the guilt, and hence suicide would most likely be an unnecessary concern from now on. So, for now, she could be expected to stand, and even profit from, the visits with her mother.

"Well, then," he said. "Let us assume that you have found life to be worth living."

"Oh, yes, for myself! Now my boyfriend knows — I told him, and — well — it was pretty hairy, but I feel like we're closer now than before. I feel very hopeful. But I feel terrible for my father — he's so lonely — and my mother. That's why I'll do anything to help."

"Good." Dr. Haynes patted her shoulder as he came around his desk and stood beside her. "Now about your mother. She naturally looks rather strange. She's thinner, and we can't often get her to let us comb her hair and fix her up. She won't be like you remember her."

Sallie swallowed and looked up into the doctor's round, friendly face. "I had thought of that," she said.

"Well, be prepared. Try to overlook that. I'll be with you all the time — at least today. We'll see how it goes. She may not even talk. But I hope that by arranging periodic visits, we can force your reality, your age, upon her. Okay?"

Sallie nodded.

"Well, then, Shall we go?"

18

Frank was getting into a routine. With Sallie home, he no longer had to cook his own meals or wash his own clothes. In a way, he was sorry for this. He had enjoyed taking care of his own needs. But the house was pretty dusty, and his culinary skills were limited, so, for the most part, he was glad to be relieved of his duties as housemaid — for the time being.

Sallie was a wonder. He couldn't get over the change in her. Before, she had been a girl, demanding attention, shy and outspoken at different times, never considered as an equal. Now he found himself talking to her as he would a friend. Her brush with death seemed to have totally re-arranged Sallie's personality, making her all at once an adult — capable of objective thought processes and genuine concern for others. This might be just growing up suddenly because of a deep trial, but Frank knew older, tried people without those qualities. It seemed to be the work of God to him.

At work, Frank began to see the light of day. All the deeds, loans, mortgages, and other various bank documents which had piled up were being worked through. In time, one got used to anything, and the first weeks of confusion after Nancy's collapse were behind him. The grumblings from the main office ceased, as the business of Frank's branch returned to normal. Well, not exactly normal. Frank had never enjoyed his work, always complained to himself at his being stuck as branch manager. Then, after tragedy struck, he had suddenly found release in his work. But the constant interruptions had kept him from realizing there was more to his job than wading through legal papers. Now, as he began to catch up on things, he saw that with a creative spirit he could lift his work from the dry, repetitive level of a clerk to the heights of personal involvement. There was a community out there. Other branches of his bank had gone out to the people, helping to establish funds for the needy, for education, and for recreation, opening new channels for existing groups and leading the way in improving the environment of their area. Frank felt excited at the prospect of being one of these leaders. Why hadn't he done it before? Did it always take an upheaval to get a man out of his dry, lifeless rut? What would their life — Nancy's and his — have been like if he had been more innovative?

Well, it was too bad he hadn't felt this way sooner, but no use wasting time worrying about it. Now was the time for action. Frank thanked God for the rebirth of his faith and the renewal of his spirit. Each day now he took time before he returned to his work after lunch to read his office Bible, long unused. It had seemed unnecessary to reread all those truths once you learned them, but now he knew he had a short memory. He guessed most people did. So, now, as he sat again at his desk, after returning from lunch at the McDonald's around the corner which he had helped finance, Frank picked up his Bible. Today he was on the twelfth chapter of Mark, and after reading it, he would contemplate it for awhile with the help of the little guidebook he had bought at the bank-financed religious bookstore. The more he assimilated old truths, and discovered new ones with the little book's help, the more eagerly he looked forward to this new discipline. He was also more aware of the good he could help accomplish through the bank.

The words of Jesus leaped out at him, "Have you never read in the scriptures: 'The very stone which the builders rejected has become the head of the corner: this was the Lord's doing, and it is marvelous in our eyes'?" How true! All the years Frank had condemned his job! All the times he had felt useless, deflated, and defeated! Now he saw how useful he could be — and surely it was the Lord's doing, for Frank himself was a pessimistic individual. It was marvelous!

Frank went back to work refreshed and planning how he would join the local Chamber of Commerce to begin his siege of involvement. Frank had never been so satisfied with his life. The only thing that would improve his situation was Nancy's return to health. He and Sallie had prayed for insight, but now he boldly asked God to heal Nancy. "Ask and ye shall receive!" Frank felt better for his brashness, as if he had done something constructive for his wife. He really wasn't concerned about how, or if, God heard his prayer. At least he was acting, and his growing faith assured him God would do His part.

The rest of Frank's day went quickly. It was Friday, one week before Christmas. He had been so busy trying to cope with the daily details of his life that he had forgotten all about shopping for gifts. Even today, as he began to feel the pressure lessening, the idea hadn't occurred to him. His mind had been toying, off and on, with the meeting at Sunshine Acres between his wife and daughter. He had thought of calling Sallie right after lunch, but had put it off. He wasn't sure when Sallie would return home — the appointment had been at ten o'clock. And too, he was hesitant to call too soon, to force a conversation upon Sallie if she were upset. He hadn't seen Nancy for a week now, not since they had moved her from General Hospital. It had taken several weeks to reach that point, and Frank had been shocked as, each day, Nancy worsened, her unkempt hair and vacant eyes bearing testimony to her deterioration. Yes, he had been shocked, and she must look even worse now. Yet maybe they fixed her up at Sunshine Acres.

Frank capped his pen and laid aside the last document. Suddenly he noticed that it had become quite dark in his room. Looking out his window he saw the pretty lights of Christmas twinkling in the crisp, clear air. People were hurrying down the dry sidewalks, lined by banks of dirty snow. A Santa Claus stood at the entrance to the dime store, bending to talk to the little children who passed in and out of the store. Frank smiled as one little girl clung to her mother's coat, turning her face away from the jolly elf. He remembered, years ago, taking Sallie to see Santa, and she had reacted in the same way.

He looked at his watch. 4:45. He would call Sallie now. Maybe she hadn't started dinner. They could go out and shop awhile after they ate. What could they buy for Nancy?

"Hello," Sallie's voice was soft, but steady.

"Hi, honey."

"Oh, daddy! I'm glad you called."

"Have you started dinner?"

"No, I guess I'm kind of lazy."

"Good." Frank noticed the withdrawn, slightly frightened quality of her voice. "How about a bite out? And some shopping?"

"That's just what I need! I didn't really feel like cooking."

"Fine. Listen, I'll finish up and be home about 5:30. You get ready. How'd it go?" Frank's heart pounded in his chest.

"It was pretty rough, and— " Sallie's voice broke off and she was silent for a moment, only the sound of her breathing coming across the wire, in gasping little breaths.

"We'll talk later," Frank said.

"Okay." Sallie's voice was hardly more than a whisper.

"Be ready, sweetie. Good-by."

"Bye, daddy."

Frank hung up the receiver and leaned back in his chair. Well, what did he expect? He should have waited till he was with her to ask her; after all, she was pretty young to have to go through this. It wasn't easy even for him.

Frank closed up his office and went out, saying good-night to the janitor as usual. How many nights had he left this building and driven home through gathering darkness? Well, tonight was different. They were all different, really. Each night a separate world of its own.

Sallie was waiting for him. She came running out of the breezeway door when he pulled into the drive. She looked heartbreakingly young and vulnerable in her scarlet coat and little plaid cap. She carried the mail with her and her black shoulder bag.

"Hi," she said brightly.

"The same to you," he returned. "What you got there?"

"Oh, mail. Thought you might want to look at it."

"Bills, mostly, I expect."

Sallie laughed. "How popular you are!"

"Not me, just my checkbook. Anything else?" Frank maneuvered the car carefully around the wall of snow at the junction of drive and road. "Wish these plows would clean up after themselves."

"Yeah." Sallie was shuffling the pile of envelopes. "Here's a letter from grandma." Grandma was Frank's mother, the only one left of his or Nancy's parents. She lived in New York with his older sister.

"Shall I open it?"

"Of course," he said, and listened as Sallie related the shock and sympathy the older Mrs. Victor felt for Nancy. Should she come? Frank had written as sparingly as he could, but the bald facts were bound to surprise his mother. Sallie finished reading the report of his sister Tracy's children and grandchildren, and laid the letter next to her on the seat.

"Should she come, daddy?"

"I don't think so. Do you?"

"No. I think she's too old to be upset by this. And we're getting along okay."

Too old. Seventy-six didn't seem so far away when you were forty. You were half-way there.

"What else have you got?"

"A letter from Sunshine Acres." A catch in her voice revealed the recent trauma she associated with the place. "It's not mommy's writing — at least not like it used to be." She was puzzled. "Who would write from there?"

Frank felt a stirring of apprehension. He drove along the divided street looking for a place to eat, so he could park.

"Should I open it?" Sallie asked.

"Well, let's get parked, and I'll look at it."

They came to a restaurant, and Frank turned in. When he had shut off the engine, he took the letter from Sallie. It was addressed to him in a feminine hand. Not from Dr. Haynes, then.

He opened it and began to read:

Dear Mr. Victor,

You don't know me, and under usual circumstances never would, but I felt impelled to write you this letter and pray that it may help you in your present situation.

I was here when they brought your wife in last week, and I recognized her right away. I'm an aid here now — have been for fifteen years. I was shocked, of course, at seeing Nancy like this, and my heart goes out to you. I've heard, by the grapevine, that she is suffering from some as yet unnamed past problem. Ordinarily, I would never write a patient's family. It is strictly against the rules. But this time I can't shake the feeling I must tell you what I know. Please talk to me before you tell your doctor about this letter. I'm not getting any younger, and I don't want to lose my pension.

If you can, meet me Monday for lunch at the restaurant in Penney's at the shopping mall just before you reach Sunshine Acres. It is important to keep this secret, and I hope I'm doing the right thing.

Faithfully,

Sara Hinkley

Frank let the letter fall into his lap.

"What is it, daddy?" Sallie's voice quavered a little.

What could this woman possibly know that could help them? Some "as yet unnamed past problem"? He looked at Sallie.

"It seems I'm to have a meeting at lunch on Monday." When was lunch anyway?

"With whom? And why?"

Frank sighed. Something told him not to tell her right now. Better wait and see what developed.

"It has to do with your mother. But I can't say more now. I'll just have to meet this person and tell you then. It's really unbelievable anyway. Probably a crank who won't show up for the date."

Sallie was curious, he could see. But he couldn't help that. It could be a crank, and Sallie had had enough for one day.

"Let's eat," he said. "I'm starved."

Monday at 11:30 found Frank sitting at an advantageously located table at the designated Penney's restaurant. He wondered why he was there. Over the weekend, he had decided not to go, but then felt foolish for wanting to avoid any possible means of help, and reversed his decision. Now he felt foolish sitting at the table in the open and obvious restaurant, with shoppers chattering, the bustle of the last days before Christmas making his vigil appear ridiculous. Everyone else was hurriedly eating, to quickly get back to the pursuit of gift-buying. Frank nursed a cup of coffee, trying to blend in with the surroundings. What if it was a crank? He could sit here till 1:30, looking like a fool all the while.

As Frank grew more restless, shifting position self-consciously, he remembered again Sallie's prayer. "Insight from an outside source." Sometime on Saturday, while they were decorating their little tree in the living room window, the words of that night had come back to him. When he and Sallie had prayed before their dinner, and she had used those words, he had been surprised and thought them rather strange. But the remembrance of them had clinched it. He would go.

Frank ordered a sandwich a little after twelve, beginning to think that, after all, it was some kind of a cruel trick. Just then, he saw a woman enter the enclosed railing that set apart the restaurant from the rest of the store. She was quite nice looking. Her hair was gray and neatly combed in a short, curly style, her slightly plump figure was pleasingly displayed in a crisp white uniform. She carried an old, but clean, black coat and a big leatherette purse. She looked to be about fifty-five — younger than he had expected, and certainly much more capable looking.

The woman looked around hesitantly, so Frank took a chance and waved to her. Seeing him, she looked relieved and came over to where he was sitting.

Frank stood up as she approached. As she came nearer, he noticed she had wrinkles on her face, and she looked tired, as if she never got enough sleep.

"You're Mr. Victor," she said as she pulled out a chair across from him. "I saw you, the day they brought Nancy in. No, please don't bother. I can seat myself."

Frank sat back down, after the woman had settled herself.

"Yes," he said. "And you're Sara Hinkley."

"Yes. Mrs. Hinkley — a widow now, but I wasn't then. I was just thirty when I first met your wife. She was a sweet young thing, and I thought I was an old married woman." Mrs. Hinkley smiled at herself. "Time flies, Mr. Victor, and I never thought I'd ever divulge any of the things I learned in the job I held then. Guess I better eat, too. I have to be back in forty minutes."

Frank beckoned a waitress, no easy job in the lunch rush, and Mrs. Hinkley ordered her lunch.

Frank didn't know what to say. Sara Hinkley appeared perfectly at ease to be sitting in the crowded restaurant, about to "divulge things." He felt only more uncomfortable.

"That must have been some time ago," he said. "That you met my wife."

"Yes, twenty-five years now. I believe she was fifteen. Your daughter is the spitting image of her." Mrs. Hinkley sighed. "I guess I may as well start at the beginning. I do hope I'm doing the right thing." She paused as the waitress set her salad in front of her.

"Please don't do anything you'll regret." Frank said in the interval. "I don't know what it is you have to say, but my wife is progressing. Perhaps it isn't necessary."

Mrs. Hinkley sighed. "I wish I could believe that. But I think your wife is suffering precisely because she has hidden, for so many years, facts that

137

alter most girls' lives. Of course, I'm no doctor, but I've been around the mentally ill for fifteen years and my previous experience only supports the necessity to bring things into the open."

Ah, yes, the open. Frank himself had said that to Sallie. Truth. Well, Sallie had survived much truth — both the telling-kind and the value-kind. But she had nearly lost her life in the effort.

"Your wife was an unwed mother at fifteen," Mrs. Hinkley went on. "No use going into who, Mr. Victor. She was officially classified as a rape. At one point in her stay with us — I worked at a home for unwed mothers that shut down fifteen years ago — she said she had foolishly struck up a conversation with a sailor just home from the war. There were plenty around in those days, aimless, looking for a pretty girl after years away. Anyway, it got out of hand. Before she could get away — she hadn't been prepared for more than talking and she was so innocent — he forced her. It wasn't too uncommon. Of course, she hid the whole episode till it was too late. In those days there was nothing for decent people to do. Her folks brought her to us — she was supposed to be visiting a distant relative. You know the story from there. She gave up the child — a little girl — and I heard she was adopted to a good home."

Frank was speechless. How did you assimilate so much at once! True, he hadn't known Nancy then. They went to different schools and churches. They had met later — at work. But this! Scattered impressions registered on his shocked brain. The extreme modesty Nancy had had when they were first married. A rape! The driving need to make Sallie have an abortion. What must Nancy have felt all those months the unwanted child, conceived in horror, grew within her? The obsessive, almost neurotic — all right, he had thought it neurotic — love and devotion to their only daughter. How she must have ached, as she grew older and more mature, for her lost little girl! And Frank had never suspected! All these years of living, eating, sleeping with this woman and never once had he suspected! Frank felt appalled at how much could go undetected in another person — the person closest to you. And he felt immensely inadequate in the face of such an enormous burden weighing secretly, horribly on Nancy's mind. No wonder the past year had been too much for her!

"Mr. Victor," Mrs. Hinkley was touching his hand tentatively. "I know this is a shock. But you must listen a minute more. This is highly classified information. We were highly screened for our jobs there at the home and at Sunshine Acres. You can see what will happen to me if the authorities at the hospital find out. I took a great risk of ruining my whole life by telling you."

"Yes," Frank managed. "I see."

"If you use this information, please, I beg of you, keep me out of it."

138

Frank nodded. How could he use it anyway? It seemed to him now, that it would take years to work through all the repercussions of this, if ever. But, yes, he could see Mrs. Hinkley's fear. No matter what, he would not bring her into it.

"Thank you for telling me," he said, out of the depths of his shock. "At least I understand a little better." Did you thank a person for shattering your whole conception of a loved one? Were you grateful for the loss of such ignorance?

"I am sorry you had to know, Mr. Victor. Don't be too hard on your years together. What good was there in your knowing before now? Poor Nancy was so humiliated, so frightened, she put it all out of her mind. Something must have triggered it." Mrs. Hinkley paused expectantly, but Frank didn't say anything. Yes, it had been triggered. Oh, yes. If you only knew, Sara Hinkley, perhaps none of Sallie's troubles would have happened, had Frank known of Nancy's traumatic experience. And he had been against the abortion! Perhaps another childless home would be no longer so, if he had known about Nancy.

"Well, I must go," Mrs. Hinkley went on. "I feel terrible being the bearer of such news. I just hope I did right."

"Please, Mrs. Hinkley. You did. I only wish I'd known sooner. So much is clear now." Frank struggled to his feet and helped Mrs. Hinkley on with her coat.

"Well, good-by, Mr. Victor," she held out her hand.

Frank took it for a moment, a small, rough hand. "Good-by. I may see you again."

"Oh!" Mrs. Hinkley was agitated. "But you don't know me!"

"Of course."

Frank watched as the woman walked away, disappearing in the crowds of gay shoppers. Then he picked up the check and went over to the cash register to pay the bill.

All he could think of was "All good things come from God." Was this the answer to Sallie's prayer? Was it good?

Somehow he would have to sort things out; he had to think of what to tell Sallie, what to do with this new information. What possible good would come from it all?

Frank left Penney's and returned to his office. At least, he was well caught up on his work. He would delay the community involvement a little. He needed time to think. And pray.

There must be a reason for it all. Somewhere, God must have an answer.

Buy why? Why did all this have to happen?

Frank remembered his grumbling former self. How different he was now! He had too many problems to waste time grumbling. If he ever made it through this, if Nancy were ever returned to him, he would never grumble again!

19

Sallie was glad she was meeting Cara for lunch. It would take her mind off all the new developments, give her a chance to just let down and have fun. They had decided to meet at the Howard Johnson's near Cara's house. Cara lived in one of the older sections of the city. It was a mixture of small businesses, restaurants, houses made into apartments, and older, neatly kept, single-family dwellings. Sallie used to live in this area, too, and often, as grade-school chums, the two girls had gone to the Howard Johnson's for ice cream. Now, as she parked her mother's late-model used Ford in the lot, she was glad to be back on familiar territory. So much was unfamiliar these days.

She was early. Her visit with her mother had been short and her talk with the doctor short, too. It was her third visit and, really, she was becoming quite calm about the whole thing. Here it was, two days before Christmas; Harvey would be arriving Monday — only four days off; Cara's wedding was next Friday evening; and on Sunday she and Harvey would return to school. Less than a week ago she had seen her mother for the first time in months, and despite the doctor's preparation, had been shocked to the depths of her being at the sight of her. Talking to her father that night had helped, and just getting out and shopping for her mother served to reinforce the hope she had felt when her mother had obviously recognized her. She had told her father about this, and that the recognition was quickly veiled and the visit had gone poorly, her mother becoming so upset Dr. Haynes had to end the meeting after only a few minutes. It was no easy thing to accept, but sharing the fear she felt with her father seemed to help.

Sallie turned off the radio and the engine, deciding Cara wouldn't be much longer. It was getting hot in the car with the heater on, so she rolled down her window, feeling the crisp air. It was melting a little today and it was sloppy underfoot, but the sun was welcome, and the cool wind invigorating.

She and her father seemed to have come a long way. Finally, last night he had told her about Sara Hinkley. Of course, she had been very curious, but his reticent attitude forestalled any questions. Instead, she had talked about the second visit on Monday, how mother had sat there while Sallie talked — talked rather desperately about college, Harvey, anything as long as it was pleasant and up-to-date. She and her father had discussed the less radical reaction with encouragement. And, after two days, he had seemed to come to a decision, and related his experience of the luncheon date he had kept on that same Monday. He told her in a flat voice that neither added to nor took away from the bare facts. Through her shock she was aware that her father really couldn't believe it. And he seemed at a loss as to how to proceed.

Sallie saw Cara approaching on foot. Her dark hair was longer, worn in a style that set off her pert face. She wore a white jacket and black pants and moved along jauntily, oozing excitement and happiness.

Time to get out of the car and stop thinking about the past, Sallie decided. Besides, it was unbelievable. Her mother ever being fifteen seemed remote; being raped and pregnant was beyond the realm of the plausible. But so was the fact that she, Sallie, had gotten involved with Cam and had an abortion. She shuddered.

"Hi," she said, waiting for Cara at the door to the restaurant.

"Hi!" Cara grinned her infectious grin and hugged her. "You look great! I'm sorry we couldn't get together sooner, but, wow! I've been running here and there and everywhere and I'm still sure I forgot something."

"Probably the cake."

Cara laughed. "Heaven forbid! No, it's probably some dumb little item that will completely throw me when I remember it coming down the aisle."

"I can see it now," Sallie held up an imaginary newspaper. "Miss Ames was divine in white organza trimmed with tiny seed pearls and a bodice of handmade lace. The only flaw to her otherwise flawless wedding was the fact that she tripped on the chancel step, thus ripping away her skirt, and exposing, would you believe, black stockings! Of course, Miss Ames was mortified, mumbling over and over, 'I knew I should have bought two pairs of the beige!' "

"Oh, for heaven's sake, Sallie. You'll have me cringing more than I am. Hey, are we going to eat or stand out here all day?"

"Eat, by all means."

The two went into the nearly empty room and found a corner booth where they could talk in privacy.

"How's your mom?" Cara asked.

"She just sits there. It's as if she knows me, but the thought of talking to me brings too many bad things to her mind."

"Like what? That's what I could never figure out."

Of course, to Cara, ignorant of all the secrets of the past year, Sallie's family looked idyllic. True, Cara had not understood why Sallie had suddenly rejected Cam, but he had been only too obviously finding interests elsewhere and that was reason enough. And what of her mother's past? Cara knew nothing of that. If only she could be completely open and honest! Ah, but she must first learn honesty in her own life, before she could safely and critically express it. God was helping her with that, but somehow, at this point, she could see no good in telling all. Rather, definite harm could come from that approach. She was still pretty shaky herself, and Cara's unbelief and shock were not experiences to be sought.

"Mom has a lot inside," she said. It was true — and general. "We just have to pray that the doctors can help her put it together right."

Cara was concerned. "I do pray for her — every night. And for you and your father, too. I don't understand why God let it happen."

God? Yes, she had blamed Him, too. But now she didn't. Mostly people going their own selfish ways had caused this to happen. And a great deal of hiding from the truth. It was one thing not to broadcast your mistakes, but another altogether not to admit them to yourself. True for Sallie. True for her mother. Some sailor's self-centered lust and the horror-stricken reaction of a young girl to forget, hide, obliterate the memory could form the basis for a weakened mind.

Sallie shook herself mentally. What had Cara said? Oh, about God.

"Maybe mom needs to do some housecleaning."

"I *have* heard that said before. But your mother was always sweet and calm. How could she need that?"

"God knows."

Cara looked uncertainly at Sallie. "I was always the one with that answer. Not you."

Sallie laughed. "Well, I have it now. You are confused, even scared by my mom's crack-up. Don't look so horrified. You wonder 'Who's next? She was so normal.' Right?"

"Well — it *is* scary. You remember, we used to worry about our parents getting a divorce?"

"Yeah." They were about fourteen, and scared of life.

"It's like that. Only your mom really did get sick."

The waitress came, a short, fat girl.

"Shrimp platter, please, and French fries," Cara said. "And a chocolate shake."

"Same here," Sallie smiled. What a combination. When they were eight it had been cheeseburgers and a chocolate shake. When the waitress left waddling away in her tight uniform, Sallie said, "I guess, I've come to trust God more, Cara. I always just slid along, you know, at church and school, just picking up the party line — never testing it. Well, trouble changes that." She could say that much.

"Yeah, but I get more scared and then I wonder why? And I'm so happy, Sal! Tim's sweet and kind. He's got a good job and we've got a swell apartment. Why can't it always be like that?"

"I don't know." Sallie thought of Harvey. They would never be as

142

naively happy as Cara was now. But already they had more depth, more understanding of each other — faults and all. Or at least, she felt they did.

"It seems to me to be unfair of God, that's all. I feel guilty being so happy, with such a bright future, and your mother's sick. Oh, I don't know, it's all mixed up."

"That's why I said God knows. Nobody else can. But don't feel guilty, Cara. Use your happiness to build on. You'll probably be tested one day, too."

"I guess that's what scares me." Cara looked around the filling room. "Hey, look who's here."

Sallie looked in the direction of Cara's pointing finger. Cam was just sitting down at a table with a cute little blonde. He did like blondes, Sallie thought. She hoped he wouldn't see her.

"You wanna say hi?" Cara asked.

"Why bother them?" Was she a little nervous at seeing him? Well, yes. Why hadn't she had enough sense then to realize that if they broke up, she would always be embarrassingly aware of their past intimacies? But then Sallie had thought she was not going to break up with him — ever. Now, as she looked at the back of Cam's head, his strong physique and good looks had no attraction for her. Thank God, they had broken up — being embarrassed was better than being stuck.

"You sure were gone on him," Cara interrupted her thoughts.

"Gone is right. I must have been nuts. Harvey is nothing, absolutely nothing like Cam." But she had hated Harvey at first! How she had changed!

"Why do you run this Harvey down?"

"I'm not!" Sallie was defensive. "Believe me, Cara, every homely inch of Harvey is pure gold."

Just then their lunch came, and both girls began eating their shrimp and dipping their French fries in ketchup.

How odd. Once Cara had been the more thoughtful and mature of the two, Sallie's mentor. Now, Sallie was the deeper one. Despite all her trouble and agony of spirit, she wouldn't trade places with Cara now. She had a feeling Cara had a lot to learn, even more than she herself had. At least, she wasn't horrified by her mother's illness, scared that the evil would spread to envelope her, as Cara was. Instead, she accepted it; she did the things prescribed by Dr. Haynes, and found that actually the proximity with mental derangement strengthened her own character. And her talks with Dr. Haynes made her own incomprehensible actions more understandable, even her suicide attempt. Of course, he had a tendency to soft-pedal the abortion as far as its being morally wrong, and refer to the whole "syndrome" as part of an experience that, had it had the proper guidance, would not have degenerated to the point of suicide.

But Sallie would have none of that. If she hadn't been sure of its being wrong when she finally became honest about it after Harvey had saved her life, she was after hearing her father's story last night. Her mother, under far worse circumstances than Sallie's, had given her baby life, but not without cost. Her trauma had led them to kill Sallie's baby. Suddenly she realized that the doctor must be told what Mrs. Hinkley had said — even it if weren't true. It might be the key he needed, the missing link. She would talk to her father tonight. Surely, he must see that no more withholding would help. Once, she had cringed from facing the truth, when her father and told her about her mother — and the other things. But you could live with the truth better than lies. Both she and her mother were testimonies to that.

"You're quiet," Cara said, slurping the last drops of her milkshake through her straw.

"Thinking, I guess. Not very polite at lunch, either. Is Tim nervous?"

They spent the rest of the meal discussing Cara's wedding and what they had gotten their families and boyfriends for Christmas. Sallie had no more time to think about the similarities and differences between her mother's case and her own. They had been victims, each of them — her mother of first a man, then repression, and ultimately of her own misguided determination; Sallie of ignorance, foolishness, and lack of foresight, the object of her mother's misguided determination. They had both overridden their feelings of right and wrong. It appeared one just didn't do that lightly.

Sallie said good-by to Cara at her house, dropping her off at the curb.

"Say hi to your folks," she said.

"You, too. See you next Friday."

Sallie drove home, feeling strangely at peace. Learning about God's laws, really learning, was a good way to live. Every inch along His way showed her more and more the value of it. Deceit bred death.

"The wages of sin are death, my girl," she murmured and felt proud of her interpretation.

"I am the way, the truth, and the life." Jesus was truth. Truth was life. Put another way, honesty really was the best way to live.

Then she thought of her mother. Poor mom! She had always stressed to Sallie the value of clean living. Sallie had deliberately chosen to ignore that, but all these years her mother had lived with being violated, with paying for someone else's uncleanness.

I guess mom always wanted to be perfect and for me to be perfect, too, Sallie thought, driving into the garage at home. That sailor wouldn't let her be, and I rebelled, too. I guess she's got to accept that absolutely no one is perfect.

Sallie turned off the car and got out. Then she went in the house and began to wrap gifts.

Christmas was lonely, but warmer than it had been for years. Sallie felt even closer to her father than she had as a child. They sat on the floor, in the early morning light, ripping off the colored wrappings and watching the twinkling lights on the tree. Later, Sallie took her mother's gifts her, leaving her father sadly behind at home. Perhaps when her father told Dr. Haynes about the past, they would be able to alleviate the fear Nancy felt at the mention of Frank's name. Meanwhile, it was sad, but at least Sallie had gifts to give from Frank, and all they could do was wait and hope.

By the time Sallie mentioned to her father that Dr. Haynes should know what Mrs. Hinkley had said, it was Christmas Eve, and her father had brought up the subject himself. She had put it off, not knowing how to tell her father what to do. As it turned out, he had come to that decision himself and so they had merely discussed how he would do it. Of course, Mrs. Hinkley had to be protected, but Sallie thought her father could tell the facts without endangering her job.

With Christmas over, the gifts delivered, bringing tears to her mother's eyes as she unwrapped them (a good sign, Dr. Haynes had said), Sallie prepared for Harvey's arrival.

After church on Sunday she aired out the den and put clean sheets on the hide-a-bed. She could hardly wait to see him. She would wear the new red slacks and white turtleneck her father had given her. It seemed ages since she had last seen Harvey. And so much had happened! Now she eagerly looked forward to talking everything over with Harvey. How nice to have someone to share everything with, without fear of rejection. Yes, that bridge had been crossed. A tough crossing, but crossed.

Sallie baked a cake and made fudge. She knew Harvey would appreciate the special food. He loved to eat. She planned Monday's dinner and discussed the details with her father. It seemed that never before had she anticipated anything more. It was hard to be too subdued, but for her father's sake, she tried.

Finally, Monday afternoon came and it was time to meet Harvey at the bus station. All at once, she was nervous. Would he be there? What would they talk about? Silly! All those fears had died with Cam. Now, surely, after the closeness of mind between them, she would not be nervous with Harvey.

But, of course, they had nearly a week together — alone a good deal of the time. Always before there had been people around. It wasn't sex, either, although she felt a little ghost of apprehension, a half-felt hope that she wouldn't be tempted. It was being alone, talking, eating — well, really living together. At night her father would be home, but she hadn't given much thought as to how they would spend the days.

Why had her father been so agreeable about the visit? Never a whisper of warning. This was puzzling, but, anyway, she was glad Harvey was coming.

She waited on the ramp where the buses came in. She had on her scarlet coat and plaid cap. Her heart beat quickly and her throat was stiff and dry. At last, the big bus rolled in, belching smelly fumes and making Sallie step back.

Harvey was the first one off. He was eager, too. He wore his duffel coat and his one decent pair of dress slacks, carrying a small battered suitcase. He spotted her right away. How could he miss her in her red coat? His face glowed and she knew hers must also.

"Hi, Miss Sallie," he whispered in her ear between hugs.

She felt the familiar wiry strength of his this arms, the hardness of his chest.

"Oh, you feel good," she said.

"You, too! Where's the car?"

"Over here." They walked arm in arm to the car and Harvey stowed his suitcase in the back seat.

"Well," he said. "Did you miss me?"

"And how," she said. "But I've been so busy. There's so much to tell you. Oh, I'm so glad to see you! I thought you might not come."

She threw her arms around him again.

"Why not?"

"Oh, I don't know. Maybe you reconsidered. Maybe you don't love me enough. Maybe I'm scared you're not real."

"Do cows give milk?"

"Silly."

"So are you." He squeezed her tight, then helped her into the car and went around and got in on the passenger side. Once in, he pulled her to him and kissed her thoroughly.

"But for you I might have gone through life hating the doers as well as the evil," he said. "I've done a lot of thinking, Sallie. I want to be a missionary," he smoothed her hair away from her face, knocking her cap off. "I feel God gave you to me — after you'd had time to make your mistake. Don't interrupt. Who knows how or why? But think of all the people getting fouled up! And all I've done is condemn them. Sure, I've worked hard at the orphanage — giving love and moralistic preaching. But how could you stand me?"

"I couldn't. You were a self-righteous snob."

"Well, you changed all that."

"Thanks," she said dryly.

He laughed and kissed her. "You know what I mean."

"No, I don't."

Harvey released her and sat away from her a little so he could see her. She looked hurt and a little confused.

"If I hadn't loved you the way I do," he said gently, "I'd never have learned we're all human. Jesus loved all of us — still does no matter who we are or what we've done. I was so hung up, I couldn't see that. You changed it."

Sallie did see. But what about the future? Suppose he got rigid or she got lost again? Then what?

"I guess I do see, but I was scared you couldn't love me. I feel pretty unlovable when I look coldly at the whole thing. But I also feel a lot wiser and not so likely to get taken in again, and I get a little mad when I'm the reason for your — " she searched for the word, " — weakening of your standards."

"You shouldn't be," he said. "It's crazy, Sal. I'm glad you got in trouble — even had an abortion. I know it wasn't fun for you. And I'm still against killing babies. But now I see that the way I was would turn people off rather than help them when they needed it. God doesn't want that. He wants us — you and me — to help people to know His forgiveness so they can be what He meant them to be."

Sallie started the car.

"How can you be so sure?"

"He forgave us, didn't He?"

Sallie remembered the infirmary, the feeling of God's never-failing love, the fact that Harvey's had indeed wavered, the desire to go first with God from then on. Yes, they both had failed, and in the failure had climbed higher with God.

"Yes," she said, backing out of the station.

"Well, it's up to us, each of us who have known the miracle of renewal to be as open and forgiving as He is. It's a simple, old Sunday school lesson. The Golden Rule, in tolerance."

"Yes," she said. "Oh, who cares? I'm just glad you're here!"

They rode along through a light snow, talking of other things. Harvey was full of Christmas, how they had managed a bike for a nine-year-old, and a real talking doll — donated — for a six-year-old. Sallie delighted in hearing about the happy children discovering an orange and nuts and candy in their stockings — all twenty-one of them. She stole glances at his face as they headed home, recalling with fondness every irregular feature. But now he looked handsome to her. His face suited him and when he smiled it was beautiful.

"You know," he said as they turned into Hilltop Acres, "faith had done a lot at the home. That and work and prayer. We manage to make those kids feel loved. I'll hate to leave them." He stopped talking as she pulled into the garage and switched off the motor. She turned to look at him and he was

147

swept by a feeling of happiness so great he thought he would burst. "But," he went on, "there's more to it than faith — or the love that faith brings. Where faith leaves off, God takes over. So many times we've given up on someone — a teen-ager, maybe, who's rebelling. And not always, but often when our faith runs out, when we're defeated, a miracle happens. Something breaks in the kid, or something happens, completely unexpected, and suddenly there He is, healing, redirecting. God Himself seems to do what we gave up on." Harvey looked at Sallie's rapt face in the dim light of the garage. Two tears were running zig-zag courses down each cheek.

"What's wrong?" he asked.

"I wish He'd do that for my mother."

"Oh, you poor honey! I've been rambling on and haven't even asked how it's been."

Once started, the tears spilled in earnest and Sallie felt the comfort of his embrace. All the pent-up tension, the trying to do her best, flowed out in a torrent of words and hiccups. It was good to be able to rest in Harvey's arms, to let it out. She hadn't even known it was wearing on her, but it had been.

"Well," she spluttered at the end. "Why doesn't he heal her? All these things ganged up on her — some were her fault, most just dumb fate."

"You say your dad's going to tell the doctor about what happened twenty-five years ago?"

"He was supposed to today."

"Well, that's all you can do, honey. I'm going to contradict myself and say don't give up faith — not yet. Doctors heal, too, you know. Even when they don't know it, God can work through them."

"Maybe if we give up," Sallie sniffled, "it'll go away. Oh, Harvey, she used to be so strong. It's awful to watch her — groping for something she can't find."

"That's just it. You can't fake giving up. Like your jumping in the river — that was real. You gotta hold on till you can't and then pray for strength to see you through the despair. Maybe your mom has to give up herself. You can't boss God around. You just have to try to do your part, and believe that at the right time He'll do His part."

Sallie felt better. Harvey was good. She was lucky to have him to rely on. Most of the time he'd be there. And always God was there. She felt more able to cope. The tears seemed to have washed away the fear and tension and the excitement at seeing Harvey. They would have a good week, after all.

20 Nancy tried to pull the comb through her hair. She had been given permission to have a mirror — to get ready. She didn't recognize the face that stared back at her, the sunken eyes, the hollow cheeks, the lifeless, tangled hair. She really wasn't too concerned about the way she looked, but she supposed she ought to be. That would be healthier.

Finally, gaining a semblance of smoothness, she put the comb down, laying the little hand mirror beside it, and went to the window. The bars had been swung out, the window raised with only the screen between her and the ground two floors below. She wondered now why they always so carefully barred the windows. It wasn't high enough to kill yourself. Ah, but she shouldn't think thoughts like that. She was better.

Why was it so depressing to be better? It was almost preferable to be sick.

Oh, well. It was pretty out today. Winter was really gone. It had seemed endless, especially after Sallie stopped coming.

That was the beginning, she guessed. She wasn't so far gone that physical evidence could be rejected. Nancy drew in deep breaths of the sunshine-warmed air. You had to recognize your own daughter and remember — whether you wanted to or not. Ah, but some didn't. One was crying quietly next door now. The sound drifted in through the gently billowing curtains. But Sallie had been there often. And at last she had remembered — or, better to say, she had separated this daughter from another unknown one — one she believed dead, killed by her own hand. But that had been Sallie's — not hers. How had they dug it all up? She had never mentioned it — not once. She had pushed it all away.

Which was why she was in a clean dress now with her hair combed, awaiting Dr. Haynes to bring Frank. Poor Frank! They said she had become terrified at mention of him. Why? It would be a long time before she understood, but Dr. Haynes said not to worry about it. She was doing fine.

But still she was sorry enough to have put him through this alone, without blaming and hating him, too. It all seemed to get clearer when Dr. Haynes hypnotized her and probed her past. Bits and pieces came at first. Then whole chunks, segments of horror relived. Then she had recognized that aid, Sara Hinkley, and she knew it was true. But, no, she hadn't killed her baby — no, she had suffered through to the end and somewhere a twenty-five-year-old girl, a wife maybe, and even a mother, lived because of her and a drunken sailor. Perhaps that was it. Everything had been so mixed up without base or time — perhaps she had feared and hated Frank because of that drunken sailor.

She thought about these things with a sense of detachment, of watching someone else struggle with the truth of her own life. Yet, there was one thing that burned still, seared her heart and turned her stomach. The abortion. She had been determined to spare her daughter — the only one she had on whom to lavish love — the hell she had been through. But the very going through of that hell had made her strongly for life, like the poor boy who made good on his own. If she had suffered the indignity of rape and had the baby, then what were these flimsy excuses being offered for abortion? Oh, she had kept it mostly to herself, and spoken up only on occasion. But it was there. And it tore her apart to go against it to save her girl the agony.

Nancy felt the cool breeze drying the beads of sweat on her lip. The sun sparkled off Frank's car as he parked it. He walked with a spring in his step, as if the rare March warmth had infected him. She remembered him as tired and silent, or bitter and angry. Sometimes stoic, and always concerned for Sallie. How was he now, after five months of her illness, and several months before that of misery? She felt more depressed at the prospect of being released in a few weeks to the old, sadly unhappy Frank.

She stood at the window a few moments longer looking at the matted brownish grass, looking at the bare trees, wishing she could stay in this peaceful place with Dr. Haynes to help her always.

"Mrs. Victor?"

It was Sara.

"Nancy to you."

"Nancy, then. But it's our secret, right?"

"Well, everyone knows now. And I'm glad. It's been so lonely."

"All right, dear. But let's go now. Your husband's downstairs to see you. My, don't you look nice!"

Nancy looked down at her once smart A-line suit dress of beige and brown to accent her blond hair. It hung on her and the jacket kept falling open and sliding on her shoulders. They always said you looked nice. Good therapy.

"Thank you. I'm ready."

They left the room together and went down the broad hall to the stairway. Frank was sitting on the bench in the hall below. She felt a little like a movie queen, making her entrance down the gently sloping, red carpeted stair.

For a while they just looked at each other. What did you say after years of drifting and then the final boiling over of so much? At last, Dr. Haynes, appearing from nowhere, took them each by the arm, directing them to the visitors' sitting room.

"Come along in here, where you can relax," he said. "Don't look so grim, Nancy. You have plenty of time."

Time? Yes, perhaps she could stay for quite a while yet. No need to rush.

150

Frank waited till Dr. Haynes left, leaving the door partly ajar.

"Well," he said at last. "It's been a long time."

She looked at him.

"Won't you sit down?" she said. They sat on the rose-printed sofa, stiffly apart, facing each other.

"Well, Sallie will be home next week for Easter. You'll see her then." Frank crossed his leg, then put it down and leaned forward a little, holding his hat in his hands.

"I guess so. I lose track of time."

"Only natural."

"Yes."

They sat silently for a while. How nervous Frank was! She was only dull, not really caring.

"You're fine?" she asked.

"Yes, I'm fine." Then, as if he were afraid he'd hurt her, he added, "But, of course, I miss you."

"Of course."

She fiddled with her jacket, trying to get it to hang right.

"Nancy?"

"Yes?"

"It's not easy to talk after all this time. Perhaps it's enough for now."

Nancy felt a little stab of pain in her chest. No! Let me get used to you again! I need time to get you straight in my mind.

"Stay a while," she said, a little breathlessly. "What have you been doing?"

"Oh, work. Things are going well at the bank. I joined the Chamber of Commerce and I've helped sponsor a drug clinic in the area. It's very interesting."

Was this Frank? He sounded enthusiastic, leashed in, as if he were afraid of saying too much.

"You like it?"

"Yes," he twirled his hat. "Yes, I like it very much. There's so much to tell. So much has happened."

"Well, I know Sallie has a boyfriend. What's he like?"

"He's nice, Nancy. Not like — " he broke off.

Nancy clasped her hands tightly.

"He's decent? They're — "

"I trust her with him. He's what she needs. They plan to marry when he graduates from college next June."

"Maybe by then . . ."

Frank covered her tense hands with his, letting his hat fall to the floor.

"You'll be home long before that. God's healing you, Nancy. I know He is."

This sounded like the Frank she had met twenty years ago, nearly twenty-one now. He was always talking about God.

"He's taking His time."

"We need time. And we have it. Dr. Haynes says you're much better. Soon you'll be home for a visit. God will help us through each step."

"I'm afraid I don't believe that, Frank. Each step will be gotten over by sheer hard work."

"Don't worry about it, Nancy. Just trust a little. In me, if you can't in God."

"It's not easy to reassemble a life that was so confused to start with."

Frank pulled her tense hands open and clasped them in his.

"Even if God doesn't take away the confusion, He makes it bearable."

"That's easy for you to say." Then she realized how she sounded. Yes, she had been the object of a meaningless attack in her youth, going on through pure will power, but Frank's life hadn't been too clear, either. Especially lately.

He took his hands away, retrieving his hat.

"Well," he said. "We'll talk more next time." He stood up.

Why didn't she just say she was sorry? How often had she neglected those words? She stood up, too, trying to gather courage. Well, maybe it was easier for Frank to say. Maybe life was bearable to him. She reached out and touched his arm.

"I don't mean it's been easy for you, Frank. I just can't find any reason in it all and that makes me want to hide forever. I tried to force orderliness in our lives, but chaos always reigns in the end."

"That's why I leave it to God to decide what's good and orderly. Perhaps He has a reason. I couldn't live any other way, Nancy. We tried. We followed the trappings, but left God out. We ordered, and planned, without regard for a higher order. I can't do that any more. And having admitted I'm incapable of making my own order, I've never been happier. Perhaps you think it's immature. But I feel that by trusting God and letting His rules be my guide, I'm free — free from all the old worry and defeat. Free to carry on a meaningful life, knowing I don't define the meaning. You should do that, too."

Nancy felt rebuked, like a small child. Frank wasn't angry; he wasn't storming at her. He was calmly telling her the way it was.

Frank clapped his hat on his head in a motion that said he had given all he was going to this time. To him, Nancy seemed completely unlike the quiet and authoritative wife he had known. She was like one of those kids at the drug clinic, lost and groping, and no amount of talk would help until she began groping in his direction. That might never happen, but until and if it did, he would show by his own life that his theology worked. Even now, seeing her eyes, haunted by the memories and resultant horror of her "chaos," he could not feel personally threatened. In a way, it was sad. For the old Frank had reacted at her every action, had stormed, or pouted, or just turned her off, but now, he was immune. His new relationship with God, his putting into practice his Christian faith, had changed all that. He still loved her, in fact his love was more universal, more objective, less demanding and competitive, but never again would she run him or overrule him or cause him to slip away from the meaning God gave.

For how long they stood, she with the stricken eyes, he with pensive ones, they didn't know. But, at last, Frank bestirred himself and bent his head toward her and kissed her lightly on the lips.

"See you next week — with Sallie."

"Yes, I'll be here." What a silly thing to say, Nancy! Where else would you be?

"Don't *worry*, Nancy. Just rest."

"Yes." Like a schoolgirl. So obedient. Ah, but so peaceful, too.

Frank turned and went out, leaving Nancy standing by the sofa, brown jacket askew, her hands clasping nervously.

Dr. Haynes met him in the hall.

"Well, well! How was it?"

Frank shrugged. "She's different."

Dr. Haynes laughed. "What did you expect?"

"Nothing. But when you live with what you thought was her personality all these years and then meet a new, entirely different one, it's hard to get used to."

"Naturally," Dr. Haynes ran his chubby hand across his glistening dome. "But you will in time. In a few weeks we'll try a weekend at home, eh?"

"Yes. But what will she be like? What should I do?"

"There's time to think about that yet. Do you still love her?"

Frank sighed. Did he mean by the old definition or the new? Who cares? The new was better.

"Yes."

"Then you'll help her, that's all. She'll put you through a lot, but I believe in time you'll see a truly stronger woman."

And God? Frank wondered. Will she ever come to see that God makes peace out of confusion, order out of chaos?

"Thank you, doctor."

As Frank went out into the sparkling spring day, he heard Dr.

Haynes jovial voice boom, "Well, well! How was it, Nancy?" He smiled a little to himself.

"Well, well, Frank," he said aloud as he got into his car. "How was it?"

Nancy went back to her room alone. Dr. Haynes stayed downstairs to wait for a patient. She noticed he avoided climbing the stairs any more than he had to.

When she got there, she saw the mirror was still there, where she had laid it down. Supposing she shattered it and slashed her wrists? Her stomach lurched. For what reason? To what end? Quit kidding yourself, Nancy. Stop these games! You were glad to see Frank. Oh, yes, you were! You want to go home again. Not right away, but soon. You want to live. Surprise! There is still the wish to live.

Nancy picked up the mirror and examined her face. She must begin a beauty program. Had Sallie seen her like this? Well, not again. Next week, when Sallie came, she would look better. How many pounds could you gain in a week?

Nancy tried a tentative smile in the mirror. It looked pretty sick, straggly, and it only emphasized the sunken look in her eyes. Well, she couldn't do it in a day. She put the mirror down and returned to the window. She let the sun warm her face, felt the warmth spread, seeping through her. Yes, maybe life was possible after all.

Sallie reclined against "their tree." She scribbled across her long, yellow pad. A few more paragraphs and she would be done. One more theme for English finished. Distantly, she could hear the choir practicing. She could, or thought she could, discern Clara's high, shrill soprano trilling out an "alleluia." She stretched contentedly and put her pad down on the grass.

Oh, what a beautiful day! The buds were beginning to open, heralding the arrival of warmth to stay. In three more weeks school would be out, she would go home for the summer to work in the bank. How sad to miss the most beautiful time on campus! And Harvey. Well, that would be hard. But there would be the visit in July to the orphanage. Who knows? Maybe she would be so taken with it that they both would stay on, work there after they were married.

Married! She was going to marry Harvey. Maybe they could move it up to next Christmas, only seven months away. If mom were home to stay.

She thought of the weekend in April, mom's second weekend home, when she had gone home, too. There had been dinner cooked by Nancy, there had been the first shy probing of conversation, not the one-sided speeches Sallie had given at Sunshine Acres at Christmas. For the first time, Sallie really began to believe what Harvey had said, "Where faith leaves off, God takes over." It seemed that despite their mutual strugglings, God was healing, not as quickly or dramatically as they, Sallie and her father, had hoped, but more slowly and completely.

Now Sallie could luxuriate in her own happiness, without guilt. If it hadn't been for the new hope given her in her hour of despair, no amount of happiness could have eradicated the guilt. And she still bitterly regretted the death of a child whom, if she hadn't had the ability to keep, she could have at least given the opportunity of life — even at a place like Harvey's home. Maybe good had come out of it all; undeniably it had. But what of her poor, dead baby? She could only hope that God, in His wisdom, was caring for the soul that never had the chance to see this world. You couldn't blame yourself forever, and to be forgiven, you had to accept the forgiveness — and pass it on.

Where was Harvey, anyway? Sallie turned on her side, sliding down a little on the soft turf to get away from the bark of the tree that was suddenly poking her. This was where Harvey had spoken to her the day they had gone into town. How different they were! In eight months, they were completely changed. Sallie smiled at their previous selves. She had been so cocky and defensive, he had been so superior and judgelike. By what miracle had they been brought together? By deep calling to deep — going around all those surface images?

There he was! He walked with a light step. He's happy, too, Sallie thought. He's got that stupid grin on his face, which means he's just aced another test.

"Well, what have you done this time, Harvey?"

Harvey threw himself unceremoniously down at her side, flipping a paper at her in the same motion that he kissed her forehead.

"See, Miss Sallie! I told you so! I, very calmly and logically, proved that my theory of reaching the deprived child was better than Prof. Isaac's was. Oh, it's painful to be right all the time!"

Sallie looked at the paper. A "C" was crossed out and replaced by a "B+."

" 'B+'? Why not 'A−'?" Sallie loved him in this mood.

"Pride my dear. A professor of our higher halls of learning does not change a 'C' to an 'A' no matter how wrong he was!"

"You're a slob! Just because you have an inside track on deprived kids you take some unorthodox approach and prove poor Ike wrong!"

"Terrific, isn't it? Sometimes my brilliance positively scares me!"

Sallie turned more toward him. "Show me your brilliance at kissing, Harvey, if you're so great at everything else!"

"Here! In front of the whole school?"

"Ah-ha! You aren't so brave then! Professors, but not peers, huh?"

That was why Clara's foot ended up gently kicking their heads, which were joined together in blissful oblivion to their environment.

"Hey, come on, you two! I thought you didn't go in for this sort of indecent display."

Harvey opened one eye and managed to glare at Clara. "Go away," he mumbled against Sallie's mouth.

"Not on your life, creep. You're helping me on my English paper, remember?"

"He's not a creép!" Sallie yelled, sitting up and pulling a few strands of hair out of her mouth.

Sitting up suddenly, he said, "Okay, kid, where's the work of art for your mentor to improve upon?"

Clara glared at him, then, opening her notebook, produced several sheets of a hurriedly written paper. Sallie sat back, dreamily staring at the buildings and distant hills, as Harvey and Clara discussed, relishing the kiss that still lingered on her lips. It was pleasant to sit in the sun with her best friend and her fiancé and think of nothing but the moment. It was good to be content and to enjoy the here and now. Perhaps the savoring of the good moments helped prepare the heart for the bad. Perhaps, if her mother had known that, she would not have been so driven to avoid the bad. Perhaps she, Sallie, would store up strength from these good times, always remembering that they came from God to give a firm foundation from which to work. Just as mistakes forgiven led to deeper insight, perhaps learning to appreciate happiness would lead to deeper strength.

Life — very complicated, yet very simple. Depending on your viewpoint, your mood, your faith. "Only a child can enter the kingdom of heaven." Yes, you must trust as a child trusts — wholly, without fear of the future, knowing that God will provide. Then you could enter heaven. At that moment of faith.

But sometimes it took a lot to get there — trial and error. And sometimes it was difficult to stay there, when fears grew and pressures increased. Believing in God wasn't always easy, especially when you or someone you loved got off the track. But it was still preferable to trying to go it alone, without God.

Sallie shuddered in the warm sunlight, suddenly feeling the cold memory of the river in December. She watched some boys tossing a football around on the commons, shouting, and generally enjoying themselves.

It was good to sit under a tree with those you love, and think of nothing.